FRACTURE

Matt James

SEVERED**PRESS**

FRACTURE

Copyright © 2025 Matt James

www.SeveredPress.com
www.MattJamesAuthor.com

ISBN: 978-1-923165-56-4

ALSO BY MATT JAMES

The Jack Reilly Archaeological Thrillers
The Forgotten Fortune
The Roosevelt Conspiracy
The Dorado Deception
The Undying Kingdom
The Venetian Pursuit
The Lost Legion
The Relic Syndicate (2025)

The Relics of God Trilogy
The Blood King
The Fasle Prophet

Stand-alone Novels
Fracture
Cradle of Death
Sub-Zero
The Dragon

The Zahra Kane Archaeological Thrillers
Empire Lost: A Prequel
The Anubis Plague
The Sixth Seal

Other Stories
The Cursed Pharaoh
Broken Glass
Plague
Evolve
Midnight Mass

The Charlee Flynn Archaeological Adventures
The Cursed Thief
The Golden Tiger
The Jaguar Blade

The Dark Island Trilogy
Dark Island: The Definitive Edition
Dark Island 2: Into the Abyss

The Unseen
Origin
Desolation
Perseverance
Inferno
Nightmare: A Short Story
Petrified: A Short Story

The Dane Maddock Adventures
Berserk
Skin and Bones
Venom
Lost City

The Hank Boyd Adventures
Blood and Sand
Mayan Darkness
Babel Found
Elixir of Life

Praise for Matt James

"The words of a Matt James story flow like the best rivers. Smooth and subtle at times, interrupted by danger and thrills at every churn of whitewater. This guy is the real deal!"
—Ernest Dempsey, *USA Today* bestselling author of POSEIDON'S FURY

"Matt James is my go-to guy for heart-stopping adventure and bone-chilling suspense!"
—Greig Beck, international bestselling author of TO THE CENTER OF THE EARTH

"Matt James is the gold standard for archaeological thrillers!"
—Luke Richardson, international bestselling author of THE TITANIC DECEPTION

"If you enjoy globetrotting adventures jampacked with over-the-top action, then you'll love Matt James' work!"
—Nick Thacker, *USA Today* bestselling author of THE ENIGMA STRAIN

"If you're looking for a fast-moving tale with action to spare, give Matt James a try!"
—David Wood, *USA Today* bestselling author of SERPENT

"Searching for relentless action and harrowing adventure in dangerous locales? Look no further than Matt James!"
—Michael McBride, international bestselling author of CHIMERA

"Matt James is a must-read! The thrilling action, unexpected turns, and rip-roaring chases across the globe are fantastic adventures every time! You won't be disappointed."
—Andrew Clawson, bestselling author of THE ARTHURIAN RELIC

"Matt James writes thrillers that define the genre! Neck-breaking speed and hairpin plot twists. Top notch!"
—Craig A. Hart, bestselling author of SERENITY

"Matt James reminds devotees of Indiana Jones and Nathan Drake why their love for rock-solid action-adventure springs eternal!"
—Rick Chesler, international bestselling author of ATLANTIS GOLD

"Matt's novels need a pause button. They do not stop!"
—Lee Murray, *Bram Stoker Award*-winning author of INTO THE MIST

"Matt James is the Michael Bay of thriller authors! He loves action, suspense, and making things go boom!"
—Richard F. Paddon, author of CASH IS KING

A Note From the Author

If you wish to know more about the animals used in this novel, there is a brief summary of each one after the last chapter. Wait until you've read the story to check it out to avoid spoilers.

Thanks, Matt

For Sam Neill, and his portrayal of Dr. Alan Grant.
This novel wouldn't exist without either of you.

-

For Dr. Kenneth Lacovara, paleontologist, and
the real-life discoverer of *Dreadnoughtus schrani*.

-

And, of course, for all of you out there who never
outgrew your love for dinosaurs.

This one is especially for you.

FRACTURE

Matt James

**When time fractures,
chaos reigns.**

1

It had been a long time since Noah Clark had been in any part of New York City. Half of his reasoning was on purpose. Noah wasn't a big fan of overcrowded, metropolitan cities—or boroughs, like Manhattan. While they offered residents and visitors an eclectic atmosphere, mostly because of the variety of people roaming the streets or riding on the subway, Noah would've rather been back home in Norman, Oklahoma.

He didn't mind traveling. For the majority of his life, it had been part of his job. No, Noah just really didn't like New York City. Case in point, the passersby that were shouting vulgarities at one another from somewhere behind him. He'd been standing on the eastern steps of the American Museum of Natural History for a few minutes now, both marveling at the building's front façade, and preparing himself for what awaited him beyond it.

The only reason he was here was because of a rather

out-of-the-blue phone call he had received three months ago. An old family friend, and the current director of the museum, Constance Farr, had invited him to be part of an upcoming exhibit called, "Prehistoric Titans." But it wasn't only that she wanted him to speak at the opening, Constance, "Connie" to very few, including the Clark family, also wanted the exhibit to feature Noah and his father's most well-known discovery. Kenneth Clark had been a *titan* in his own right within the paleontological world.

Dreadnoughtus schrani, the monstrous sauropod, was one of the largest that had ever been found, even though the animal had been immature and still growing when it had died. Noah had been floored by the offer—and surprised. The specimen had been at its home in Argentina for the last decade, per the country's laws stating that all fossils pulled from its soil remained in the province where they were discovered.

The only time the bones had been somewhere besides Argentina, specifically the Padre Molina Museum in the Santa Cruz Province, had been during its initial examination—an examination that had occurred here in the United States. That examination had ended in 2014 when the species was officially recognized by the scientific community. And once Noah and his father had finished their time with it, the *Dreadnoughtus* had been shipped home to Argentina where it was put out on display.

That had been a sad day for Noah, but he also understood, having worked alongside the Argentine government throughout the entire process. He had known what was coming and had been ready for it.

"But now you're here," he said to himself. "Somehow, you're here."

Constance had pulled some pretty impressive strings to get the Argentine authorities to agree to her offer to headline her exhibit with their dinosaur's remains. Noah let out a long breath, feeling a bit uneasy. Behind the front doors of the Theodore Roosevelt Memorial Hall stood his discovery. He was incredibly excited to see it again—and nervous as all hell. It had been his greatest achievement, the crown jewel of a near-two-decade-long career as a paleontologist, as well as a professor of the same subject.

Almost twenty years now, Noah thought. It was hard to believe that it had been that long.

As the commuters' shouts faded, Noah's senses picked up on the soft breeze pushing down Central Park West. He glanced behind him, holding his gaze on the trees to the east of the bustling roadway. Central Park was an oddity to Noah—an expansive, and expensive, one at that. The land it took up was worth hundreds of billions of dollars, probably even more than that. But he respected the city for keeping it intact instead of selling it off bit by bit to building, yet another, skyscraper.

"Did you hear?" a female voice asked.

Noah turned his attention back to the museum to find a young couple standing only a few steps up from him.

"What about?" the guy with her asked back.

"Some star millions of miles away went supernova eons ago. The blast is supposed to hit Earth soon."

"Really?"

The girl faced her friend. "Yeah. I guess it's kind of a big deal to the NASA nerds since it's never happened before."

The guy faced her now. "Wait. So, no one knows what's going to happen to us?"

She grinned, obviously enjoying his reaction. "Nope. No one. Super spooky if you ask me."

"Definitely," the guy said looking around nervously. "I'd really like to be inside when it happens."

"Yeah," she said, snorting a laugh, "I'm not sure it'll matter."

Then they were off, heading up the steps, while continuing their interesting conversation out of earshot. Noah looked up, examining the afternoon sky for a moment. It was late spring, so the weather was perfect. It wasn't cold, but nor was it hot. A car horn blared behind him, prompting Noah to get moving. He climbed the steps, entering the museum just behind the young couple. He slipped inside the museum's iconic turnstile doors and prepared himself to see *it*. When he did, he stuttered to a stop.

"Hello again."

The *Dreadnoughtus* would've taken up nearly the entire space, filling the Roosevelt Rotunda, had its bent pose not cut down on its length. Still, it was an imposing sight to say the least. Its skull was directly above where Noah stood now, and it had been positioned so it was turned to the side a little, making it seem like the dinosaur's vacant left eye socket was staring at whomever entered the museum. Noah craned his neck back and smiled wide.

"Just as beautiful as I remember."

A set of feet stopped beside him.

"You fall in love?"

Noah peeled his eyes off the skeleton and found a man standing three feet from him. He guessed the newcomer was around six-inches shorter than he was—so, around five-eight. The stranger was Noah's age, black, and possessed cropped, salt-and-peppered hair, and a light beard. He was athletically built and wore gray jogger pants, running shoes, and a form-fitting, black t-shirt.

Noah smiled. "As a matter of fact, I did."

"Well, right on," the other man said. "I fancy redheads myself. What's your girl look like?"

Noah turned and faced him. "She used to be covered in a leathery hide, but now she's all bones."

The stranger scratched his head, attempting to process Noah's *interesting* description of his *girl*. But the only thing he could do was shrug and say, "To each his own, I guess."

"Noah Clark," Noah said, holding out his hand and introducing himself.

His offer was accepted and they shook. "Mike Dillon. So, what's your story?"

"I'm a paleontologist."

"Really?" Mike asked, eyebrows raised. "Dig up anything neat?"

Noah simply pointed straight up, at the *Dreadnoughtus'* skull.

Mike followed his finger, opening his eyes wide when he saw what Noah was gesturing to. "Damn!" He lowered his eyeline back to Noah. "You know, in hindsight, I should've seen that coming. Impressive work, Doc."

"What about you? What do you do?" Noah asked.

"Well, I try to be a cop, but it's become harder and harder to want to go to work these days."

That was a painful reply. "I'm sorry to hear that." Noah looked around. "Come here often?"

Mike nodded. "I do, yeah. It's a great place to wander and

think."

"Think about what?"

Mike shrugged again. "Quitting and moving to South Beach."

"I can respect that," Noah said, smiling, "though I'm more of a cabin-in-the-mountains kind of guy."

"The mountains are pretty too, but they're missing one thing."

"And what's that?"

Mike winked and grinned like a teenager. "Bikinis."

"Wouldn't know. I've never worn one."

"Noah!" Both men turned to find a tiny, pale, black-haired woman wearing a tight black, knee-length dress, with oversized, black-framed eyeglasses waving at them—at Noah—from across the rotunda. "There you are!"

Noah held out his hand again, and they shook. "Gotta go, the boss is looking for me. It was good to meet you, Mike."

Mike gave him a quick wave as Noah turned away. "Likewise."

2

Sarah Rakestraw was at her wits' end. She'd gone to the bathroom five minutes ago, and in those five minutes, her son had already lost his sister. Then again, Sarah shouldn't have been all that surprised. Kyle wasn't exactly the epitome of responsibility. All he wanted to do was listen to music, play drums, and watch music reaction videos on YouTube. The family's therapist had said several times that his behavior was typical for that of a rebellious, sixteen-year-old boy.

Then, consider what their family had been through over the last four years...

Still, Sarah expected more from her son. Kyle had once been a straight-A student. He'd routinely been at the top of his school's honor role. But then, once he'd begun to go through puberty, and after his father was forced out of the picture, Kyle's grades had begun to suffer, and his attitude had dramatically changed.

"Come on, Kyle, really—already?" Sarah looked around the

Roosevelt Rotunda. "Where's your sister?"

Kyle rolled his eyes and paused his video, actually annoyed for having to do so. "Relax, Mom, she's right there." He tapped the screen of his phone with one hand and pointed toward the middle of the room with the other, never once looking at her.

Sarah turned her head and found Becca standing beneath the gargantuan dinosaur skeleton taking up most of the space. She wore her usual attire: weathered overalls, an unmatching long-sleeve shirt beneath them, and a beat-to-death pair of Converse shoes. Her strawberry-blonde hair was pulled back in the messiest ponytail Sarah had ever seen...since the day before. And unlike her brother, Becca had not yet shown signs of maturation, even at twelve years of age.

But, then again, Becca wasn't your average preteen.

"You're supposed to be looking after her, not let her wander off while I use the toilet."

Kyle shrugged, and this time, he looked up at his mother. "Give me a leash and a shock collar, and I will."

"That's not funny," Sarah snapped, finding her hips with her hands.

The corner of Kyle's mouth turned upward. "It was to me."

"And therein lies the problem." Sarah looked around, discovering an unclaimed bench behind her. "See that?" she asked, pointing to it.

"Yeah?"

"Park it while *I* go get your sister."

Kyle shrugged. "Fine by me." He headed away and added under his breath, "I'll never say no to a break from babysitting duty."

Now alone, Sarah closed her eyes and let out a long breath. At forty, she would still be regarded as a looker to some. But when she stared at herself in the mirror, all she saw was a worn-out woman with crow's feet and a touch of gray invading her blonde hair. A friend had recently said that she should treat herself to a *mani*, a *pedi*, a makeover, and a pushup bra.

"It'll make you feel great about yourself, Sarah!" Viv had added.

Sarah had chuckled and replied with, "Yeah, we'll see about that."

Of course, she did none of it.

"You okay, ma'am?"

Sarah opened her eyes to find a man standing six feet in front of her.

Surprised to be asked, and a little embarrassed that she was obviously looking like she needed help, Sarah didn't know what to respond with other than, "Sure?"

The man stepped closer, smiled, and quickly flashed a police badge at her. "Just in case you're wondering why a stranger is asking if you're okay."

Sarah smiled softly, happy to see that random people still cared about one another. "Thank you, and yes, I'm fine. Just have a lot of Mom stuff going on right now." She glanced down at her feet. "It's my kids, mostly."

"You lose them?" he asked, looking around.

"No, we're good. I have one happily sitting over there glad to not be helping with his sister. She's over at this big dino."

He glanced behind Sarah, easily picking out the "troubled youth" with the mope of blonde hair and the backward baseball cap. Then he brought his attention back to her. "You sure you're okay, ma'am?"

Sarah relaxed. "Yes." She stepped forward and held out her hand. "And it's Sarah."

He shook her hand. "My dad named me Mike, so we'll go with that." That made her smile. "If you need anything, just scream as loud as you can."

This time, Sarah actually laughed a little. "Thanks."

"You're welcome, and take care of yourself."

Mike gave her a nod and left. As she followed him to her left, she met eyes with another man. This one was tall and well-built. He wore jeans, sneakers, a flannel shirt with sleeves rolled up, and a dirty baseball cap.

And, boy, was he handsome.

The statuesque figure caught her staring from across the room, making Sarah spin around and blush heavily. She glued her eyes to the floor and headed for her daughter over at the exhibit. It shouldn't have surprised her that Becca was glued to it. Dinosaurs, well, all prehistoric life, were the constant things in her life that brought her joy. Becca wasn't a terribly sad person, but a developmental disorder had robbed her of having what most would call a "normal childhood."

Now, Rebecca Rakestraw was seen as awkward, and to those that didn't know her, off-putting since she rarely took part in a typical conversation. She kept to herself, unless of course, the discussion involved the lives of creatures that had been dead for tens of millions of years.

Sarah stepped up next to her daughter and took a deep breath, figuring out what she wanted to say before opening her mouth. Very little got through to Becca in the way of parenting. Again, she wasn't a bad kid, she just didn't understand things in the same way her brother did.

"Becca, you know you can't just—"

"*Dreadnoughtus schrani*," Becca interrupted, "discovered by Kenneth and Noah Clark in 2005 in the Cerro Fortaleza Formation in the Santa Cruz Provence of Argentina. Sadly, the elder Clark passed away three years ago at the age of seventy-one."

"Becca, I don't—"

"*Dreadnoughtus* meaning, 'fears nothing' and *schrani*, named after Adam Schran who financially supported the excavation."

Sarah opened her mouth to say something else, but didn't get the chance. Once Becca was in the zone, it was best to just let her finish what she had to say.

"At eighty-five-feet in length and weighing in at well over one hundred *thousand* pounds, *Dreadnoughtus schrani* is easily one of the largest land animals to have ever existed—some say it was—others, possibly jealous of the discovery, have long-disputed the claim. One thing is clear, though: this *Dreadnoughtus* was a behemoth, and includes the most complete skeleton of any titanosaur ever found."

Becca was breathing hard now, having spit out facts about the creature in record time.

Sarah smiled. She couldn't help but be impressed with her daughter's mind. She motioned up to the dinosaur. "Something that big would've definitely 'feared nothing,' right?"

But Becca didn't reply. She had already pulled back into her own head and shut down. Sarah frowned that, once more, she had been unable to get through to Becca.

"Probably would've moved like an AT-AT, huh?" she asked, trying again. Surely some *Star Wars* talk would work, right?

Still, she got nothing from her daughter.

"I really wish you'd open up to me again, Becca," Sarah said, sighing. She never felt more alone than in situations like this. Her daughter barely knew she was alive, and sometimes it felt like her son didn't care if she was or not.

"Well," Sarah said, looking over her shoulder at Kyle, "at least you still talk to your brother, Becca. Even if he doesn't want to talk to you..."

Then, suddenly, Sarah felt the pinpricks of static electricity. Her limbs quickly went numb and her head pounded. She felt her stomach churn as the room grew cloudy—and a murky orange—but she figured that was just her mind being unable to process what was happening. Why would the room be turning orange?

What's...happening?

"Ugh," she moaned, falling to her knees and snapping her eyes shut. "Becca? Your brother... Find him."

Then she blacked out.

3

Noah awoke to screams and the thunder of running feet—a stampede of sorts. He was groggy and his head was killing him. He sat bolt upright and tried to remember why he was on the floor of the Roosevelt Rotunda. He looked up at his dinosaur, but could barely see it through a strange, orange, smokey miasma.

No, not smoke, he thought. *It's fog.* He looked around. *But inside?*

Then a spark ignited overhead. The quick flash morphed into a bolt of lightning and it streaked across the vaulted, arched ceiling of the room, but in super slow motion. He expected it to detonate when it eventually struck the far wall, but it didn't. The lightning, if that's what it was, just continued into the wall as if it weren't really there.

"A projection?" he asked, struggling to get the words out.

He climbed to his feet and took in the state of the rotunda.

Nothing had exploded, but that didn't keep the visitors, and staff, from panicking. People stepped on one another as they rushed for the front doors, filing into and through the turnstiles at capacity. Noah didn't, though. With no immediate threat present, he stood still and caught his breath. His head began to clear too—some. But even Noah went wide-eyed as the fog grew denser, smelling of ozone. Something else was coming. He could feel it.

To hell with this!

He joined the fray and waited his turn to enter the turnstile. It had already been a slightly claustrophobic experience, and now, it absolutely was. The other people with him must've been feeling the same thing because they huffed and pushed harder and harder until everyone spilled outside together.

Noah caught himself before he could fall, and as one person after the other bumped by him, all he could do was take in the state of Central Park. It was right there, across Central Park West, and yet, he couldn't see it. The fog was too thick, and even out here, it crackled with fervent, slow-moving electricity.

A bolt lanced out at him. Noah covered his head and closed his eyes, but nothing happened. He opened them to find it moving as slow as the others, only this one was passing straight through his gut. Noah stood in place and twisted his upper body around to confirm as much. The bolt of lightning had exited his back and entered the front of the museum, also passing through several other, equally frightened, people.

Noah simply sidestepped out of the midway point of the bolt, just for his own sanity.

"What the hell is going on?"

Just as the words came out of his mouth, the flashes of

lightning began to wane and the fog started to slowly dissipate. And just when the strangeness of the event had seemingly concluded, the most amazing, and terrifying thing happened.

A woman rushed down the steps and onto the sidewalk, fifty feet from where Noah stood. Then she looked south and screamed. Out of the fog came a herd of living and breathing *Gallimimus*. The ostrich-like creatures screeched at her as they sprinted by, moving like a coordinated flock of flightless birds, trampling several people as they moved. With nowhere to go, the woman ducked in place, going into a catcher's squat, and covering her head with her hands. Once the animals were gone, she stood, no doubt counting her lucky stars—only to have a mammoth set of jaws snap shut on her, and cut her in half at the waist with the single bite. Noah's eyes bugged out of their sockets as the owner of the jaws slipped out of the fog next: a *Tyrannosaurus rex*.

"Oh, my God."

It swallowed down the top half of the innocent museum patron, turned, and roared right at Noah. The paleontologist backpedaled toward the doors. His face was frozen in shock, his brain still trying to process what he'd seen—what was happening to New York City, and possibly the world.

He reached behind him, blindly swiping at the door, searching for it, unable to pry his eyes off the prehistoric invasion unfolding before him. And that's what this was. Somehow, animals from the Cretaceous Period, an era of time dominated by some of the largest, fiercest animals to ever inhabit planet Earth, had been brought here, to the modern day.

A faraway cry turned his attention skyward, but the fog was still too thick in places to see much of anything above ground level. But then, it appeared, diving straight at Noah. The *Pteranodon* dropped almost right on top of him. It had its legs out and its talon-tipped feet spread open, ready to snag Noah as if it were a bear catching a leaping salmon.

At the last second, it opened its wings to arrest its fall, but Noah was already diving inside the enclosed turnstile. With Noah out of reach, it landed and shoved its six-foot-long head into the rotating entrance, including its three-foot-long beak. Noah leapt to his feet, flattened himself against the other side of the turnstile, and sucked in his gut. The *Pteranodon* jabbed at his stomach with the pointed end of its beak but found nothing. Noah drove his weight into the door, rotating and closing it on the animal's neck. It freaked out and yanked its head free, letting loose an angry caw at its escaping prey.

Noah fell through the opening behind him, back into the museum. He landed flat on his back but didn't notice his lack of wind. He already couldn't breathe because of the last handful of minutes, let alone the hard fall. For now, he just lay there and took in what he saw, replaying it in his mind.

None of this could possibly be happening. The only explanation was the fog.

"Gas leak..." he said, between heavy inhalations. "Has to be..."

But somehow, Noah knew this wasn't just some *run-of-the-mill* hallucination. It was only his brain trying to process and cope with the events. People were dying outside, and it was because of dinosaurs.

He let out a long breath and leaned up on his elbows. "What the hell, man."

Noah pushed himself off the floor, stumbled forward, and

caught himself on the frame of the turnstile door. He let out another long breath, then turned, only to have a fast-moving blonde run into him. The top of her head smashed against Noah's chin, causing him to bite his lip and draw blood. For her efforts, she rebounded off his chest and went sprawling to the floor in a heap. He licked his lip, but paused when he saw who had just assaulted him.

"Oh, hey there."

He had met eyes with this one not too long before the cosmic storm hit. Noah had just been called over by Constance Farr, the museum's director, for a very unemotional, overly formal hello. But that was Constance. Emotions had always played second fiddle for her, which was precisely why her husband had left her. She had even admitted as much. Constance had given Paul zero animosity when he had asked her to sign the divorce papers. The two went about the proper proceedings, and Paul left. Just like that.

It had stunned Noah to hear, but who was he to judge?

The blonde looked up at him, blinking her eyes hard. "Uh, hi..." Noah was pretty sure she had thumped her head against the floor.

"Sorry about that. You were moving pretty fast."

She blushed, obviously embarrassed by her actions. "It's...fine." Noah reached down to help her up, and she accepted. "Sorry about the lip." Once she was back on her feet, and steady, she tried to slip around Noah and into the turnstile.

He gripped the back of her arm to stop her. "Whoa there. You don't want to go outside."

She tried to pull out of his grip but couldn't. "But—my kids! I have to—"

"Do you trust them?" Noah asked, stopping her outburst mid-sentence.

"What?" she asked with a look of confusion.

Noah loosened his grip on her arm. "Are they smart?"

"Yeah, I guess..."

Noah let her go this time. "Wow, not much confidence there."

She gave Noah a glare and turned on him. "Look...whoever you are...it's been a rough couple of years, okay? I'm not very 'confident' about anything anymore."

Awfully grim of her, he thought.

"Look, it's chaos out there. If your kids aren't complete bricks, I'm sure they stayed put indoors." She looked over her shoulder at the door, then seemed to relax a bit. "What's your name?"

"Sarah, Sarah Rakestraw."

Noah held out his hand. "Noah Clark."

She cocked her head to the side and squinted. "*Doctor* Noah Clark—the paleontologist who found, well, that?" Sarah pointed at the *Dreadnoughtus* without looking away from him.

"You know who I am?" he asked, impressed, and slightly uncomfortable. Noah wasn't used to being picked out of a crowd.

"*Pff*, only because my daughter knows everything about dinosaurs from its era, yeah." Now it was Noah's turn to tilt his head to the side and stare. "Believe me," she continued, "she does."

A small smile crept onto Noah's face. "Congrats. Sounds like you have a future paleontologist for a daughter, though I do have to warn you, it's not a *glamorous* lifestyle."

Sarah's expression morphed into one of amusement for a split second before returning to its earlier, ultra-serious form. "Yeah, I'm not so sure of that. Becca doesn't exactly like, you know, people."

Noah chuckled softly. "Sounds like my kind of girl." As soon as the words left his lips, Sarah's right eyebrow rose. Noah rolled his eyes at her reaction. "You know what I mean..."

"Not much of a people person yourself?"

Noah turned and faced the skeleton. "I prefer the company of things that have been dead for sixty-five million years."

"*Touché*." She looked up at the dinosaur again. "Becca's different, though. She has a developmental disorder, and only ever thinks about dinosaurs. We call her brain the 'Sponge of Infinity.'"

"Forgive me for asking, but is she on the spectrum?"

Sarah nodded. "Asperger's, yeah. You familiar with it?"

Noah nodded. "Sure am. I have this cousin back home in Oklahoma, he's sort of the same way as your daughter, but with car engines. Lord knows he can't work on them, but he can tell you everything about them."

Noah and Sarah paused and met stares. They each looked away. Noah cleared his throat and returned his attention to his dinosaur. Sarah's face flushed, she tucked a loose strand of hair behind her ear, looking at the floor as she did.

"So," Noah said, breaking the awkwardness, "your kids?"

Sarah glanced at the front doors, then back, deeper into the rotunda. "Please, help me find them."

"You try calling them?" he asked, covering all bases.

Sarah pulled her phone out of her pocket, tapped the screen, then flipped it around so he could see it. "No service. Whatever happened, it fried the network." She pocketed it and looked him over. "You haven't tried yours?"

"I've been a little preoccupied," he replied, shrugging. "What about their father, is he here?" Sarah didn't reply with anything except a hard stare. "Right, touchy subject. The only reason I asked was because of the ring..."

Sarah slipped her hands into her front pockets, effectively ending anything else to be said about her wedding band.

Oookay.

Noah looked around, then listened to the garbled noise coming from outside the museum's doors. "Sure, why not?" He stuck his thumb out, aiming it at the doors to his back. "It's not like I'm going back out there anytime soon."

"That bad?" she asked, eyeing the nearest turnstile.

"Yeah." He pointed at the *Dreadnoughtus*. "Imagine those—but with skin. All of them. Even the ones with sharp teeth and a less-than-cheery disposition." He let out a long breath. "A couple seconds before we, uh, *met*, I watched a real-life *T. rex* eat someone."

Understandably, Sarah's lower jaw hit the floor. She faced the doors. "What the hell is happening, Noah?"

"I have no idea..." he replied, voice trailing off. He stepped away thinking.

"What's wrong?" she asked. He glanced over at her. "Besides the world ending."

Noah removed his ballcap and combed his fingers through his overgrown mop of brown hair. When he replaced it, pulling it down tight, he faced Sarah and explained.

"Earlier today—when I first came in—I overheard two people outside. They were talking about a star that had gone supernova. They said its remains were supposed to hit Earth," he looked down at his watch, "a few minutes ago."

"Oh, God," Sarah said, eyes going wide. "I read about that last night. No one at NASA had any idea what was going to happen, either. What *did* happen..." She rubbed her face with both hands. "Didn't think anything of it 'til now."

Noah got moving, heading toward the rear of the rotunda, toward an entrance leading into the Hall of African Mammals.

"Think that's what caused all this?" Sarah asked, falling in line next to him.

"I think it's pretty clear that it did. And now, the animals from the Cretaceous Period are here—with us."

She bit her lip and looked over her shoulder. "Think it's a global issue?"

"I seriously doubt it's just Manhattan that was affected."

"Right," Sarah said, blowing out a long breath, "even we don't have that kind of luck."

Noah glanced over at her, but she was lost in thought—in a memory. The *we* didn't include him. That had obviously been reserved for her and her family.

What the hell happened to these people?

4

Three tall archways served as exits out of the Roosevelt Rotunda. The right-hand exit led out into a hallway that ran left-to-right. Directly across from the archway itself was an exhibit labeled, "The Butterfly Conservatory." But if you made the left, and took the long, tiled corridor, you passed beneath a sign for the "Rose Center for Earth and Space." The rotunda's left-hand exit led patrons into the Hall of Asian Mammals, and like the prior corridor, it also contained a tiled hallway that would lead you deeper into the museum—to other exhibits.

Noah and Sarah didn't head for either. They continued straight across the room, toward the Hall of African Mammals. They passed between two, long ticket counters on their way to it. Noah nearly stomped past them without looking, but a whispered voice caught his attention.

"Noah."

He paused and turned right, in the direction of the voice. A slight figure crawled out from beneath one of the ticket counters, pushing a rolling office chair aside as she did. Then the person stood on trembling legs.

"Connie?" Noah asked. He headed straight for her and embraced the older woman. "You okay?"

The museum director's eyes were wide and wild. She nodded and replied, "No, you?"

Noah shook his head, then looked back at Sarah, getting an idea. "We could actually use your help with something." That seemed to focus Constance.

"What with?" she asked.

Noah held out his hand, inviting Sarah over. "Sarah Rakestraw, this is Constance Farr, director of the museum. We need to find her kids, Connie, and no one knows this place better than you." He tipped his head back toward the rotunda's exit. "Think you can guide us along?"

Constance glanced at Sarah, then back up at the *much* taller Noah. He absolutely towered over her. "Sure. Yes, of course." She cleared her throat and brushed off her dress.

"Right," Noah said, facing Sarah, "so where do you think they may have gone? Any guesses?"

Sarah bit her lip again. It was clear to Noah that it was her thinking face. Then she re-tucked the same strand of hair behind her ear. "Yeah, the dinosaur halls. They're Becca's favorite."

Constance took a deep breath. "Okay. That would be the fourth floor, but..."

"But what?"

She lowered her voice and said, "The reason we were hiding," Noah looked past her and discovered more people hiding beneath the subsequent ticket counters. Something had spooked them into hiding, "...is that there's something in here with us."

Noah stood tall, his mind going a million miles a minute. "Describe it. Be thorough."

The retired paleontologist scoffed at the notion. "It's like you don't even know me..." She blew out a long breath. "Smallish theropod—a little shorter than me—about eight to nine feet long too. Oh, and it was feathered."

"Theropod?" Sarah asked, looking back and forth between them both. "Can one of you give me a quick refresher?"

"Yeah," Noah replied, nodding his head softly, still lost in thought. He blinked then explained, "Essentially, it means 'wild beast foot.' It's a broad dinosaur clade that sports three-toed feet and three-clawed, uh, hands, if that's what you want to call them."

"Carnivores?" Sarah asked, looking around nervously.

"Some of the most famous ones were, yes."

"Like your rex?"

He nodded again. "Uh-huh."

Sarah's shoulders sagged. "Wonderful."

"What do you mean by *his* rex?" Constance asked, eyeing Sarah.

She gently placed her hand on Noah's shoulder. "Tell her what you saw outside."

Constance whirled on Noah, and a little too loudly asked, "You saw a *Tyrannosaurus* outside?"

"Shhh!" Noah and Sarah hissed in unison.

The woman flinched, but apologized with a nod.

"Oh, I saw a lot more than *just* our rex."

Noah quickly recounted what he saw, describing it in vivid detail. It was hard to forget, after all. He also knew that it was something that would haunt him for some time—forever, more than likely. He had never seen anyone lose their lives. Even his own father had passed away without Noah being by his side. The one major difference with Kenneth Clark's death was that it had been expected. The woman who had been cut down by the rex, her death had been sudden—unexpected—and brutal.

"Well, whatever it is you saw here," Noah said, shaking off his rising nerves, "let's hope we don't run into it." He took a step away, but stopped, and looked back at both women. "And let's hope it isn't a carnivore."

Constance peeked into the central exit, then wiped a bead of sweat away from her forehead. "Follow me, please." She stepped away. The sound that her heels made was like repeating gunshots in the still air of the museum.

Noah grabbed her shoulder and looked down at her feet. "Wait." Constance faced him, then also gazed down at her feet. "Gonna have to ditch those, Connie."

The director looked up at Noah, then back down at her feet. Her shoulders dipped slightly, but she didn't argue and slipped out of them. Now she was even shorter, if that were even possible. Constance bent over and snagged the heels, intent on bringing them along.

"Another question," Sarah said, speaking softly. "Since dinosaurs are now here, with us humans, are there fossil records to support activity like this in New York City?"

"I've been thinking the same thing," Noah replied. "And no, I don't think so. Connie?"

She shook her head, causing her short bob to follow suit and sashay back and forth. "I've lived here all my life. Even wrote a paper on the subject eons ago." She waved her hand

and explained. "Unsuitable bedrock conditions, erosion, ancient glacial activity, urban development... I know, for a fact, that there have never been any dinosaur bones found in New York City. None of this makes any sense."

"Which part?" Sarah asked.

Constance shot her a glance. "All of it."

"I know, right?" Noah added. "I just saw a herd of *Gallimimus* running from a *T. rex*. Then I got chased indoors by a *Pteranodon*."

"Would that have been unusual sixty-five million years ago?" Sarah asked.

Noah slowed as they neared the hallway beyond the rotunda. He leaned around the corner and took a look just as the lights began to blink on and off.

Come on, really?

As a result, half of them stayed off, casting some interesting shadows everywhere.

He turned and faced Sarah and explained what was bothering him. "Okay, so rex and the flyer would've had contact. They were both from the same area here in what would eventually become North America, specifically Utah, Wyoming, the Dakotas... But *Gallimimus*—its remains are found on the other side of the planet, over in modern-day Mongolia and parts of China."

"Oh, but how?"

Noah scratched his chin and shrugged. "No idea. But whatever caused our prehistoric friends to be thrown into the future—supernova or not—it didn't care what their original locations were."

"It looks to have scrambled them up," Constance added, nodding in agreement.

"Which also means that territories and behaviors will be scrambled too."

Sarah glanced back into the rotunda nervously. "That can't be good, right?"

"No," Noah replied, regaining her attention, "it can't. Every living thing brought here will be hyper-disoriented, and worst of all, on edge and angry."

"Including the big herbivores, I bet," Constance said.

"Yes, even them. Like a hippo is today, the herbivores from prehistory were some of the most dangerous creatures to ever exist."

"This just keeps getting better and better," Sarah muttered, sighing.

Noah stepped out into the hallway. "That all depends on what else was dropped into the city," he pointed at the floor, "including inside the museum."

Sarah kept close to him, as did Constance.

"Anything terrible come to mind?" the mother of two asked.

"Yeah," Noah replied, nodding.

"Care to share?"

He gave her a quick look. "No, I'd rather not magically speak them into existence." Then Noah eyed his long-time friend. "Connie, if you would?"

She nodded. "Alright, the stairs are this way."

5

Kyle was livid. When whatever happened had happened, he had caught a glimpse of his sister bolting through one of the rotunda's exits. Knowing that he'd be the one to blame for her leaving, he had decided to follow her, fighting waves of nausea and blistering headaches as he did.

At first, he had trouble keeping up with her. He listened for her hurried footfalls as they clambered up and up flights of stairs. Kyle had even called after her, hoping she would, but betting on that she wouldn't, reply. And, of course, she didn't. Then it had dawned on him, and he slowed. He knew exactly where she was going and had no reason to rush.

It was then that he noticed that he was missing an earbud.

"Stupid girl," he said growling and looking around his feet. "That's coming out of your allowance."

He readjusted his backwards trucker hat, one featuring a stylized, half-mechanical oni-demon from Japanese folklore.

The only reason he knew anything about them was because it was the symbol for a fictitious band that was featured prominently in his favorite video game *Cyberpunk 2077*. The band, one fueled by piss, vinegar, and revolution against the suffocating corporations of the game's world, was called Samurai.

Kyle slowed as he reached the fourth floor. He was winded and angry, but some of the latter had burned off with time. Now he was more annoyed than anything—annoyed that it was always him who was saddled with looking after his baby sister.

Why me...

He now stood within the David H. Koch Dinosaur Wing. To his left, and at the end of one of several maze-like halls inside the museum, was the "Dino Store" gift shop. And six feet before the store, there was an opening leading into one of two dinosaur-themed halls—exhibits. But the Hall of Ornithischian Dinosaurs was not where he'd find Becca.

Kyle headed to his right, then took another quick right. He passed two elevators. Both looked to be down for the count.

"Hmmm," he mumbled, curious if it had been the weird fog that had caused it. Or maybe it had been the trippy light show; lightning that phased in and out while also speeding up and slowing down, yet seemed to cause no damage.

Kyle had gotten high a couple of times in his life, with friends his mom didn't approve of, and he had never experienced a trip like what he had experienced only a few minutes ago.

Thirty feet past the elevators, Kyle stopped and turned left. He looked up at the sign, reading it to himself.

Hall of Saurischian Dinosaurs.

Kyle had no idea what *Saurischian* meant, nor did he know

what the hell *Ornithischian* meant. The only reason he could even pronounce them was because they had been here more times than he could count.

Let's see. Twice a year for forever equals...

Kyle wished his mom would do stuff like this for him occasionally, but no, Becca and her "disorder" came first. Always. No matter what.

He sighed and stepped through the entrance. There was an odd, banner-like display almost as soon as you entered. He stepped around it, instantly finding who he was looking for: Becca. Seeing her reignited his earlier rage. He narrowed his focus on her and stomped over.

"Dammit, Becca," he growled, "you are in *so much* trouble."

And, as expected, she just stared up at the specimen, an admittedly impressive *Tyrannosaurus rex* skeleton. Kyle stepped up next to her, glaring at her with angst. But all she could do was stare up at the carnivore.

"Did you hear me?" he asked loudly. He stepped away and stopped next to another nearby case. "Something weird just happened and the only thing you could think to do was run off to your boy, Rex, and his other dumb, dead, dino buddies!" Kyle pounded his fist on the second display case. He turned away and stomped his foot. "God, I hate this place!"

When he faced his sister again, a single tear ran down her cheek. The sight instantly made Kyle feel like a prick.

"*Albertosaurus*," she finally said, still not looking away from the creature. Then, she pointed up at it. "This is a *T. rex.*"

Kyle took in his sister closely now. Her leg was twitching, as were her hands. She was terrified, but didn't know how to express it properly. So, she had run, to the one place in the entire museum that Kyle knew would calm her down—make her feel safe—make her happy.

"Crap," he said, rejoining her. He gently wrapped his arm around her shoulder, then patiently waited for her to initiate the next step. It took her a second, but she eventually leaned into him a little, though her eyes remained fixated on the rex.

"Look, I'm sorry," he apologized, meaning every word. "It's not easy looking after you, you know?" Kyle looked up from the top of his sister's head and to the dinosaur, blowing out a long, pain-filled breath before speaking his next words. "Not since Dad died..."

"I miss him," she said softly, focus unwavering. The zones—trances—she could get into were creepy to witness sometimes. Being "dead to the world" was something that Kyle knew all too well when it came to playing video games or listening to music, but Becca's *zones* were downright spooky at times.

He squeezed her harder. "Yeah, I know, me too."

The two Rakestraw kids stood in silence for a while, just enjoying one another's company. Despite Kyle's longing for a normal life, he and Becca still had moments like this on occasion. He was pretty sure he understood why too. *He* was the only man in her life, and he was closer to her age than their mom was. But more than that, Becca understood deep down that the two of them were bonded for life. She trusted him, and he needed to remember that.

Kyle also needed to remember that she was not a normal twelve-year-old girl. Her needs were much different from those of other girls her age. Becca didn't need to be parented by her older brother. The only thing that was required of him was to be there for her, which he sometimes wasn't.

Damn, maybe I am a prick?

But there was no maybe about it. Kyle knew, deep down, that he sometimes could be one, and that those sometimes had been a lot more often recently. He wiped a tear from his eye, wishing his father was standing there with them to console them both. Kyle needed him more than ever right now.

A noise made both kids hold their breath and snap their heads around to the left, back toward the entrance. The only way Kyle could've explained what he'd heard was that it was an animal of some kind on the prowl in the hallway outside this hall.

A snarl?

Then, a second noise caused them to jump back—the sudden scream of a frightened man, wailing as something attacked him. A heavy *thud* followed, then more shouts. After three heartbeats, the agonized cries turned to wet gurgles and gasps.

Finally, the worst sound imaginable: the sound of a large predator of some kind eating—eating the remains of a human being. The munch and crunch made Kyle gag and force down his rising vomit.

"We need to get out of here and find Mom," Kyle whispered, looking around.

"We can't," Becca said, staring at the hall's entrance.

Kyle looked away from it and down at his sister. "Why not?"

"Because..." she looked up at the *T. rex*, "it's here."

"What is?" he asked, likewise gazing up at the tall, bipedal carnivore.

Becca returned her attention to him, staring into his eyes and said, "A dinosaur."

6

"Nearly there," Constance said, leading them onto, yet another, landing between stairs.

Noah nodded and took in the last flight with discomfort. They had made it this far without conflict, which was beyond a blessing. Noah had expected Constance's feathered friend to show its ugly mug at some point. Regardless of what animal it truly was, carnivore or not, he figured it'd be able to pick out their scent easily and come look for the oddball animals it was smelling.

They stopped on the bottom step of the last flight and took a moment. Noah rested his knees, while Constance massaged her lower back. She was almost twenty-five years older than he was, and he doubted she used the stairs all that often when traveling between floors.

Noah's discomfort wasn't from his youthful days. In fact, his knees were bothering him because of his current profession.

Hiking through unstable terrain and kneeling and lying down on coarse, unyielding stone had nearly destroyed his lower body. Luckily, he was able to maintain a solid foundation when it came to his physique. Noah was still in great shape, all things considered, though a touch heavier than he'd been in college.

Easy, Noah, he thought. *You're in your forties, remember.*

"Anyone else see the lightning?" he asked.

Constance nodded, but Sarah shook her head.

"Must've missed it when I was out cold."

Noah shrugged. "It was...something." He tipped his chin up the steps. "Ready?"

Both women confirmed with small nods and they got moving. They reached the top moments later, but suddenly paused four steps short.

Noah held up his hand. "Hang on. Let's figure out where we're going before we step into the unknown."

Constance turned to Sarah. "Where will your daughter be, the Hall of Saurischian Dinosaurs or the Hall of Ornithischian Dinosaurs?"

Sarah bit her lip, then replied, "Whichever one has the *T. rex* skull."

"That would be the Saurischian exhibit," Constance said, motioning to the right-side of the neighboring hallway. She took a step forward. "This way."

"Connie," Noah said, gently touching her arm. "Let me have a look first, okay?"

The museum director nodded and backed down two steps, giving Noah room. He stepped up to the fourth floor and peeked left, seeing nothing out of the ordinary besides more of the now deserted museum. Then, he leaned around to the right, looking

180 degrees, back the other way, and there, lying on the floor in a pool of blood, was a ravaged human corpse. He swallowed back his bile, stared a moment longer, taking in the body's clothing and hair color, then returned to Sarah and Constance.

"What did you see?" Sarah asked.

He faced her, feeling his face flush with grief. "Your kids... What were they wearing?"

"Why?" she asked, giving him a confused look.

Noah preemptively held up his hands in a calming gesture, knowing her reaction wasn't going to be good. "There's a body on the floor just outside of where we're going and—"

Sarah ducked beneath his right arm and sprinted up and around the corner. As soon as she saw the body, she staggered away, holding her hands to her mouth, eyes releasing tears down her cheeks.

Noah helped her sit. "I'm so sorry."

Covering her mouth still, Sarah shook her head. When she lowered her hands, she let out a soft sob, then calmed. "No, it's okay. It isn't one of them."

"Oh, thank God," Constance said, visibly relaxing.

Noah blew out a long breath of relief. "Okay, good, well, except for whoever that was." He faced Constance and asked, "There's another way into that area, isn't there, from the back side?"

"There is," she replied. "It's a bit of a walk, though."

Noah glanced over his shoulder and looked at the right-hand wall of the stairwell. He visualized the body lying on the floor just outside of their destination. There was no way in hell he was going that way.

"Lead the way," he said, turning and looking at her. "I'd prefer to avoid whatever it is that killed that person."

"Same," Constance said. Her eyes shifted over to Sarah. "You alright, my dear?"

Sarah nodded. "Yeah... Seeing the body made me think about what could've happened to my son and daughter. My mind showed me them lying there instead. It...broke me for a second." She looked up at Noah. "What about you?"

Noah held out his hand and helped Sarah to her feet, shaking off the question. "I'm fine. Connie?"

The museum director nodded and tiptoed out into the hallway, heels in hand, heading left, toward the Dino Store and the other exhibit. Sarah went next.

Noah hung back for a moment. He let out a long breath and held up his hands, watching them shiver. He curled his fingers into fists and squeezed, then relaxed them, shaking them out vigorously. He was scared. There was no denying it. The prospects of an event like this, humans and dinosaurs somehow coming together, was one of the reasons he loved the area of study. As a kid, he used to imagine what it would be like. Noah knew it would be terrifying to live alongside Earth's prehistoric rulers, but he never thought it possible, even through genetic engineering.

Nothing could've prepared him for this, not even that same overactive imagination. Surviving in a world like this would be nearly impossible despite mankind's technological achievements, especially if this "invasion" was truly global. Noah still believed it was, and he'd continue believing it until proven otherwise.

They made it to the arched opening that served as the entrance to the Hall of Ornithischian Dinosaurs. Constance

36

arrived first, but did not step through. Noah and Sarah joined her and waited. From what they could tell, the entire hall was deserted, like much of the museum, not that they had explored every nook and cranny of it. But Noah recalled hordes of people rushing past him as he dealt with the crippling discomfort caused by the storm, wondering why it had affected him, and even Sarah, so badly.

Noah took a peek inside the gift shop, just to make sure it had also been deserted, but as he leaned inside, he heard something coming from back down the hall. He slowly stood erect and turned. The lighting was still out of whack. Some lights worked, others didn't. In this case, a shape was quickly coming into focus in the way of a hunched shadow, and it was coming from the direction of the body.

Whatever creature had killed that poor soul, it was still here with Noah, Sarah, and Constance.

"Come on!" Noah whispered sharply, ushering the two women into the store.

No one argued. They ducked inside just as the shape fully emerged—not that the human survivors saw what it was. They were too busy looking for somewhere to hide. Unfortunately, the shop was small and offered few places. It was a rectangle as big as an average-sized living room with a single items rack at its center. All of the other wares were either stocked on wall-mounted shelves or over on the counter containing the cash register.

That'll have to do, Noah thought.

He grabbed Sarah's wrist and hauled her behind the waist-high counter. Constance was hot on their heels. Noah sat with his back against it. Sarah knelt to his right and Constance gingerly got down on both knees and dipped her head as low as she could.

Light footsteps built up louder as their owner moved closer. Noah pushed himself off the floor enough to look over the counter. He gazed up at the top of the doors, seeing a rolling gate. If he could shut it, they'd more than likely be safe.

But they'd also be trapped.

He sat back down and turned to Constance. "Is there a way out of here—or even a stock room?"

She looked past him, toward the back left corner of the room. There, not twenty feet from their current position, was an unlabeled, closed door. Noah cursed himself for not taking an extra second to look around. They could've been inside, behind a solid barrier, not here, praying their hunter didn't simply lean over, or even around, an indefensible counter.

He pushed himself off the floor again. If he was going to die, he wanted to see what was coming before it could tear out his throat. But as he locked in on the store's front door, his eyes dropped to something sitting atop the counter. There, acting as enticing point-of-sale merchandise, were three six-inch-tall figures. And since they were inside the "Dino Store," those *toys* were obviously of the dinosaur variety.

It's just an animal. Noah plucked the middle figure from its place, a *Brachiosaurus*, and returned to his hiding spot.

"Get ready to move for the back door," he said softly.

"What are you doing?" Sarah asked.

Noah simply held up the toy. The non-answer caused Sarah to glance at Constance. The museum director could only shrug.

Footsteps grew even louder. Noah could tell that their owner was now right outside the door. The animal began to sniff deeply. He pictured an enormous dog testing the air. It knew they were here, but couldn't tell exactly where they were.

Then it happened. The beast entered the Dino Store in search of its next kill. Noah took a deep breath and waited, visualizing the storefront. From the sound of the animal's steps, it was on the opposite side, possibly behind the centrally located items rack. Depending on how tall it was, it wouldn't be able to see Noah as he quietly climbed to his feet.

When he did, he froze, seeing the back third of the...dinosaur. *Oh, my God.*

It was a theropod, as Constance had described, and it was covered in feathers everywhere except for around its feet, just like a modern-day bird. But that's where its similarities to its descendants ended. Regrettably, the paleontologist couldn't see its midsection or head, so properly identifying it would be impossible. But that needed to take a backseat to their survival—and it did.

Noah chucked the *Brachiosaurus* toy out through the door then slunk back into place between Sarah and Constance. The result was instantaneous. The beast growled, then shifted its weight and, presumably, looked the other way. Noah watched it happen in his mind. The dinosaur's clawed feet pivoted then dug into the tiled floor, making a harsh scraping as they looked for purchase. The bottoms of its callused feet did the same, rubbing against the floor like sandpaper on stone.

Sarah and Constance both had their heads tucked into their chests, covering the former with their hands. But Noah didn't. He was too invested in what was happening behind him to do so. Yes, he was slouched down a little, but his eyes were wide, staring through the wall in front of him. He would've given anything to see what was going on...other than his life.

And the lives of others.

He let out a long exhalation, getting himself under control. Noah wasn't familiar with helping others in the same way a police officer or soldier might've been, but he had been raised to look after those who couldn't fend for themselves. As a kid, that meant smaller, shyer classmates. Back then, Noah had a knack for putting bullies in their place.

As an adult, it hadn't been the same. He didn't go around beating up jerkoff grownups, though he had met plenty who needed a good ass kicking. No, Noah just tried to help anyone that needed it, in a way he knew how. Like now, with Sarah and Constance. Taking care of them had been the right thing to do, so here he was.

The animal's footsteps continued toward the door, then after a moment of sniffing—probably investigating the inert, tiny *Brachiosaurus*, the theropod carnivore was gone.

"Sounds like it's bypassing the Hall of Ornithischian Dinosaurs," Constance said with hope in her voice.

Noah closed his eyes and nodded. His own brush with death came to the forefront of his mind. That mountain lion had come so close to a meal that day.

Not now, Noah.

"Probably heading back to its kill," he said, letting out a long breath.

"You okay?" Sarah asked.

He opened his eyes and smiled. "Yeah. Got lost in the moment for a second. Nerves are on fire. Feels like I just scored a game-winner."

"Basketball?"

"Football," Constance replied. "Our Noah was quite the athlete growing up. Went on to be a highly touted, college recruit."

Sarah's right eyebrow rose a little. "And yet, you've been a paleontologist for the better part of your life. I—"

Noah raised his hand to stop her. "*I* will tell you later. Come on."

Before either of the women could add anything, he pushed himself up. Constance happily accepted his help off the hard floor, but Sarah got up easily on her own. Noah placed a finger over his lips and stepped lightly toward their exit. As much as he wanted to crawl into the stockroom and hide, they still had a mission. They needed to find Sarah's kids.

Before it's too late. He peeked into the hallway, seeing nothing. Then, he glanced back at Constance and Sarah, holding the latter's eyes for a split second longer. He waved them forward. *If it's not too late already.*

1

Kyle didn't care that the dinosaur had bypassed their exhibit and continued down the outside hallway. He had grabbed Becca's hand and half-dragged her further and further away. Becca had kept her head on a swivel the entire time, and not because she was worried about dying. Kyle knew she just wanted to see which dinosaur it was, more than anything, even over concern for their wellbeing.

But Kyle didn't want to die—not now at sixteen—and not mauled to death by some prehistoric shithead. If he were to die young, he figured it would be because he partied too hard while on tour or after too many fourteen-hour days in the studio, like some of his favorite vocalists—not that he had any interest in hardcore drugs.

He'd grown up listening to his father's favorite bands: Alice in Chains, Soundgarden, Stone Temple Pilots... Nineties grunge had always been Kyle's favorite "genre." But unfortunately, that era of rock music had also produced a lot of drug addicts and alcoholics, as did the Seattle music scene where heroin was incredibly easy to obtain, and to afford.

Coincidentally, the singers of his three favorite grunge bands were all dead. Lane Staley, Chris Cornell, and Scott Weiland had all died tragically from substance abuse problems and suffocating depression. Some people say it had been their lifestyle that had influenced their sound—their art. And maybe, it was. But Kyle had no plans to follow in their footsteps in that way. His father, Mark Rakestraw, had taught him better than that.

Pot was fine, so were the gummies. Kyle hadn't experimented with booze all that much, nor did it really interest him. He'd hung out with a few girls that loved the sugary, froufrou drinks, but not Kyle. Anything harder than feeling a "relaxed high" was something he didn't want to mess with. His mind had been bent enough following the death of his father. He didn't need a high-octane narcotic to do it for him. Honestly, he was afraid of what might emerge from the anger he'd been squelching.

Are we really doing this now, brain? he thought, struggling to maintain his grip on Becca's wrist.

They hurried deeper through the Hall of Saurischian Dinosaurs, passing an impressive Apatosaurus specimen. The big herbivore was built similarly to the others Kyle knew about from his sister...and his father. His father had loved dinosaurs too, and he knew that it was *their* shared love that had driven *him* away from the subject. Becca needed special treatment, and their father, like their mother, had spent his fair share of time working with Becca.

And it had pissed Kyle off.

It had also made him resent himself as he'd gotten older.

A low, guttural sound picked up behind them. Both Rakestraws skidded to a stop, unable to keep themselves from looking back and seeing what had created the noise. The animal looked like a feather raptor, but it was much bigger. Even Kyle knew how much Hollywood had overstated the size of a *Velociraptor*. This wasn't a raptor, though. It was thickly built and stood as tall as he did.

"Oh, shit."

"It's a—"

He didn't let Becca go into one of her info-tangents. He yanked her through the exhibit's exit, much to the displeasure of their hunter. As they hooked around to the left and into the next exhibit, the animal called out with a sound that resembled anger and frustration. They ran, zooming by a handful of fossils on their left, and several racks of merchandise on their right. A cash register followed up on the left, as did an emergency exit. For a split second, Kyle thought about diverting their path and using what he figured were stairs on the other side.

But what if there was already something waiting for them beyond the door? Kyle had no interest in finding out. Plus, he wanted to keep them on the fourth floor.

Where are you, Mom?

The oddly positioned gift shop ended on the right with a set of doors. They leapt through, then Kyle slammed them shut. Then he went to lock the doors, but couldn't. The deadbolt's thumb turn was on the other side. The only thing they had here was a slot where the key fit inside.

"Keep moving," he said, once again grabbing Becca's wrist. She resisted him for a moment, but quickly fell in line beside him when the doors were hit from the opposite side.

They turned and fled into the Hall of Vertebrate Origins. This room was huge and filled with displays that rivaled those of the *T. rex* room. The animals here weren't all dinosaurs, either. There was a section dedicated to prehistoric flyers in the *Pterosaur* family on the left. The first area on the right was dedicated to the ancestors of modern-day crocodiles and alligators.

Crocodylotarsians, Kyle read as they passed, not even attempting to sound it out loud.

They hurried beneath a giant turtle that was suspended from the ceiling, as well as its neighbor, a *Plesiosaur*, one of several species that cryptid enthusiasts believed could've been the Loch Ness Monster. Next were fish of all kinds, and Kyle's favorite ancient animal, the *Megalodon*—the jaws of one, anyway.

There was also a streak of blood on the floor. Kyle protectively stepped in front of Becca, but she had already noticed it. Whoever the trail had belonged to had been killed and dragged behind a sign designating that the area belonged to the animals of the Chondrichthyan family.

Kyle's hands shook as he read the small print beneath the clunky names. *Sharks, rays, and their relatives.*

Thankfully, the pounding behind them had stopped. They turned away from the gore, then leaned against a nearby wall, catching their breath. Kyle looked away from the exhibit, finding doorways on either side of him and Becca.

"Eh, screw it, come on," he said, stepping toward the men's restroom.

"Ew, no!" Becca argued. "I am not going in there."

Kyle wheeled on her, but quickly relaxed. "Why not? It'll smell like pee. Might mask our scent, right?"

Becca shrugged. "Or the smell will attract it even more."

"Yeah, good point. Let's keep looking."

They exited the Hall of Vertebrate Origins and entered the next room in the maze that was the fourth floor, the Miriam and Ira D. Wallach Orientation Center. Kyle recalled sitting through a film about what to expect in the fossil halls. To his right were rows of benches and a large projection screen that had been mounted to the wall. The exit was to their left, but at the center of the space was the single biggest skeleton cast he had ever seen.

"*Patagotitan mayorum*," Becca said, staring up at it. "Considered the largest animal ever to exist at 122 feet long and 70 tons."

"What about the 'fears nothing' dino downstairs?" Kyle asked, remembering the car ride here. His sister hadn't been able to shut up about seeing the thing.

"*Dreadnoughtus schrani* is the most-complete titanosaur skeleton ever recovered, and very important to the scientific community because of that. It's just another reason why people like Kenneth and Noah Clark are so revered."

Kyle followed the creature's impossibly long neck toward, and through, their exit. The animal's head, as well as its first two vertebrate poked outside the room, making it look even larger. They followed it and left, pausing when they came upon a stairwell and a pair of elevators. There was also a spot to get some food here, *Café on 4*, but Kyle was too focused on not dying to think about the last time he had eaten.

He shifted his weight back and forth in place, contemplating abandoning his plan to stay put on this level.

"What do we do?" Becca asked, looking around.

A human scream echoed around them. Its origin was

unknown, which made matters worse to Kyle. He backpedaled beneath the immense dinosaur's skull.

"We could try the library," Becca suggested.

He faced her. "The library? Why?"

"It has heavy glass doors and sturdy locks."

Kyle's eyebrow crawled up his forehead. "Why do you know that?"

"Why don't you?" Becca asked back, shrugging.

Kyle flashed her a grin and said, "Because I'm not a weirdo, like you."

"Jerk," she said, scowling at him hard.

"What? Come on, Becca. You're twelve and you know what kind of doors and locks the museum's library has. You don't think that's weird?"

More noises got them moving again. This time it was the call of an unknown animal. It may have been the same one that was looking for them, but there was no way to know without seeing it.

"The library, where is it?" he asked, relenting to his sister.

"Back the other way," she said, pointing into the orientation center. "We passed it on our way here."

"What?" he asked, flustered. "Why didn't you say anything about it then?" The only reply he got was a subtle lifting of her shoulders. "Dammit, fine. Let's go. Lead the way."

She did. They hurried back through the space dominated by the titanosaur, then reentered the Hall of Vertebrate Origins. Kyle half-expected to be greeted by their feathered friend, but it didn't happen. They were alone here.

Thank, God.

Halfway into the exhibit, Becca led Kyle over to the left-hand wall, and there, built right into it, was a pair of heavy glass doors. And yes, even their locks looked stout.

Well, I'll be...

"Bingo," he said, gripping and opening the right-hand door. Unlike whoever else had used them last, once he and Becca were through, Kyle snapped the lock shut to keep anything from following them inside.

The corridor was painted in an ungodly shade of turquoise. Kyle instantly wanted to slap the person who had decided on the color. He and Becca descended a short ramp toward a second set of heavy glass doors, continuing past another elevator in the process. The doors to this one were open and the car was stuck between floors. Someone had pulled the doors open to escape, that much was certain.

Next was a water fountain. Becca helped herself. So did Kyle. He then stepped up to the second set of glass doors, seeing a full-blown library on the other side. He had no idea this had been here, even with as many times as he'd been here. He gripped the right-hand door and greedily pulled, but nothing happened.

It was locked.

"No," he said, looking around. "You've gotta be kidding me," he said when his eyes landed on a metal box with a printed note attached to the wall above. "Swipe ID for entry," he read. He faced Becca. "Really?"

She shrugged. "Mom has our membership card."

"Then why did we come here?" he shouted, making her flinch. He let out a long breath and knocked. "Hello, anyone in there?"

But there was no movement.

Kyle banged on the glass harder this time. "Hello?"

Suddenly, a balding, spectacled man did his best prairie dog impersonation and popped up out of hiding from behind the main desk—the librarian's desk. Then, two more people stood and took in the frightened youths.

"Uh, Kyle?" Becca said, voice soft.

"What?" he asked, pounding on the door again. "Let us in!"

Becca pulled on his sleeve and whispered his name, "Kyle."

"What?" he snapped, frustrated.

"Look." Becca's voice was soft and tense.

He looked over his shoulder as a shape stepped into view on the other side of the locked glass doors. The bipedal animal was the same species as before and it stood there, staring at them. Then, it tested the door with its forehead, pushing on it slightly.

"*Moros intrepidus*," Becca said, identifying the dinosaur.

"Is that bad?" Kyle asked.

She nodded. "Very. *Moros*, from the Greek term meaning 'an embodiment of impending doom,' and *intrepidus*, from 'intrepid,' referring to the wide dispersal of their population across North America."

"Thanks..."

She glanced up at him, then back to the dinosaur. "You're welcome."

Kyle rolled his eyes, then stepped back as the *Moros intrepidus* pushed on the door again—harder this time. Then, it struck the door with violence.

Kyle *and* Becca spun and began frantically slamming their fists on the door. "Let us in!" Kyle shouted.

The glasses-wearing man looked at the others he was with and motioned for them to stay put as he stood. He hurried over and slapped a button on the wall just inside the doors. There was a click and the bolt released. Kyle shoved through the door, nearly taking the other man out as he and Becca entered.

"Thank you," Kyle said, breathing hard. "There's...a dinosaur...out there."

The stranger's eyes went wide and he looked past Kyle and back toward the first set of doors. Kyle followed the man's glassy stare but found that their feathered hunter was gone. Both men now stood as still as statues, waiting. But it didn't show itself again. Not yet, at least.

"Is there another way out of here?" Kyle asked, still looking at the other doors.

"Not without a staff member's keycard," he replied.

Kyle faced him. "You don't work here?"

"No," he replied, shaking his head. "I was reading when everything happened."

"Where's the librarian?"

He shrugged and pointed the way Kyle and Becca had come. "Out there somewhere. She ran—left us behind."

Kyle thought back to the voices he had heard, wondering if one of them had been the missing librarian.

"Are we stuck?" Becca asked, looking to her older brother for answers.

Kyle decided to be honest with her. "Yeah, we are," but he quickly added, "for now."

8

Noah, Sarah, and Constance slowly made their way out of the gift shop and into the Hall of Ornithischian Dinosaurs. All was quiet now. The thump of the predator's feet, and the tick of its clawed toes, had vanished along with it. The humans were alone, or so they hoped.

"Why the two exhibits?" Sarah asked softly.

"It's all in the hips," Noah replied.

Sarah glanced at him and cocked her head to the side a little. "Did you just quote Chubbs Peterson as an answer?"

"Who's Chubbs Peterson?" Constance asked.

Noah waved her off, then gave a real answer. "Never mind... Traditionally, dinosaurs are broken into two major groups, Saurischia and Ornithischia. And yes, it really is all in the hips."

Sarah glanced at Constance. "What?" the older woman said. "He's right!"

"Saurischian dinosaurs, like rex and the raptors, possess hips that resemble modern-day lizards," Noah explained, "where the pubis bone points towards the creature's belly. Ornithischian dinosaurs possess the opposite. Their pubis bones point backward, towards the tail, making their hip structure similar to that of a bird, as the name suggests. 'Ornithischian' literally translates to 'bird-hipped.'"

"And Saurischian?"

"It means 'lizard-hipped,'" Constance replied.

"That's it?" Sarah asked.

Noah shrugged. "You seem surprised."

"I am," she said. "I was expecting it to be something...cooler, I guess."

"Hollywood..." Constance muttered with disdain in her voice. "Movies have made this profession out to be something it isn't. It's science, not entertainment."

Sarah nodded and looked around. "I agree. I don't find any of this entertaining."

"Which part," Noah quickly slid in, "the job or the death-defying escapes from real-life dinosaurs?"

"Both," she said slyly.

Noah and Constance slowed and stared at her, but Sarah did not stop. Noah enjoyed Sarah's sense of humor when it showed itself—which was, understandably, not all that often.

"But, to be fair," Noah added, "Hollywood has helped usher in more youthful energy into the subject."

Sarah shrugged. "So, it hasn't been all bad, huh?"

Constance gritted her teeth and forced out, "I suppose not."

The displays here were littered with some of the most popular dinosaurs of all time: *Stegosaurus*, *Triceratops*, *Ankylosaurus*, *Iguanodon*...

Noah was impressed when Sarah noticed something unique about the animals on display.

"They're all herbivores?"

"They are," he said, grinning. "Nice catch. Ornithischian dinos were all herbivores, but the other hips, the Saurischia, featured herbivores *and* carnivores."

"But, why?"

Constance looked at her. "Evolution, my dear. This is what the world chose. Simple as that."

They finished the trek through the hall, coming up on the next leg of their search in complete silence. Noah looked up at the red banner, quickly reading it to himself.

Lila Acheson Wallace Wing of Mammals and Their Extinct Relatives. Then below it, the banner read, *Ahead to: Café on 4* and *Miriam and Ira D. Wallach Orientation Center.*

They were now in the southeast corner of the museum, and thanks to the wall of windows, and their elevated position, Noah could now see over the tree line on the other side of Central Park West and into Central Park. It was complete chaos outside. He would've given anything to rush over and watch what was happening. There was movement everywhere; on the ground and in the sky.

"Noah?"

He blinked and turned, finding Sarah and Constance ten feet away. They had headed right, toward yet another exhibit. Noah glanced down at his feet. He hadn't realized that he'd stopped.

"Sorry," he said, rejoining them. "Let's keep looking."

Constance gave him a soft smile and rubbed his arm. "I know how you feel, Noah. It's a lot for people like us."

"You're a paleontologist too, right?" Sarah asked.

"I was, yes, though long since retired," Constance replied. Sarah opened her mouth to ask another question, but was stopped. "We'll talk later—somewhere safer than here." She motioned to the room.

Sarah didn't complain. She just nodded and allowed the dinosaur experts to lead the way.

The trio left behind fossils belonging to the ancestors of the modern world's most beloved animals, including *Gomphotherium*, an early elephant-like mammal. There was also *Toxodon*, a massive herbivore that looked sort of like a hippopotamus, but was actually related to rhinos and tapirs. Then there was *Glossotherium*, a 2,200-pound ground sloth. But of the specimens on display, Noah's favorite non-dinosaur from prehistory was also here: the *Smilodon*, the 800-pound saber-toothed cat.

The next room, the Paul and Irma Milstein Hall of Advanced Mammals, was as big as the Hall of Ornithischian Dinosaurs and contained just as many fossils and information cards. Under any other circumstance, Noah would've stopped to give it all a look, even though the animals here were *not* dinosaurs or even prehistoric reptiles. Paleontologists were often linked exclusively to digging up dinosaur bones, but that just wasn't the case. Paleontologists studied fossils of all kinds. Noah just so happened to specialize, and focus on, dinosaurs.

Noah especially enjoyed the mammoth remains on display here. They were at the other end of the hall from what he could remember. It had been years since he'd been here—since before his father had passed. The museum changed displays often, but there were some, like the mammoths, that had become permanent fixtures.

"Kyle, Becca?" Sarah whispered as loudly as she could. Noah glanced at her. "What? How are they going to know we're looking for them if we don't let them know?"

Noah didn't like the idea of drawing attention to their position, but she was right. The kids could be nearby and would have no way of knowing Noah, Sarah, and Constance were looking for them. But as they drew closer to the hall's exit, Noah gripped Sarah's shoulder, getting her attention. Once again, his finger went to his lips as they stepped out next to a flight of stairs, two elevators, and the beginnings of an enormous sauropod.

"The competition?" Sarah asked, staring up at it.

Noah nodded, then shook his head. "Sorta. *Dreadnoughtus* might not be the biggest animal of her class ever, but it's the most complete."

"And a very important discovery for us," Constance added. "*Patagotitan mayorum*, while impressive, does not come close to what Noah and his father have given us."

"And what's that?" Sarah asked.

Constance looked at Noah and smiled, "Insight. Something everyone in our community can be proud of. Studying *Dreadnoughtus* has given us priceless research into the entire family of dinosaurs, not just the one."

They scurried through the orientation center, past its bathrooms, and entered the Hall of Vertebrate Origins. Noah made it five steps in before stopping and discovering something awful. Sarah and Constance joined him, taking in the scene—the blood trail.

"Looks like it continues behind the, uh, shark signage," Noah said.

Sarah nodded quickly, biting her lip. She stepped forward,

but Noah slammed on the brakes in the form of his arm. He snapped it up in front of Sarah's chest, stopping her cold.

"But—" she started.

"It's not them," he countered quickly. "We keep looking, then come back to it if we have to, okay?"

Sarah looked back at the streak, then up at Noah again and nodded. "Okay."

As she stepped away, Noah and Constance met eyes. The other woman's look matched what Noah was feeling inside: dread.

The center of the hall featured the *Anaschisma browni,* an interesting creature from the Late Triassic. It was essentially a crocodilian-shaped amphibian. Noah thought it looked like a giant salamander because of its flat skull and wide mouth. He took his attention off the flat, cylindrical, glass case long enough to spot a set of doors to his left.

"What about that?" he asked, staring at the entrance to the museum's library.

"Oh, God. Poor Kyle," Sarah said.

Constance faced her. "Excuse me?"

"Becca loves libraries. He *hates* them. But..." she let out a long breath, "we might as well have a look."

A raspy bird-like call picked up somewhere ahead of them. Noah shoved the two women forward. They all rushed the doors, but found them to be locked.

Sarah pounded on them. The impacts were loud enough to get the desired reaction. Noah watched as two people appeared behind a second set of glass doors built further down the corridor on the other side. The teenage boy wore a backwards, flat-billed hat, and the girl wore overalls. The girl slapped something on the wall out of sight, then yanked open the doors and sprinted to them. The boy was right on her heels.

The girl then snapped open the deadbolt on these doors, but it was Sarah who flung them open. She was slammed into by the two children—her children.

"Oh, thank you, God. Thank you, thank you, thank you..." Sarah cried out, weeping hard, and squeezing them.

Becca and Kyle were okay, but none of them would be for long. The tearful reunion needed to continue somewhere else.

"We need to hide," Noah said, forcing everyone back inside.

He closed the doors and relocked them as Sarah and Constance were escorted to the library. Her kids rambled on about everything they had seen and been through. And as Noah had expected based on what he knew about them, Becca focused mainly on the specimens she had come across, as well as the animal that was hunting them—everyone really.

Moros intrepidus, damn.

The feathered carnivore matched Constance's description perfectly. Also add to it what Noah had seen in the Dino Store and there was no doubting the creature's identity.

They continued to the library. The entrance doors were locked automatically thanks to a trigger mechanism built within them. Noah could see several other survivors inside, which was a wonderful change of pace. An older man with glasses gave the group a curt wave from a sofa positioned halfway into the forty-by-sixty-foot space. Noah returned the wave with one of his own, then refocused on his own people, as the other man quickly got up, came over, and let them in.

"What is that?" the stranger asked as he opened the door.

Noah turned and found their dinosaur stalking past the glass doors. Noah grabbed the man's shirt and pulled him out of the animal's sight line.

"That," Noah explained, "is a very deadly, carnivorous dinosaur."

"It is?" he asked, wide-eyed.

Noah nodded. "Yes, and it would do everyone a great service to not go rushing toward it, okay? Not unless you enjoy being torn to ribbons."

The stranger nodded, his open lower jaw flapping as he did.

"Good. Now why don't you go relax for a bit."

The older man nodded again, then edged around the outside wall of the room on his way back to the central sofa.

Noah blew out a long breath then faced Sarah and the others.

She now sat between her kids, in one of six cushioned chairs off to Noah's left. Constance sat across from her. At the center of the chairs was a square, faux-wood coffee table holding several books. Based on their subject, he doubted they belonged to Kyle or Becca. One was about birds and the other one was entitled *Catalog of Fishes, Volume 2.*

Noah stepped around behind the Rakestraws, patting Kyle on the shoulder as he did. "Good to see you two still kicking," he said, "I'm—"

"Dr. Noah Clark!" Becca shouted, leaping to her feet. She zoomed around the chairs, stopping a foot in front of him. She craned her neck back and stared at him. "Professor of Paleontology at the University of Oklahoma, co-discoverer of the *Dreadnoughtus schrani* alongside your now deceased father, Dr. Kenneth Clark, another man I greatly admire."

Noah was taken aback by what Becca had just said. "You admire me?" No one, besides maybe Constance, had ever said that, especially not a twelve-year-old girl.

"Very much, yes." She stepped back, straightened her posture, then held out her hand. "May I shake your hand, sir?"

The gesture and respect touched Noah greatly. He smiled and got down on one knee. "I'll do you one better. After what I've seen, I sure could use a hug. How 'bout it?" He glanced over at Sarah. She had a huge smile on her face.

Becca bounced up and down on her heels, full of nerves and excitement. Noah knew that some people who were on the Autism spectrum had issues with being touched, in any way, by people, even loved ones. The main reason he was offering to embrace Becca was to show her that he could be trusted, but there was also a small piece of him that wanted to show Sarah that he could be trusted with them.

Becca stepped forward, leaning just her forehead closer to Noah. But then, she shook her head and stepped back, once again holding out her hand. Noah happily accepted the offer and they shook. Sarah frowned in his periphery, but he didn't react to her.

"Put her there," he said. "I look forward to many lengthy discussions with you."

"I would be honored, Dr. Clark."

Noah smiled. "*But* only if you call me Noah."

"Yes, sir," Becca said, bouncing up and down again. "I mean, okay, Doctor... Yes, *Noah*."

When he stood, Sarah faced him and nodded appreciatively. Noah gave her a wink, then turned and made sure Kyle was okay.

That's when he noticed the kid's hat.

"Oni-cyborg, nice."

Kyle perked up. "You play *Cyberpunk 2077*?"

Noah waggled his hand. "A little. My schedule doesn't exactly let me game late into the night." He grinned. "Judy Alvarez, am I right?"

Kyle visibly blushed and looked away.

"Who is Judy Alvarez?" Sarah asked.

Kyle was about to say something but Noah beat him to the punch. At the very least, it would deflect the conversation back to him.

"No one important," he glanced at Kyle, "right?"

The teen nodded feverishly. "Yep. Just—a b-character. No one important. Not hot at all."

Noah dipped his head and sighed. That was exactly what he was trying to avoid.

Sarah only shook her head, then returned her attention to Becca.

Kyle mouthed, "sorry" to Noah, then flopped back into his seat.

It's fine, kid. It's fine...

9

They waited over an hour to test their exit. Noah had wanted to get moving again sooner, but his mind was still stuck on what he'd seen. The *Moros intrepidus'* existence here had rightfully spooked the paleontologist, even more than the *T. rex* had. Something about the rex being *safely* outside comforted him. Here, inside the museum, he and the others were being hunted by something infinitely more dangerous than the "King Tyrant Lizard." While the rex was much more imposing and terrifying to look at, the smaller *Moros intrepidus* would be faster, more agile, and worse, indoors.

Noah and Constance crept forward, closing in on the outer set of heavy glass doors. Noah had been keeping watch for movement for the last twenty minutes. Having seen nothing, he had come up with this idea. He and Constance, the two dinosaur experts, would quietly move closer, even open the doors and have a look.

Well, the 'adult' experts, he thought. He had no doubt that Becca could hold an intelligent conversation with Constance and him. Based on his own experience with his engine-obsessed cousin, Noah knew that Becca's knowledge was legit.

But, right now, he and Constance needed to confirm if their hunter was still here or not. Worst case, it was, and they would retreat into the library and wait it out longer. Eventually, the *Moros intrepidus* would get bored—frustrated even—and leave to find an easier meal.

More people.

The thought made him sneer in disgust. Once again, his younger self's imagination returned. He had pictured what it would be like to be hunted like this—mostly dreamt about it. But like most kids growing up in the late-eighties and early-nineties, he had been scared by the fictional prospect of *Velociraptors* chasing him, not an animal such as *Moros intrepidus*. The latter didn't possess anything unique to evolution, like a raptor did with the elongated claw on its hind feet, but it did have a size/speed combination that concerned Noah deeply.

"*Moros intrepidus,* huh?" he said quietly.

Constance shook her head. "Unbelievable." She glanced at him. "What do you know about it? My memory of them is a little fuzzy. Been out of the game too long."

"Other than it being intelligent and a tyrannosauroid theropod, not much. The only thing I do remember, however, is its feet."

"Its feet?" she grinned. "Didn't take you for a foot guy."

Noah rolled his eyes. "I'm not. T and A, all the way."

The statement made Constance snort out a laugh. "Good to

know... So, what about its feet do you remember?"

"That they are closer to that of an ostrich than all other carnivores from its era," he replied, peering through the glass.

"Right," Constance said, working it out. "Balance and power."

Noah looked away from the hall outside the door. "But in a package that is smaller, and therefore, much more agile. The perfect, small-game hunter."

She sighed. "So, what you're really saying is that we're screwed."

Noah shrugged. "Honestly... Yeah." But he quickly added. "*Unless* it's gone, that is."

"Nice save," she said, facing the glass again. "See anything?"

"No." He reached for the lock and carefully turned it. "Let's take a closer look, shall we?"

Constance was understandably nervous, but she nodded and helped Noah push through the door. They stepped lightly, helping the assisted-shutting doors close. There was no sound made by them, or in the room. If the dinosaur was still present, it had stopped and was standing in place somewhere out of sight. Unfortunately, the Hall of Vertebrate Origins was packed with beautiful displays. It meant that Noah could see very little beyond a dozen-or-so feet in any direction.

He held out his hand, signaling for Constance to stop.

She did.

Noah continued further into the room, pausing in front of the squat cylindrical case containing the oversize salamander-croc from earlier. Here, he could see down the entire length of the room in both directions.

There was nothing here with them from what he could see

and hear. Nothing moved. The only discernable sound was that of his own breaths. He took in one long inhalation, calmed some, then faced Constance and nodded. The museum director relaxed. So did he.

Noah returned to the glass doors and waved the others forward. Sarah led Kyle and Becca through the second set of glass doors. They were the only ones too. The other survivors, including the older man they had met, were staying put. He instinctively thought that was a mistake, but he was also okay with it. His group had just increased by two. This was not a numbers game—more wasn't merrier here. If anything, a larger group could only make things harder. More could go wrong with more people to look after. He had quickly become the de facto leader of his party, which meant he bore the responsibility of keeping them alive.

No pressure, he told himself. Then he sighed. *They sure as hell didn't cover this in class.*

Noah was just being realistic with their situation. He was the most qualified person of them all to lead. So, here he was. He gladly did it too, because in all honesty, he didn't trust anyone else to get him out of here in one piece—not even Constance. She knew her way around here, sure, but she wasn't one to dive into the unknown. Constance had been an academic her entire life. Noah had always liked to think of himself as an adventurer who'd been trained to dig up dinosaur bones.

"And now you're leading a search and rescue operation," he muttered, shaking his head at the ridiculousness of it, "while being hunted by a dinosaur. That's something..."

"What now?" Sarah asked quietly, stepping up next to him.

Noah looked to his left, then back to the right, seeing the

enormous titanosaur's head protruding from the orientation center's entrance. He mapped out the way in his head. From there, you came to the stairwell and dual elevators. Across the hall was the exhibit featuring the mammoth display. Beyond that, was the room containing the southeastern facing windows. Outside the windows was an unobstructed view of Central Park.

He turned toward them. "We get a lay of the land. Come on."

One by one, they followed him back the way they had come—back the way he, Constance, and Sarah had originally come. Kyle and Becca had come from the opposite direction, though Noah had no idea how much of the fourth floor they had explored in totality. For all he knew, they had gone straight to the library. The question hadn't come up during their downtime together. Everyone had mostly just sat in silence—happy to be reunited and still alive.

They were all wary of attack, but pushed forward, returning to the room with the ancient rhinoceros remains, as well as Noah's *Smilodon*, the Hall of Advanced Mammals. Across the centrally located display was a wall of windows, but that's not where Noah headed. Instead, he went to the southeast corner of the room, to a place called the Astor Turret.

The circular observation room wasn't all that big, maybe twenty-five feet across and half that in height. Three floor-to-ceiling windows gave the group access to the world outside. Noah and Constance stood before the central window, while the Rakestraws huddled in front of the left-hand window. Noah picked up movement in his periphery, watching as his lifelong friend set down her pricey heels. He rolled his eyes, then gave Manhattan his full attention.

Flying reptiles soared through the air. They were mostly

Pteranodons, but there were also others further out. Noah couldn't quite ID them. He even saw a few with long tails. He dug deep into his brain but couldn't recall any of the flying reptiles from the Cretaceous Period possessing long tails. By then, evolution had shortened them into what could be found on classic pterosaurs.

More secrets from the ancient past.

On ground level, he watched another herd of *Gallimimus* zoom by. Or, it could've been the same one from before—the group that had been running from the *T. rex*. The rex was nowhere to be seen, but the aftermath left behind by its entrance into the modern world was. There were car wrecks everywhere, bodies and blood too. The people directly outside the museum, and on the streets, had been given no chance to find cover once the fog had rolled in.

"The cloud—and lightning," Noah said, not looking away from the window. "What was that?"

"I...don't know," Constance replied. "But it definitely had something to do with our situation. Maybe it resulted from our two worlds colliding?"

He lifted his left hand and leaned against the window frame. "Yeah, probably. Think there's any going back?"

Constance looked up at him. "I don't see how, no."

"Same. I think this is our world now."

"Which means you're both out of the job," Kyle said, looking at them.

Sarah opened her mouth wide and hissed out, "Kyle!"

Noah pushed away from the window and folded his arms across his chest. "Humanity must—"

"Evolve?" Becca finished.

Noah smiled. "Yep. Mankind will survive, but it'll take some time to figure out where we belong. Are we still the dominant species on Earth? Personally, I have no idea." He gave the world outside one last look, then turned his head and looked over at the Rakestraws. "We ready?"

Sarah and Kyle nodded, but Becca didn't. She wasn't facing him or the window, either. Her eyes were wide and glued to something behind him.

"Shit," he said, knowing exactly what had happened. They had been so transfixed on the cityscape that they allowed their hunter to sneak up behind them.

He slowly turned around to see an inert *Moros intrepidus* standing there. It was as still as a statue. The only movement was its eyes as they darted around, sizing up its cornered prey. Constance, then Sarah and Kyle turned around next. Each one shrank back against the fourth-story windows. With nowhere to go, Noah needed to come up with a plan—and do so quickly.

He did, and luckily for him, he wouldn't have a problem living with the regret of it.

Because Noah Clark was about to die.

10

The only way out of this was for the *Moros intrepidus* to focus on one person instead of all five. And since Noah wholeheartedly believed in the classic mantra of "women and children first," it was his life that was about to be forfeited. He stepped forward and brought his arms out wide to his sides.

That alone caused the animal to lock in on him. It lowered its head and widened its stance. Noah's eyes flicked down to its featherless feet. They really did look like they belonged to an ostrich.

"Get ready to run," he said softly.

"What, no?" Sarah argued. "We'll figure something out."

"Oh, yeah, what?" he asked, glancing at her. Sarah opened her mouth to say something, but nothing came out. Her face saddened. "Exactly. This is how it's going to go," he continued. "Sarah, you, Kyle, and Becca are going to sidestep left, behind me, while I slide right, and away from Constance."

"Noah," Constance started, "we—"

"Don't," he snapped. "Just do this, okay?" He looked at her. "Get them out of here."

The museum director nodded, fighting back tears.

Noah stepped to the right, all while talking to the prehistoric predator. "Come on, uh, boy, eyes on me." He had no idea if the animal was male or female, but calling it a boy felt right. "Follow the nice, juicy meal."

He stepped to the right again, as the Rakestraws stepped to the left, slipping behind him as they did. Sarah's hand found his right shoulder as she led her kids around to Constance. She dragged her fingers across his back to his left shoulder, digging her nails in, as if refusing to let go.

He blinked away the feeling of her touch and refocused his attention on his would-be murderer. "Hey, there, boy. You're, um, much angrier than I had hoped."

It snarled at him, then shifted its gaze to the others.

Noah stepped forward and clapped his hands. "Hey!" The *Moros intrepidus* snapped its head around and growled. "Right..." His next words came out as a question. "Good boy?" This wasn't what anyone wanted, but it was what Noah wanted now.

"Get ready to run."

The creature lowered its head, like a 170-pound cat about to pounce on a man-sized mouse. Its eyes narrowed and its lips curled. Noah heard its claws dig into the floor as they scraped against the tile. That would be his only way out of this. If the animal somehow lost its footing...

"One... Two... Th..."

It attacked.

The *Moros intrepidus* squatted low—then took three rounds to its left flank. It shrieked and squealed, falling, writhing in pain. Mike Dillon, the off-duty, redhead-chasing, New York cop stepped into view, pistol clutched tightly in both hands. Like Noah, his eyes were as big as saucers. He rushed forward, aimed his gun at the back of the twitching carnivore's head, and swiftly put a bullet in it.

The dinosaur immediately fell still, dead.

Mike sneered. "That is one ugly ass animal." Then he winced and looked away. "Smells awful too."

Noah's hands found his knees as the built-up adrenaline took over, causing him to shake uncontrollably. "Mike..." Noah said, sounding almost angry. "What the *hell* are you doing here?"

"Saving your ass, apparently," he replied, patting Noah on the shoulder. "You good?"

Noah stood and shook his new best friend's hand. "I'm not dead, so, yeah."

"You two know each other?" Sarah asked.

Mike faced her. "Hello again, Sarah."

Noah looked back and forth between them. "Do *you* know each other?"

"We met downstairs," Sarah explained, "just before the world went to crap. How do you know each other?"

"The same," Noah said, shrugging. "We met right after I walked in."

"What about you two?" Mike asked.

Noah pointed to his busted lip. "We met *after* everything went to hell."

"She hit you?" Mike asked, shocked.

"No!" Sarah replied. Then she thought about it for a second.

"I guess I did, sorta."

"With her skull."

Mike scratched the back of his. "So, you became friends *after* she headbutted you in the face?"

Noah looked at Sarah and they both shrugged. "Yeah, actually," he replied.

Constance cleared her throat. "Are we done here? I'd really like to get moving again."

Noah nodded. "Yeah, we're done." He faced Mike. "Coming with?"

"Hell yes, I am," he replied. "Being alone in here sucks." Mike took in Kyle and Becca. "Happy to see you found your kids, Sarah."

"Thanks to Noah here," she said. She motioned to Constance. "And Dr. Farr, of course."

Noah looked over his group. It had grown from three to six in the matter of an hour. *But* they had found Sarah's kids, *and* now they had someone with a gun they could trust. Noah would take the downside of herding along a larger group with what he'd been given.

Noah faced Constance. "Shall we?"

"One thing," Mike said, garnering everyone's attention. "If something else nasty shows its face, duck. I don't need one of my core memories being shooting one of you accidentally."

Everyone gave him a curt nod, then the two paleontologists got the group moving. Mike hung back and took up the rear, gun in hand. Sarah, Kyle, and Becca kept to the middle of the group. When they got to this room's exit, Constance stumbled to a stop.

"What is it?" Noah asked, worried. He looked around,

waiting for something to jump out.

"Left my heels."

Noah squeezed his fists tightly. "Forget your damn heels, Connie."

"Not with how much those things cost!" she snapped, appalled by the thought. "Plus, I'm going to need shoes once we get out of here. I don't know about you, but I'm not about to go gallivanting through New York City barefoot."

Mike stepped up to them. "She's right, Noah. Do you know what we find on the streets during our day-to-day?"

Noah did know, and it was one reason he despised cities like this.

He rubbed his face hard, trying to force out his frustration. "Fine, but make it quick."

"Look who's the boss now," she poked, smiling as she turned and headed back to the Astor Turret. "Just give me a sec."

Noah watched Constance like a hawk. She tiptoed back to the southeast corner of the fourth floor, edging around the very dead dinosaur lying in the entrance to the Astor Turret. She grabbed her heels and held them up for Noah to see. He responded with a quick wave of his hand, motioning for her to get back to them.

Constance gave him an "okay" sign with her fingers and started back to the group. She exited the turret—and was immediately bowled into by a second *Moros intrepidus*. The animal had leapt out of cover from behind a display, taking the much smaller woman off her feet. The two slid across the tile out of sight.

Constance Farr only got out a brief cry before it was turned into a wet gurgle. It was obvious what had happened. The predator had gone straight for her throat.

"Connie!" Noah shouted, stepping forward and in shock.

Mike rushed to his side and pulled him back by his arm. "Come on, Noah. We gotta go!"

"But—Connie?"

"It's too late, Noah." Mike pulled Noah so hard, that he nearly dragged him to the floor. Sarah joined in, and together, Mike and her got Noah moving. "I'm sorry, but she's gone."

"Where are we going?" Kyle asked, clutching Becca's hand.

Noah had no idea what to do next. Luckily, Becca did. "Back to the library!" she said.

Mike and Sarah led Noah there without another word. They re-entered the outer doors, locked them, then shambled down to the second set. The same man from before opened them. Noah collapsed upon entry, hyperventilating. Constance was dead, but he couldn't process it. It had been the same when he witnessed the *T. rex* kill the woman out front.

Noah was back inside the alien fog, unable to see, unable to put together the puzzle of the recent events. He just sat there, on his knees, staring at the carpeted floor. A hand found his left shoulder. It squeezed hard. Just by the size and touch, he knew it was Sarah. He knew it was the same hand as before, the one that had touched him after he had decided to sacrifice himself to save her and her children.

He reached his shaking right hand up to hers and laid it atop it. Noah applied a small amount of pressure, holding it in place. He needed her touch—her comfort—right now. He'd known Constance Farr for two and a half decades. She had become an aunt of sorts. She had been instrumental in Noah's growth as a paleontologist and had even helped him when he had had course questions during college. His dad had been there too, but she had been an amazing source of outside assistance.

She would be irreplaceable.

"Dammit," Noah said, feeling tears streak down his face. "I'm sorry, Connie."

11

Everyone, not just Noah, had been affected by Constance's death. But clearly, he had been hit the hardest. She'd always been there for Noah over the years, especially since his father died. He still couldn't believe she was gone.

"How well did you know her?" Sarah asked.

Noah looked up from his folded hands, seeing something in her face that he desperately needed: compassion.

"Really well. She and Dad knew each other for almost thirty years by the time he passed. Even though paleontology is a global profession, it's a surprisingly small, tightknit community."

"So, you all get along okay?" Kyle asked, sitting next to his sister. Sarah sat on the other side of Becca, gripping her hand tightly. Noah and Mike sat across from them. The group had happily fallen into the plush chairs, once again, taking up the space to the left of the glass doors.

"I never said that..." Noah replied. "It's very competitive and there are a handful of real losers out there who are more focused on fame than digging in the dirt."

"Like Jonas Miller," Mike said, speaking up for the first time.

"Who?" Sarah asked.

Mike looked around. "You know, from *Twister*. Cary Elwes' character. That asshole was more focused on stardom than science."

"Interesting reference," Noah said, "but yeah, exactly like that." He let out a long breath. "Connie was one of the first people to call Dad and me and ask us about our discovery. She had been genuinely excited about it. Before that, she and Dad had only known each other through social circles. After that, we all stayed in touch regularly."

Noah pushed aside the memory of her being attacked and continued. "She worked for the Smithsonian at the time. Then a few years later, she retired after her ex-husband hit it big on some tech stock."

"Wait," Mike said, looking around, "you call this retirement? This is a pretty meaty gig for someone trying to retire."

"Sure was," Noah replied.

"Damn," he said. "That woman sure did love her work."

Noah looked away. "Yeah, she did..."

The room went silent.

"Aw, look, man, I didn't mean anything by it."

Noah waved him off. "No, I know. It's fine. Connie loved what she did, but she *hated* to travel. Coming to work here was a no-brainer for her. She was a New Yorker through and through, and she adored all of history's layers, not just the paleontological side of things." He sighed then looked around. "Hmmm."

"What is it?" Sarah asked.

Something had just struck Noah. "Wasn't the museum pretty busy today?"

Sarah looked around. "Yeah, now that you mention it... Where is everyone?"

"You mean, besides hiding behind locked doors and libraries?" Kyle asked.

"Yeah, exactly," Noah replied. "I seriously doubt they all went running outside, right?"

Mike shifted in his seat, suddenly looking extremely uncomfortable.

"Something you'd like to add?" Noah added.

Mike looked up from his feet. "I think so, but I'm not sure if what I saw was real."

"Uh, okay," Noah said.

Sarah met eyes with Noah then said, "Just tell us. What could be weirder than dinosaurs time traveling into the future?"

Mike locked eyes with her. "What I'm about to say."

Once more, the room went silent.

"Tell us what you saw, Mike," Noah said. "There's no judgment here, right?"

Sarah and Kyle nodded. Becca just stared at Mike, waiting for him to spill the beans.

"Okay, so, I was wandering through the Birds of the World hall down on two."

"Birds?" Kyle asked, confused.

Mike looked away sheepishly. "There was a, um, nice-looking redhead eyeing the Gobi Desert diorama."

Sarah and Kyle both looked at Noah. He shrugged and said, "What? He likes redheads." He reached out and patted Mike's arm. "Keep going."

"Anyway... When I finally turned to say something, that fog hit us. Once the nausea and headache subsided, I looked over, and she just went and blipped out of existence like that purple bastard snapping his fingers."

"Thanos?" Kyle asked.

Mike nodded rapidly. "Uh-huh."

Noah got to his feet and began to pace back and forth. "My God," he said, stopping. He faced the others. "They were traded. The dinosaurs were traded with creatures from this era."

"Which includes *Homo sapiens*—" Mike jabbed a finger into his own chest, "us."omo *Homo*

Sarah covered her mouth. "Oh, no."

The realization that people had been traded for prehistoric animals had shocked everyone into silence. What could anyone say? Noah tried to picture winking out of existence in the modern world only to blink your eyes and suddenly be 65 million years in the past. The same thing had happened to the creatures here, but Noah doubted the mental effect had been the same. Dinosaurs and other ancient reptiles were built on instinct and habit. Were they thrown for a loop once they got transported into the future? Sure, but the result wouldn't last as long as it would for a human.

"What happens next?" Mike asked to no one in particular.

"You mean, *if* we get out of here?" Kyle added.

Mike threw his hands in the air. "Come on, kid, glass half full!"

"I seriously doubt we can just drive our way out of the city," Sarah replied, skirting Kyle and Mike's back-and-forth.

Noah agreed. "Not if it's as bad as we think."

"It must be utter chaos out there," Sarah said, "besides what's going on outside the museum."

"Yeah, well, I hate to break it to you, Mom," Kyle said, "but it's not much better inside it."

Noah couldn't argue with him there. They had all witnessed Constance's demise, after all. "First things first," he said, "we need to get out of here—out of the museum. We'll worry about the next part when it comes." He looked everyone over. "For now, let's take a few more minutes, okay?"

Everyone replied verbally or with a nod—except Becca. Noah didn't want to leave her out, so he posed a question specifically for her.

"Becca?" he asked. She swiftly looked up at him. "Is there anything you can tell us about *Moros intrepidus*?"

She sat bolt upright. "It was a Late Cretaceous theropod. First remains were found in 2013, in present-day Utah, making it a very new species—in the Stormy Theropod site of Emery County."

Mike nodded, impressed. "You're like a real-life Encyclopedia, aren't ya?"

Becca didn't reply. She didn't even look at him.

"Okay. I see..."

Noah lightly punched his shoulder. "Don't take it personally. She..." He glanced at Sarah. "She's *particular*."

Mike folded them across his chest and pouted, still not accepting their explanation.

"You'd love Lindsay Zanno, by the way," Noah said, looking at Becca. "She's amazing."

"You know Dr. Zanno?" Becca asked, eyes focused.

Sarah looked at them both. "Who is Lindsay Zanno?"

"She was part of the team that helped to identify and name

Moros intrepidus," Becca replied quickly.

"What about the fact that Moros was supposed to pre-date animals like *T. rex* by tens of millions of years?" Noah asked, curious what Becca would say.

"Wait," Kyle said, perking up, "so that thing isn't supposed to be here at all?"

Noah smiled. "Or...maybe history was wrong and *Moros* lived later into the Cretaceous Period than we originally thought?"

Becca smiled wide. "Cool."

Noah could've extinguished the girl's excitement by reminding her that one had just killed a close friend of his, but he let it go. Becca was engaged and enjoying herself, and he wasn't about to ruin it for her.

Sarah must've understood what Noah was doing. She gently rubbed Becca's back but looked at Noah as she did it. She gave him a heart-filled look and mouthed the words, "*Thank you.*"

Noah gave her a quick wink, then stood. "So, how 'bout we find a way out of here?"

Kyle stood. "How?"

"Well," Mike replied, also standing, "there is one way to avoid the streets and still get out of Dodge."

Noah stared at the man, then it hit him. "No, absolutely not."

"What are you guys talking about?" Sarah asked.

Noah sighed. "He's talking about using the subway tunnels that run directly below the museum."

"Look, I know it sounds sketchy as hell," Mike said, raising his hands in an attempt to squelch a second rebuttal. "But if we follow them south, we can pop out at Lincoln Tunnel. That'll take us out of the city, across to the Jersey side of the

Hudson—to the mainland."

Noah looked to Sarah for her opinion, but all she did was shrug. She didn't have a better plan.

So, Noah relented. "At least it'll limit our exposure to flyers."

"Sounds like a good place to get trapped," Kyle added.

"Yep, there's also that," Noah said. That had been the source of his original reaction. There'd be zero places to hide while underground. It was bound to be dark too. None of that comforted him especially with animals that survived by hunting prey using sound and smell, not just sight, in their midst.

Mike rubbed his hands together and faced the group. "Look, I may not be some dinosaur expert, but I know what I don't want, and that's some prehistoric bird coming down and pecking at my eyes or snatching my ass off the ground."

"I...agree," Noah said. The prospect of being attacked from above spooked him too. "The subway may not seem like the best option, but it's the best of what we have right now."

12

Leaving the library—for good this time—had been proven easier than Sarah had expected, not that she knew what to expect. The dinosaur, the one that had killed Constance, seemed to have moved off. No one went to check to see if it was in the next room, feasting on the woman's corpse, or even that of its packmate. They knew Constance was dead, and that was enough.

She followed Noah alongside Kyle and Becca, holding each of their hands. Mike dutifully watched over them from behind, doing his best impression of an owl. His head constantly rotated around, checking to make sure nothing was sneaking up on them. If that were Sarah, she knew, without a shadow of a doubt, that her neck would be a mess afterward.

Noah led them past the mammoth display, exiting the Hall of Advanced Mammals without a word being spoken. They all knew the goal. They needed to make it down to the subway station, which meant that they had several floors to descend to get there.

Noah slowed as he passed a door with a red sign and white lettering reading "FIRE HOSE INSIDE" in all capitals. He reached for the handle and pulled, quickly examining what the small cubby contained. Sarah couldn't see what he had found, but it must've been something useful for him to reach deeper and pull.

A hose? Sarah thought, honestly having no clue what he was doing.

When he leaned away and shut the door, he lifted his find for all to see.

"A fire axe?" Mike asked.

Noah shrugged. "Better than nothing."

"That's a Pulaski axe," Becca said, "invented by Ed Pulaski in 1911. Its signature head features a traditional cutting edge, but the back side also sports a sideways blade called an 'adze,' an ancient cutting tool used as far back as Ancient Egypt."

Noah looked back and forth between Becca and Sarah, understandably confused by her knowledge of the axe type.

"How does she know that?" he asked, settling on Sarah.

"Yeah," Mike added, "I thought her thing was, you know, dinosaurs."

But it was Kyle who answered, not Sarah.

"Our dad was a firefighter," he said, looking away.

"Was?" Noah asked.

Sarah nodded. "Mark... He died four years ago in an apartment fire in Brooklyn." That phone call still haunted her. The station's captain had been on the other end, and Sarah knew there was no reason for him to be calling her directly unless something had happened to Mark. She had expected to hear that he'd gotten hurt, not killed.

She glanced up at Noah, seeing a look on his face that resembled understanding. His shoulders relaxed, and his face softened.

"I'm sorry to hear that," Mike said. "NYFD is as tough as they come."

"Not tough enough, apparently," Kyle said under his breath.

Sarah wheeled on her son. "Kyle!" She had wanted to scream his name, but had smartly hissed at him with an aggressive whisper instead.

Noah stepped forward a little. "Back down in the Roosevelt Rotunda, when I asked you if their father was here... You gave me a stern look and then said that it had been a rough couple of years for you all. *This* is why?"

"Yeah," she replied, feeling her heart rate soar. "Kyle..." she glanced at her son, but he refused to meet her eyes, "he's distanced himself from me ever since, and Becca won't even talk to me unless it's on her terms." Sarah hadn't felt this alone in years. Some days, it felt like all she had was her thoughts, and those could sometimes be too dangerous for her to focus on.

She expected Noah to say something, like apologize, just as Mike had. But he said nothing. Mike, the New York cop, was the one who spoke next. What he said threw Sarah for a loop.

"When my marriage fell apart, I thought my life was over. Jasmine and I had been together since high school. We got hitched a few years after graduating and stayed together for another twenty years."

"What happened to you two?" Kyle asked, shifting uncomfortably in place.

"Found her sleeping with a divorce lawyer," Mike replied

sheepishly. "I know, pretty ironic, huh?"

Sarah couldn't help but smile. Unfortunately, Mike noticed.

"I'm happy to see that my misery amuses you, Sarah."

She blushed and looked down at her feet. "Sorry." When she looked back up at him, Mike was smiling wide.

"Look, it's fine. That was two years ago now. I've moved on the best I can. I focused on me—got back into shape, started eating right—"

"Started looking for redheads?" Noah slipped in, earning a smile from Mike.

"Yeah, that too." His expression turned serious again. "My point is that life sucks sometimes, but then you stand tall and keep moving forward." He held up his free hand. His right hand held his drawn pistol. "I won't pretend to understand what it's like to lose my father as a kid, but what I do know is that your mom is still here, and she needs you."

This time, Kyle looked at Sarah. Becca didn't, but she did squeeze her mom's hand harder.

Suddenly, a raspy chirp picked up somewhere behind them. Sarah guessed it was back near Constance's body.

Damn.

"Alright... Where were we?" Mike asked, resetting his grip on his pistol.

"Getting the hell out of here," Kyle replied, earning a look of contempt from Sarah. She didn't like it when he talked like that, but here he was, sixteen and fighting for his life. What could she possibly say?

Noah patted Kyle's shoulder. "Exactly." He gave Sarah a quick look, including a nod, then faced their exit.

To their left were the elevators, and to their right were the stairs. Sarah wanted to take the elevator. Something about being in a steel box comforted her. But they had no idea what was waiting for them on the other side of the doors once they got to the main floor. There could be a big predator waiting for them, licking his lips as it waited for the doors to open. That's when an elevator could quickly transform into a coffin.

Never mind. No thanks.

Noah headed for the stairs, immediately descending as quickly and quietly as he could. Sarah was right behind him with her kids. She wanted to move faster, but she understood why they couldn't. Running made too much noise, and noise could bring trouble.

As they rounded the staircase down to the third floor, Sarah spotted the entrance to the Hall of Primates. She'd only been in it once before, and couldn't really recall much about it other than it contained an impressive array of the world's species of, well, primates. Noah didn't stick around long enough for her to contemplate it further. He swiftly began their descent down to the second floor. Sarah remembered the first time she had visited the museum. She had been confused to find out that the famous entrance leading into the Roosevelt Rotunda was actually on the second floor.

"We did just climb a bunch of stairs," her husband had once said, lightly jabbing at her. "What did you expect?"

Her only response to him was, "Shut it."

Sarah, Kyle, and Becca slowed as they stepped onto the landing between floors, allowing Mike to join Noah at the front of the group. Together, the two men descended to the second level. Noah checked their right as Mike checked their left. They must've been satisfied because they both relaxed and waved the

Rakestraws forward.

"Which way?" Noah asked, looking left and right. "Do we keep going down?"

Mike pointed to their right. "Not yet. Through here, I need to show you something first," he replied, pointing into the Hall of Birds of the World. He stopped and gave the room a good, long once-over, then faced the group. "This is where I watched that redhead vanish into thin air." He pointed at a specific window, a life-sized diorama containing birds of the Gobi Desert. "Right over there." He headed for the window, leading the others over. "I stood here," he explained, standing over near the left-edge of the display, "and she stood there." He pointed at the floor to his right, at the middle of the window.

"There's nothing you could've done, Mike," Sarah said, not knowing what else she could say.

He nodded softly. "I know, but..." His shoulders sagged. "I know..."

"Must've really freaked you out, huh?" Kyle asked.

"That's one way of putting it, yeah," Mike replied, snorting out a quiet laugh. He raised his left hand and held his forefinger and thumb an inch apart. "Was this close to having the actual shit scared out of me."

Sarah couldn't help but smile. Mike caught her again, and this time, *she* was prepared for it. "Yes, Mike, your misery still amuses me."

Noah and Kyle smirked. Becca reacted by stepping closer to the window and taking it in.

"We should keep moving," Noah said.

Sarah nodded and gently rubbed Becca's arm. "Becca, sweety, we need to go."

She expected Becca to resist. Becca moved on Becca-time, no matter the situation. But her daughter turned and stepped away, aiming for Noah. Sarah realized that it had been his words, not hers that had swayed Becca into moving. That saddened *and* impressed her. Becca had quickly taken to Noah, a stranger, but a stranger she knew very well because of her thirst for knowledge.

They picked up their pace, exited the Hall of Birds of the World, and descended another flight of stairs. This one ended at the first floor. There was no access to the lower level here, that much Sarah knew. The museum could become an inescapable labyrinth if you weren't careful. Even with the signage pointing you in the correct direction, it was very easy to get turned around.

At the bottom of the stairs, and to the right, was the Hall of Human Origins. Straight ahead was the appropriately named *Café on One*. But Mike led them to the left, into the Grand Gallery, a large room that once featured an equally large canoe, "The Great Canoe," in fact. The 63-foot-long, 8-foot-wide, dugout canoe had been relocated to the Northwest Coast Hall a few years ago. Sarah's favorite tidbit about it was that the entire sea-faring vessel had been carved out of a single western red cedar.

Mike must've seen her staring at where the canoe had once been because he quietly said, "It's too bad, right? That thing was here, in this room, for sixty years."

Yeah, too bad, Sarah thought.

They exited the Grand Gallery and hurried into the Hall of New York State Environments. As they did, a familiar raspy, bird call echoed past them. But no one stopped to examine the source of the noise. If anything, the sound helped them put on a touch more speed.

Moros intrepidus, Sarah thought, feeling her spine tingle.

Kyle asked the only question that mattered. "Is it following us?" The answer was clear—so clear that no one replied. He just looked back and said, "Oh, right, of course, it is."

They zoomed past another staircase, as well as an additional pair of elevators. Both of the lifts were jammed open and wholly inoperative. Mike led them forward, weaving the group past window after window of dioramas and display cases.

"How do you know where you're going?" Kyle asked quietly.

Mike glanced back at him, then flicked his eyes down. "Look at the floor, kid."

Sarah and Kyle both did, seeing red and blue stickers with forks and knifes on them. The survivors came to an intersection of sorts. At the center of it was an immense mosquito behind glass, fake of course. The creepy creature was 75 times its actual size, showing off just how truly horrifying, and ugly, the insects were. Had it not been for the red and blue food stickers, Sarah would've been utterly lost. But they continued around to the left, and so did Mike.

Next was the Hall of Biodiversity, then Theodore Roosevelt Memorial Hall. Sunlight peeked in through the members' entrance, and Sarah half-expected someone to go check it out, but they didn't. Neither Noah nor Mike gave the exit a single glance. They just pushed onward and past the statue of a seated Teddy Roosevelt. Beyond this room was a hallway, as well as the entrance to the Hall of Planet Earth. Mike leaned around the corner, then stepped into the hall, forgoing the exhibit and continuing left.

Sarah saw why. There was a red sign hanging from the ceiling that pointed guests downstairs to the Lower Level. This was the first staircase Sarah had seen that serviced the basement level of the museum. She knew that most of the elevators did, but only a handful of staircases would take them there.

They quickly made their way to the stairs, then started down them.

"Next stop, the subway," Mike said.

Another familiar call found them. Sarah glanced at Noah.

"Go," he said, "we need to hurry."

13

The dinosaur calls continued somewhere behind them. Noah knew, for a fact, that there were, at least, two more *Moros intrepidus* hunting them. It wouldn't be hard, either. The scent of five, sweaty and fearful, fleeing prey would be easy for any gifted predator to track. But he tried to not pay attention to them, hurrying alongside Mike as they descended to the lowest level of the museum and into the Hayden Planetarium.

At this point, they weren't waiting to be caught from behind. They jogged around to the right and toward the subway entrance. Noah tried to pay attention to the world in front of him, not the one above him, but he couldn't keep focus. The calls were getting closer. Not only had he and the others picked up their footspeed, but so had their hunters.

They hustled along, nearly at a sprint now. They bolted through the security checkpoint, seeing sprays of red on the walls to either side. The sight caused Noah to stumble, but he caught himself and kept moving. He glanced back at Sarah, watching as she dragged her bewildered kids along.

"You okay?" he asked.

"No, but better than whoever that belongs to," she replied, tipping her head toward the blood.

A set of stairs led them up to a wall of glass-paneled, wood-framed doors. Even from his lower vantage point, Noah could see the subway turnstile gates on the other side. They were almost there now.

Multiple shrieks startled everyone into stopping. Noah turned and backpedaled at the sight of three, not two, *Moros intrepidus*.

"That was fast," Noah said, staring at the animals coming up behind them. Then he grabbed Sarah and pushed her forward. "Go, go, go!"

They hauled butt up the stairs as the triplets charged forward, heads down, teeth bared. It was a truly terrifying sight to behold. Noah and Mike shouldered through the worn exit doors but were unable to lock them from the outside.

Damn.

Mike faced the doors, aiming his gun at them. "The turnstiles! Move it!"

Noah nodded. Instead of these being enclosed, like the one he had used to enter the museum, the subway's turnstile gate was made of steel piping and was much more cumbersome to maneuver, mostly because only one person could use it at a time. That was the point too, in retrospect. They were a better design when it came to security.

"Do it," Noah said, hurrying along with the Rakestraws.

Mike stepped aside and leveled his pistol at the doors to the museum. "I'll cover you."

Noah patted him on the shoulder, entering first. He wanted to be the first one through, just in case something worse awaited them on the other side. As Sarah ushered Kyle and Becca into and through the turnstile, Noah checked out the other side of the checkpoint, seeing nothing—and everything—all at once. While there was nothing alive to greet them, there was plenty of death. A brawl between species had broken out between the subway gate and an immobile subway car.

The report of a gunshot, and an explosion of glass, caused Noah to jump out of his skin. He spun just as Sarah exited the turnstile. Mike backed toward it, gun still pointed at the museum exit.

"What happened?" Noah asked.

"One of them tried to push through. Don't know if I hit it, though."

Kyle backed away, stepping closer to Noah. "Let's hope you did."

"Same," Mike said, reaching behind him and finding the barred exit. All at once, the trio of *Moros intrepidus* launched themselves through the doors. Mike nearly fell, which would've been the end for him. It was quite easy to get caught halfway inside a turnstile gate, especially if you were wearing a jacket. Here, Mike almost got his foot pinned but yanked it through just as one of the dinosaurs snapped at it.

"Shit!" Mike shouted, raising his gun and shooting the animal through the bars from still inside the turnstile.

The shot had been point-blank, and in the thing's open mouth, mid-shriek. It didn't even cry out in pain. The animal was dead before it hit the subway floor. The other two creatures snarled and hissed, understandably irate over their packmate's—probably sibling's—death. Mike quickly exited but kept his weapon leveled at the animals on the other side.

"Can they get through?" Kyle asked, voice shaking.

Noah looked around for something to block the turnstile from working properly, finding it in the form of a garbage can.

"Sarah, help me," he said, stepping over.

She hesitated for a moment, but eventually rushed to his side. Together, they tipped the heavy, cylindrical object on its side and rolled it back to the gate. The pair found the bottom edge and shoved it lengthwise into the gate's exit, angling it in such a way that would make it all but impossible to dislodge from the other side.

One of the animals charged the gate, colliding with it headfirst. It held, causing the dinosaur to bounce off and spill to the floor. The other *Moros intrepidus* squawked at the first, then sneered at the escapees. It looked behind it, down a long corridor that Noah figured led to the surface. The carnivore squawked again, and after a moment of resistance, the other animal turned and sprinted down the hallway alongside its surviving packmate.

"Think that's the last we've seen of them?" Sarah asked, rubbing Becca's back.

"I sure hope so," Becca replied, earning a small smile from her mother. "That was *not* fun."

Becca's innocent reply made Noah smile.

No, Becca, it wasn't.

Mike was breathing hard, coming down from an epic adrenaline dump. He turned and faced the subway platform and car. "Oh, God."

Everyone faced it now. Noah had already seen the aftermath

of some great, subterranean conflict, where both human beings and prehistoric kings had lost their lives.

"This was a mistake," Kyle said softly, eyeing the carnage.

Noah looked over his shoulder, staring at the museum exit. "Yeah, it was," then he faced Kyle, "but what choice did we have? They'd have caught us if we had stayed."

Kyle didn't have a comeback because there wasn't one. The surface would've been infinitely worse since the event had only just occurred. Maybe after a few days, once the ash and blood had settled, things would be more manageable.

Maybe.

As far as this side of the turnstile gate was concerned...

Directly across from Noah and the others was one of several open doors of a subway train. But the car in front of them held something the others didn't. A herbivore lay on its side, with its backside still half inside the car. Its remains were ravaged with bite and claw marks. Based on the pattern of the wounds and the number of them, Noah guessed it had been attacked by multiple assailants.

But what?

"*Parasaurolophus,*" Noah announced, looking up and down the platform as he identified the dead herbivore. "Looks like it got trapped down here with something else."

"Para-what?" Mike asked.

Becca stepped *toward* the dead animal. "*Parasaurolophus,* a hadrosaur, first found along the banks of the Red Deer River in Alberta, Canada. Playfully referred to as a 'duck-billed dinosaur,' the genus' most notable feature is not only its flat, duck-like mouth but also an elongated, bony crest that protrudes from the top of its head, flowing backward like a bulbous car antenna."

"Looks like they got pretty big from the looks of it," Mike said. That much was obvious. This specimen was huge.

"They did, well, compared to us humans," Noah said. "They grew to about thirteen feet tall, thirty feet long, and weighed over 10,000 pounds. Still, that's not very big when you compare it to other species."

They edged closer. As he did, Noah now saw that its throat had been slashed and bitten. Its eyes stared blankly at the ceiling, and its tongue hung from its open, duck-like mouth. Noah tried to picture the animal's entrance into this world, suddenly blipping to existence inside a metal box on wheels. He wondered how many people it had killed, imagining the thing rampaging around inside the car like a rodeo bull loose inside a tiny barn full of clowns.

What about the slashes?

Something else had appeared down here along with it, and it wasn't the *Moros intrepidus*. It was clear to Noah that they had spawned to life inside the halls of the museum. Unfortunately, there was no way of knowing if that had been all of them. There could be dozens more right outside, waiting for them.

Bodies greeted them no matter which way they turned. A second *Parasaurolophus* lay off to the north, as did several human bodies.

"South, right?" Noah asked, looking at Mike.

The cop nodded, mouth agape. He swallowed and blinked. "Y-yeah, south."

Mike led them away from the deceased herbivore and they snaked their way through the remains of seven people. There was blood everywhere—and pieces everywhere else. It looked like a bomb had gone off. Noah was barely keeping himself together. There was so much death, and none of it was anyone's fault. The universe had decided that Earth was in need of a change—a drastic one at that.

How many people are dead worldwide?

There was no way to know for sure but with seven billion people inhabiting the globe, he guessed it was in the millions, at least. Then there were the people that had been traded and sent back in time to the Cretaceous Period. How many of them had been blipped? Was it an equal number with the dinosaurs brought here?

Does it even matter at this point?

"We may have a problem up here," Mike said from further ahead.

"What's wrong?" Noah asked, looking at Sarah for a moment. She returned his nervous look with one of her own.

Mike pointed at the southern edge of the platform. "The train stopped short. We can't get down to the tracks this way."

"What about from inside the last car?" Sarah asked.

Kyle pointed at one of the blood-splattered windows. "In there?"

The only answer his mother could give him was a shrug and a sorrowful look.

Noah blew out a long breath and stepped over to the rearmost car's door. He tilted his head at it and leaned his Pulaski axe against the outer hull of the car, getting Mike's attention. "Give me a hand."

Mike nodded, holstered his gun beneath his shirt, then did as Noah did and dug his fingers into the crevasse between the doors. Noah pulled on the left-hand door, while Mike pulled on the right-hand door. It resisted for a moment, but finally ground open. When it did, a body flopped to the platform between their feet. They both looked down to find the ravaged face of a very dead woman.

There was nothing left.

"What the hell is down here?" Mike asked, wide-eyed, staring at her. "Looks like she was attacked with a handful of razor blades."

Noah blinked, then brought his eyes up to him. "I don't know." He released the door, happy to see that it didn't quickly rebound shut, not that the dead woman would allow it. He reclaimed his axe, raising it high enough for Mike to see. "But we aren't defenseless." Noah glanced down at Mike's pants. "How's your ammo looking?"

"We're okay, for now." He drew his gun and double-checked. "Glock 17s have seventeen round magazines, plus one in the chamber." He expelled the weapon's magazine and looked it over. "This one is about half full, and I have another full one in my pocket. As long as we don't run into anything armored, or with a super thick hide, we should be alright."

"Oh, I can think of a few things," Noah said. "But let's not focus on that."

"Yeah," Sarah said, stepping closer with Kyle and Becca, "how about we focus on getting the hell out of here instead?"

Noah gave her a curt nod of the affirmative. "My thoughts exactly."

Noah and Mike removed the body from the doorway. Noah stepped inside first, keeping his axe out in front of him. The lighting was dim, but most of the lights were still working well enough. Further up the car to the north, surrounded by more human bodies, was a feathered lump in the floor. Even from here, Noah could see the knife sticking out of its side. Someone had killed it, but not before it had slaughtered several others.

Upon initial examination, Noah had thought it was another *Moros intrepidus*, but he quickly dismissed it because of the animal's size. It was much smaller.

Unless it's a juvenile?

"What is it?" Sarah asked softly.

Noah shook his head. "Not sure. It's facing away from us. Can't get a good enough look at it." He glanced at her. "Plus, it's not like I've ever seen these things with skin or feathers. The only pictures of them 'alive' are nothing but interpretations—educated guesses."

"I don't care what it is," Mike said. "I'm just happy it's dead."

"Same," Kyle said, facing south.

They all did. The rear door of the car was just ahead, only ten feet from them. And thankfully, the way was clear of bodies. But not blood.

There was plenty of blood.

14

Not being able to identify the smaller predator was bothering Noah. Regardless if it were true or not, he felt that his usefulness was tied to identifying the animals and then using his knowledge of their biology to keep everyone alive. Right now, he felt wholly unneeded except for moral support.

He descended the subway car last, giving the feathered mystery one last look before facing their next challenge. Most of the tunnel's lights were out, casting it into near-complete darkness. This was exactly what Noah had hoped to avoid. He remembered the tunnels being dark the last time he had ridden in them, but not to this degree.

"What's wrong?" Sarah asked, gently grabbing the back of his arm. "You look lost somewhere."

"I am," he replied.

"Where are you?"

He thumbed over his shoulder. "Back in there, sitting next to the unidentifiable carnivore. It's bothering me that I don't know what it is."

Mike and Kyle were a little further ahead, looking over the tunnel in the beam of a small flashlight. Mike must've carried one with him. Becca was between them all, mumbling to herself.

"Okay, then. Well, talk it out." She smiled in the dim light. "I'm here for you."

Noah gave her a small smile back. "If we're to assume that whatever killed those people—"

"What about the duck-billed dino?" Mike asked.

Noah shook his head. "No way could that thing have taken it down by itself."

Mike faced him. "I didn't ask if it was by itself. What if it was a pack of those things?" Noah was about to say something but Mike beat him to it. "Come on, Noah, you saw the bite marks. They weren't caused by one animal."

"Yeah, I know," he said, unfortunately agreeing with him. "So, if it—or they—were from the same area as the *Parasaurolophus*, then the killer could be a number of things, even if it wasn't the smaller predator onboard the subway."

"Like what?" Sarah asked. "What does your gut tell you?"

Noah took off his hat and scratched the top of his head. Then he pulled his overgrown hair back and replaced the hat on his head. "For starters, something like an *Albertosaurus* or even a pack of *Atrociraptors*." He was about to go over each species' features, but decided to get the quietest member of the group involved instead. "Care to enlighten us, Becca?"

The young savant looked up at him with wide, excited eyes. No matter how dire the situation became, Becca enjoyed being included in the discussion. "Yes, of course. *Albertosaurus sarcophagus*, meaning 'Alberta lizard' because of where it was first found, and 'flesh-eating' due to it obviously being a carnivore—not a flesh-eating bacterium—was a close relative to the more popular *T. rex*, though smaller and therefore more agile."

"And the, uh, *Atrociraptor*?" Mike asked. "I'm assuming that's similar to a *Velociraptor*, right?"

"Yes, they are—" Becca began, but she slipped, then froze in place. Mike took his flashlight's beam off the tunnel and aimed it down at the ground around her and Noah. They were standing in a pool of blood and subway filth.

Becca shrank into her mother, staring at the wretched mess.

The group headed south, leaving the pool behind.

"Yes," Noah finally replied, stepping in for Becca. "*Atrociraptor* and *Velociraptor* are of the same family of dinosaurs. And despite what you think you know about them, they weren't all that big."

"How big we talking—*Atrociraptor*, I mean?" Mike asked.

"Six feet long—forty-ish pounds. Stood about *yay* high." Noah held out his hand next to his hip. "Despite that, they were still very dangerous. Possessed the same signature sickle-shaped claws on their hind feet as its cousins, and, of course, they hunted in packs." Noah looked behind him, once again picturing the dead, unidentifiable predator in the subway car. "But...it could also be something else entirely, from another part of the world, and we could be way off base."

"So, either way, we aren't in good shape, huh?" Kyle asked.

Noah could tell Mike was about to berate the kid for being negative, but he didn't. Mike jabbed a finger in the youth's face, then allowed his hand to fall to his side. He sighed and said, "I hate to admit it, but I was thinking the same thing."

"Only if it's still close by—and alive," Noah reassured. "It could be long gone by now."

"Can't be worse than those *Moros*-things, right?" Sarah asked.

Noah shook his head. "No. *Moros* is much bigger—more powerful. The bite marks suggest it's something smaller."

Mike pointed his flashlight at Noah. "It doesn't matter. We can't go back the way we came. At least, here, there's a chance we're alone."

"You're right," Noah said. "We know what awaits us back there. And all the blood is bound to attract something else."

Mike aimed his light forward again. "So far, so good, though, right?"

"For now," Kyle muttered.

"What did I say about keeping the glass half full?" Mike snapped.

Kyle rolled his eyes. "Fine, we *probably* won't die down here. Better?"

Mike turned and blew out a long breath. "A little, yeah."

They barely made it 500 feet before they heard a noise that spooked everyone. It was higher in pitch and sharper, but also somewhat similar to that of a pigeon. They stopped to listen. Noah stood straight, concentrating on the world *behind* them. In the deathly quietness of the subway tunnel, he heard the slightest noise of something—the shifting of footsteps.

"We aren't alone," he said, barely above a whisper.

"What do you see?" Sarah asked, instinctively stepping closer to her kids.

Noah shook his head and tapped his left ear. "I can hear

something behind us, but it hasn't advanced."

Mike went to swing his handheld flashlight around, but had it pushed away by Noah. "Don't." Mike just stared at him. "Don't provoke it," Noah explained, recalling a run-in he had with a mountain lion when he was thirteen. He had inadvertently caused it to attack when he had foolishly turned and made a run for it. "Whatever it is, it hasn't attacked yet." He glanced at Sarah. "Let's not give it a reason to."

They started off again at a slower pace, taking lighter steps. Now, it could clearly be heard. But all you could hear was the creature's footsteps. It did not call out at all.

It knows that we know, Noah thought. *Damn, it's smart.*

"Any thoughts on what it is?" Sarah asked quietly.

"Honestly, I have no idea," Noah replied, catching Kyle and Becca looking at him while they were speaking. "Might not even be a predator. What I *can* say for certain is that it is *not* another *Moros intrepidus*."

"What about one of those big Para-ducks?" Mike asked.

"*Parasaurolophus*?" Noah asked, thinking about it. "Could be, I guess. But we haven't seen any offshoot passages, and an animal that size couldn't possibly have fit through the subway car's rear door. The sound is all wrong too. I don't see a *Parasaurolophus* making bird noises."

The group went silent for a moment.

"What about an *Atrociraptor*?" Kyle asked.

"Could be—if it's a carnivore from Alberta. I don't think it is, though."

"Why not?" Sarah asked.

Noah shrugged. "No scientific reason. I just don't think these things traveled here together is all. Odds are that it isn't something from the same region as the dead duck-bill." He looked over his shoulder as they continued forward. "Whatever it is, it doesn't know what to make of us yet, so it's staying back, studying us, determining whether we're a viable threat."

"Or easy prey," Mike added.

"Dude, really?" Kyle asked, throwing his hands up in dismay. "You're allowed to be a Debbie Downer but not me?"

Sarah glanced at Noah then said, "He has a point, Mike..."

They made it 200 more feet before their friend made more noise. This time, Noah slowly lifted his axe, nodding at Mike.

"Get behind us," Mike said, stepping in front of the Rakestraws.

Mike started his flashlight at their feet, then deliberately traced a line down the tracks until the beam landed on their pursuer. It was feathered and of the same size as the one Noah had seen inside the subway car. But no, it was not a raptor.

"It... I think it's a *Troodon*!" he announced, with borderline excitement.

It was seven-feet-long and around 100 pounds. This theropod carnivore was a good bit smaller than *Moros intrepidus*, but would still be very dangerous if provoked. What caught Noah's attention the most were its eyes. They were slightly oversized, zeroed in, and laser focused. Its head tilted back and forth to the side, reminding Noah of a dog thinking things through.

"It's true," he mumbled.

"What is?" Mike asked.

Noah shook his head and took a step away. Everyone followed suit and they backpedaled down the tunnel. But the *Troodon* followed them, moving stride-for-stride with them.

"So, I'm guessing this thing is pretty dangerous, huh?" Kyle asked.

"Yeah," Noah replied. "Its name means 'wounding tooth,' so..."

"Do we want to know why?" Sarah asked.

Noah was going to say, "no," but Becca stepped in.

"Its teeth are heavily serrated, like the inside edge of a work knife—or some species of sharks."

"Lovely," Sarah said. Noah didn't turn to see her face, he knew she was sporting a very nervous look, same as his.

"Just keep moving away," Noah instructed. "Nice and easy."

"A second ago, when you said that it was 'true,'" Mike said, "what did you mean?"

Noah sighed. "*Troodon* was said to have an unusually large brain for its size, meaning it would've been incredibly smart. Its eyes lend to that, since they are bigger than typically seen in animals of its size."

"Don't large eyes usually signify great night vision in the animal kingdom?" Mike asked.

Noah glanced at him. "Yeah, it does. How did you know that?"

Mike shrugged and replied, "*Nat Geo*. Watch a lot of specials late at night."

"Is that why it's been trailing us and not just bull rushing us?" Kyle asked.

"Mmhmm," Noah replied. "We'll be okay, though. Just keep moving away from—"

Suddenly a clattering noise startled everyone. Noah looked back at Kyle, who was now looking at the ground beside him. Noah saw what had made the sound. Kyle had stepped back and kicked a discarded beer bottle with his heel. Even though the teen was mortified by what he'd done, Noah wasn't angry with him. It had been a mistake and nothing more.

The *Troodon* took the sound as a sign to attack—and did.

Mike sent a shot wide.

No, not wide, Noah thought. *It dodged the bullet.*

So, Noah did the only thing he could, he charged forward, hollering like a maniac and swinging his axe in wide arcs. While the *Troodon* was smart, it was significantly smaller than Noah was. But Noah didn't have serrated teeth and a blood-thirsty lust for flesh.

The pair danced around one another. Luckily, the *Troodon* was too smart. It refused to get inside Noah's reach, understanding that it could be injured by the sharp, club-like object in Noah's hands. It also knew to keep Noah in between itself and the others.

It knows Mike can hurt it from a distance. Shit.

Lost in his own head, Noah was late getting the axe head around. The *Troodon* snapped at his hands, but caught the thick, wooden shaft of the tool instead. It curled its lips, baring its shark-like teeth. Noah was amazed by what was happening, but also scared beyond belief.

"Hey, birdbrain!"

Both Noah and the dinosaur glanced in the direction of the voice. The latter was clunked in the side of the head by something, forcing it to relinquish its hold on Noah's axe. The beer bottle shattered when it hit the ground. The carnivore stepped back, shaking its head from the impact.

Noah jabbed at its neck with the axe head, nicking the animal's hide six inches beneath its lower jaw. It squeaked, took another handful of steps away, then let out another high-pitched pigeon noise, though, this time, it added some throat to it. Noah lunged at it with his axe, but the *Troodon* was already on the move—away from them, calling out angrily as it headed back to the Museum of Natural History's subway station.

"Holy crap," Noah said, blowing out a long breath. He sucked in deeply, placed the axe on his shoulder like a lumberjack, but kept an eye out for the dinosaur.

"I don't want to be down here anymore," Becca said. Her voice was impossibly small and barely audible.

"Me either," Noah said, turning and facing the group. "Mike, I think it's time to abandon this part of the plan."

The cop shrugged. "May as well see what the surface has in store for us." He pointed to the south. "The 72nd Street station is close by. Should be able to get out there."

"How far exactly?" Noah asked.

Mike looked up, thinking. "Well, we should be directly beneath the Central Park West and West 77th, so about a quarter of a mile, give or take."

That made Noah relax some. They were much closer than he had thought.

"Lead the way."

Mike nodded and got them moving. Noah hung back for a second longer to settle his nerves.

"You okay?"

He looked up from the tracks and found Kyle waiting for him.

"Yeah, sure." He patted Kyle on the shoulder as the two caught up with the others. "Oh, and by the way, nice arm. Thanks for the assist." The corner of Kyle's mouth turned upward and he nodded. "Ever think about trying out for football?"

Kyle smiled wide.

"You play at all?" Mike asked.

"A little..." Noah didn't like to talk about his college days, before he had decided to pursue paleontology. That chapter of his life was long over.

"High school?" Mike asked. He hadn't been with them when Constance had revealed some minor details pertaining to the subject.

"Yeah. Also played some college ball before focusing on my studies."

"Were you any good?"

Noah shrugged. "Yeah, you could say that..."

15

The 72nd Street station was thankfully abandoned, though not undisturbed. People had died here too, so had a pair of *Troodon*. Noah was happy to see more and more evidence of humanity fighting back with some success.

He and Mike climbed up onto the platform first, then went about lifting Sarah, Kyle, and Becca up to them. Once there, they took a moment to catch their breath. They had hustled here, jogging at a brisk pace, needing to get as far away from the living *Troodon* as quickly as possible.

Kyle stepped away and bent over to pick something up. He turned and held out what he had found: bullet casings.

"I wonder who the shooter was?" Sarah asked.

Noah was curious too, but they weren't about to go out of their way to figure it out. They headed for the steps leading up to the road, and unwillingly found the owner of the spent rounds.

"Damn," Mike said, stepping over to the deceased cop. The

man lay face down atop the lowest steps, in a drying pool of blood. Mike immediately went about the task of searching him.

"What are you doing?" Kyle asked.

"Looking for more ammo."

Noah stepped closer. "What about his service pistol?"

Mike shook his head. "Nope, it's gone." He stood. "His extra mags are gone too, not that I can blame whoever stripped him of them."

"Same," Noah said, feeling a little deflated.

It would've been nice to have a second gun. He carried one everywhere he could, but not here in New York City. The people in charge didn't think too fondly of people who carry a weapon, even for protection. What he really wanted was his shotgun from back home, a slick-looking Beretta A300 Ultima Patrol. He loved that thing.

But you don't have it, he thought. *Deal with it, Noah.*

And he did. He gripped his axe tighter and followed Mike up the steps. Even from below the surface, they could hear the cacophony of chaos raging above them. Animalistic roars mixed with small-caliber gunfire could be heard within a mixture of distances. Some were barely discernable. Others were nearby.

We need to avoid the nearby ones like the plague.

Mike was a few steps further ahead of Noah by the time they reached street level.

"My God," Mike said, shoulders sagging.

"That bad?" Sarah asked from the back of the group.

Noah joined Mike and looked over the immediate area. Then he looked back at her. "No, it's so much worse."

The five survivors knelt on the top step and gawked at what they saw. Fires raged in the form of burning cars, trees, and even a few storefronts. Noah was happy to see that no one's homes were alight. The fires hadn't spread higher…yet. However, without a working emergency team, the flames would undoubtedly spread and eat entire buildings. Noah imagined what the Empire State Building would look like completely engulfed in fire.

Then there was the dead. They were everywhere. And similarly to the subway platforms beneath them, both man and animal were represented. But, like the platforms, the dead were mostly people.

"Very apocalyptic," Sarah said.

"What, like End Times stuff?" Mike asked.

Sarah shrugged. "Well, yeah, but not in the Biblical sense."

Noah sighed. "She's right. This could very well be humanity's downfall."

"But I thought you said that you were confidant in mankind's ability to fight and take back the Earth?" Kyle asked.

Noah shrugged. "Part of me still believes that, but look at all this. This is so much worse than I ever thought."

He peeked around the corner of the three-sided barrier that protected people from falling into the hole in the ground that made up the stepped subway exit. From where they knelt, they could not be seen unless the *who* or *what* was standing directly in front of them.

A loud squawk caused Noah's spine to tingle. *Or from above.* He looked over his shoulder and up, seeing a pair of *Pteranodon* mid-dive.

They were pointed right at the five humans.

Noah grabbed Sarah and Becca's arms and pulled them out onto the road. Mike instinctively snagged Kyle's shirt sleeve and brought him along as they ran across Central Park West and beneath the trees lining its eastern side. The *Pteranodon* pulled up, cawing in frustration at losing their meal.

Noah, Mike, and the Rakestraws all huddled together beneath two trees, keeping close to their trunks as a herd of *Gallimimus* came zooming past them from the north. The ostrich-like dinosaurs sprinted by, using their long, powerful hind legs to drive their impressive weight forward at what must have been close to forty miles per hour.

"Okay, we have Sheep Meadow directly behind us," Mike said, taking in their surroundings. "The entrance to Lincoln Tunnel is about a mile and half further to the south and another half mile to the west."

"Two miles?" Kyle asked. "That seems doable...right?"

No one agreed.

"Under normal circumstances, absolutely," Mike finally explained. "But in all this...?"

"We—" Sarah started, getting cut off by the thunderous steps of more *Gallimimus* as they sped back to the north.

"More *Gallimimus*," Becca said.

"Could be the same ones," Kyle suggested.

Sarah looked at Noah. "Wait, wasn't there a herd of those things outside the museum—when you saw, you know, the *T. rex*?"

Noah nodded. "Yeah, there was." He looked up and down Central Park West. "I think it's best if we stay off the street for as long as we can." He glanced at Mike. "Keep to the trees lining the road whenever possible."

"Fine by me," Mike said. "Last thing I want to do is get trampled by a stampede of prehistoric ostriches."

A guttural, earth-shaking roar startled them all.

"Never mind," Mike said. "I'll take a stampede any day."

That's when the *Gallimimus* returned for a third time, and this time, they brought a friend, one with impeccable eyesight and a keen sense of smell.

The *Tyrannosaurus rex* stomped into view from around a wrecked school bus, clipping the inert vehicle with its hip as it did. The enormous carnivore didn't seem to notice, though. It just kept coming, sniffing the air as it moved.

This time, when the *Gallimimus* fled from the rex, they did so to the east, through the trees, and right at Noah and the others. The group shouted and leapt behind the trunks of two trees as the fast-moving herd barreled through the foliage, exiting out into the open expanse of Sheep Meadow.

The rex followed.

"Run," Noah said. No one moved. They were all locked in fear. He grabbed each one and pushed them east. "Now—go!"

Once they left the protection of the treetops, they were quickly swarmed by more *Pteranodon*. One pecked at Noah, then moved for Becca. She saw it before it could reach her and changed directions, screaming and sprinting away from the others to the south.

"Becca!" Sarah cried, but she, Kyle, and Mike were cut off by more of the flying reptiles.

Noah had made it past them and adjusted course, pointing himself right at the fleeing girl. "I've got her!" he yelled, waving back at the others. "Get to cover! We'll find you!"

Noah dug deep and willed his legs to go faster. Thankfully, he was still in great shape, and he quickly caught up with Becca in no time. But that wasn't the reason he needed to put on more speed. He looked back and saw something he dreaded. The rex was following him.

"Oh, shit!" he shouted, scooping up Becca in his arms and heading for the nearest trees. The feat was made more difficult since he was also still holding onto his fire axe. But to get there, they had to pass the carcass of an animal that had no business being in a vast, grassy field.

"Is that a *Plesiosaurus*?" Becca asked as her voice bounced with Noah's steps.

He grunted and set her back down, but gripped her hand tightly so he didn't lose her again.

"No, this one's neck is way too long. Could be an *Elasmosaurus*. Weird, right?"

Its ID was more of a guess than anything else. Members of the long-necked plesiosaur genus all looked remarkable.

"But why is it here—in Central Park?"

Noah was wondering that too. The marine reptile did not belong on land. He looked around and immediately understood what had happened.

"They were dropped wherever the storm wanted. It was all random, just as we thought."

"So does that mean that some land animals were dumped in the ocean?"

Noah grinned. "It does. And let's hope it was a lot of them."

They looped around the dead, partially eaten, thirty-five-foot-long animal and darted into cover beneath the trees to the west. Central Park West was behind them now as they searched the meadow for the others—only to find an incoming *T. rex* instead.

"Not good," Noah said, pulling Becca deeper, "we need to keep moving."

"But it'll find us. Rex could scent prey up to five miles away. We can't outrun it, either."

Noah bit his lip then said, "Believe me, I know. This is worst-case for us." He looked around. "We need to get indoors."

"But where?" Becca asked, looking around. "I only see trees and grass—and I'm not crossing the road again. No way."

Noah scanned the grounds, seeing an aberration back to the west, tucked away beneath the trees. Its shape was tough to make out since it was broken up by dozens of trees, but Noah was pretty sure he knew what it was.

Tavern on the Green, he thought.

He'd never been to the Central Park restaurant, but he had heard wonderful things about it from Constance over the years. The thought of his now deceased friend saddened him, but as Becca pulled on his hand, he knew he had to push aside his sorrow, delay his grief, and focus on keeping this little one alive.

Their escape from the rex had carried them southeast and away from Central Park West. They were currently in the corner of Sheep Meadow, near the Le Roc d'Ercé landmark. To get to the restaurant, they'd have to backtrack toward civilization. Noah gave their surroundings another look. He didn't see any other hiding spot that would work.

"This way," he said, gripping the axe handle hard.

Becca staggered to a halt and snapped her head around. "Noah? Where's the rex?"

Noah gave the meadow yet another look. The massive carnivore had vanished. "What the hell? How can we lose something that's 40-feet-long and 20,000 pounds?"

"And noisy," Becca added.

Noah couldn't help but grin. This was the most he'd heard

her speak except for when she gave one of her light-speed explanations. Something about all of this was bringing her out of her shell, and Noah wasn't about to mention it and ruin whatever progress she was making. Plus, it made his life easier if she was fully invested and not hiding inside her own head.

They walked as fast as they could, sticking to a wide, shaded footpath. Here, the treetops were healthy and dense. Noah kept his head on a swivel, but Becca did eventually zone out and stare forward at nothing. He could see her lips moving, though. He wondered what she was saying to herself. Maybe she was mouthing the words to her favorite song? Noah wanted to ask, but again, he didn't want to overstep. So, he left it alone and focused on getting to the restaurant in one piece.

They were within 200 feet of their destination when Noah noticed that something was off. The shrubs to their right contained two very out-of-place tree trunks. He slowed, studying the trees for a second longer. They grew at odd angles, and instead of becoming thinner as they grew skyward, here, in some miracle of nature, they grew thicker as they grew taller. He looked down at his right leg, picturing his calf compared to his thigh. Then he picked up Becca and hurried behind a different tree as the other two moved.

The crooked tree trunks were the rex's legs.

Becca squeaked as Noah pressed her back first against the tree. He slapped his free hand over her mouth, forcibly turned Becca's face up to look at him. He set his axe down and placed a finger over his own lips. The axe wasn't going to help them here. Becca's eyes went wide when the booms of the animal's footfalls picked up behind her. She quickly nodded as a tear ran down her cheek. Noah released his grip on her mouth, then leaned over her to create a protective cocoon around the girl.

Becca clutched his shirt then buried her face in it, breathing heavily, understandably petrified. The tree barely hid Noah. He scrunched his shoulders in toward his chest and leaned forward, covering Becca even more. A snort caused both humans to flinch. Noah could've easily looked around the tree and checked to see just how close the rex was, but he didn't. He just stared through the bark and listened.

The super predator pounded off to the west, toward the restaurant, where Noah and Becca were headed now. That wasn't good. Noah, and therefore Becca, as one, sidestepped east—in the opposite direction of the rex—keeping the tree between them and it. There was very little they could do against a behemoth as big as the rex except hope it would eventually lose interest in them, or become distracted by something else. They needed to be patient, and above all else, quiet.

It let loose a guttural, crocodilian growl, causing Becca to whimper. Noah clutched the back of her head, pulling it deeper into his body. In turn, she squeezed him harder. He didn't know what else he could do for her. He was as scared as she was.

The thunderous footfalls drew nearer, then stopped as the dinosaur stepped up to the other side of the tree. Noah pictured it standing there, staring at their hiding spot, waiting for its prey to make the first move. Noah and Becca's sizes were their only real advantage at the moment. They could move through this area better than the rex could. But if one of them tripped and fell, it would be game over for them both. Becca wouldn't survive without Noah, and he wouldn't survive without her, because he wasn't going to leave her side.

The *T. rex* inhaled deeply then let loose a roar that punched the air from Noah's lungs. The tree did very little to shield them from it. The sonic assault caused Noah to release his own set of tears. This was it. The rex was preparing its attack, attempting to stun its prey with fear before moving in for the kill.

The "fear" part was working. Noah couldn't move. He couldn't think. What broke the spell on Noah was the stench of the air. The roar had released an invisible cloud of grotesque stink, gagging him. Becca was still curled into his body. She hadn't come up for air in some time.

The rex stepped forward and after five immense footfalls, Noah and Becca's tree was bumped from the other side. The rex was right *there*. Noah's lower jaw quivered as he desperately tried to hold back his emotions.

They were going to die.

16

A low, cow-like cry caught everyone's attention, even the rex. It sniffed the air and shifted in its stance. Noah needed to know what was happening. He slowly leaned to the right so only half of his face was exposed. The *Tyrannosaurus rex* was impossibly big. The back of its head scraped against the underside of the canopy as it stood taller and taller.

But it wasn't looking their way anymore.

Noah forced himself to peel his eyes off the dark brown, lightly freckled giant and gaze past it. A small herd of *Triceratops* were making its way across the middle of Sheep Meadow. There were three adults and one calf present. The younger one was still plenty large, easily clearing more than 5,000 pounds, and it was currently being picked on by the same *Pteranodon* swarm that had attacked Noah and Becca. The behavior of the flying reptiles was so odd considering none of them could eat an animal the size of a white rhino. They didn't have teeth for starters. Animals like a *Pteranodon*—a pelican, for instance—could only eat what they could swallow whole.

It has to be the storm, Noah thought. *It's really messed up their behavior.*

One of the *Triceratops*, the largest of the bunch, the bull, spotted the rex, facing it. It swung its mighty head around and aimed its impressive horns right at its natural enemy. Then it snorted and let loose an aggravated bark-like noise. That threat was enough for the large carnivore to turn away from Noah and Becca, and face the more dangerous challenger.

Triceratops prorsus weighed around the same as a *Tyrannosaurus rex* but in a body that was ten feet shorter and a lot lower to the ground. The overall bio-package made *Triceratops*, essentially, a living and breathing battering ram. Then add in the fact that there was a calf's life in the balance, and you got a living and breathing battering ram, but with a mean streak.

The rex stepped toward Sheep Meadow, slowly exiting the trees. Noah patted Becca's back. "Look," he said.

She shook her head.

"Becca?" Slowly, she removed her wet face from his stomach and looked up at him. "You need to see this." He grinned. "Trust me."

She nodded and leaned around the tree, twisting her upper body around as she did. When she saw the prehistoric standoff between titans, she spun the rest of her body around, hugged the tree, and watched. Noah's grin widened into a full-blown smile. This was her world, as it was his world. Why shouldn't they be allowed to marvel over it, while simultaneously being scared of it?

"Incredible," she said.

Noah placed his hand on her shoulder and squeezed. She didn't shrug away from his touch. That also made him smile. He let out a long breath and looked around. The way to the restaurant was now clear.

"Come on," he said, snatching up his axe.

"I want to keep watching," she replied, refusing to look away.

Noah shook his head, but not in anger. "There could be another rex nearby."

Becca released her hold on the tree, stood straight, and faced him. "Yes, we should go."

Noah held out his hand, and she took it without question. The two dino-nerds hurried northwest now, glancing back and forth between their destination and the ensuing fight that was boiling over out in Sheep Meadow. Noah slid to a stop when a ballsy *Pteranodon* got too close to the rex and was plucked out of the sky as if it were Mr. Miyagi snatching a fly with his chopsticks. The bone-crunching bite of the rex, and the subsequent noise it created as it pulverized the stupid reptile, gave Noah the chills.

"*Tyrannosaurus rex* holds the record for bite force by any land animal based on extensive biomechanical study, peaking at around 13,000 pounds per square inch," Becca explained.

Noah nodded. "But did you know that a *Megalodon* carried a bite force of 40,000 psi?"

"Not a land animal—and *not* a dinosaur," Becca quickly replied. "And...I don't like sharks."

"Me either."

Becca looked down at her feet. "My stupid brother likes the *Megalodon*."

Even though she had just insulted Kyle, Noah could hear the worry in her voice.

"We'll see them again, very soon," he said. "I promise."

Becca simply nodded, then the pair picked up their footspeed, breaking into a jog until they reached Tavern on the Green.

They continued around to the side of the restaurant, trying the first door they stumbled upon. But it was locked.

Damn.

They kept looking, finding another door around the back. Due to its lack of decoration, and a pair of nearby dumpsters, Noah figured this was the kitchen entrance. He ushered Becca forward, grabbed the handle, and pulled. It opened.

"Thank heavens," Becca said, earning a snicker from Noah as they slipped indoors.

"Yeah, looks like one of the staffers left in a hurry." He looked down at Becca for the first time since they'd been at the tree and noticed that she was crying again. He knelt in front of her as the door shut behind them. "Hey, kiddo, it's okay now, we're safe."

She sniffed in hard. "I didn't like that, Noah."

"Yeah, that was pretty intense, wasn't it?"

Becca wanted none of him right now.

"It *was* pretty scary, huh?" he admitted. Then he leaned in closer and lowered his voice. "Truth be told, I almost peed myself."

Becca's frown deepened. "I did a little."

That broke his heart. "Oh, that's alright. Happens to everyone now and again." He glanced at the backdoor, thinking about locking it. But then, his mind went to Sarah, Kyle, and Mike. What if they tried to get in and it was locked?

Becca turned her head and looked at the closed door too.

"Think that was the same rex from when the storm hit?"

"Yeah, could be," he replied. "I bet it's scoping out its new territory, getting a lay of the land."

"Does that mean we can't ever leave?"

Noah gently placed both of his hands on her shoulders, but she wouldn't look at him. "Hey." Still nothing. Becca definitely did things on her own terms. "Becca, I know it's hard for you sometimes, but I really need you to look at me, okay?"

Slowly, she dragged her eyes off the door, and the world beyond, meeting Noah's eyes. "There you go," he said, smiling softly. "See, that wasn't so hard, was it?" Becca looked down and shrugged, but returned her attention to him. That also made him smile. "I need you to trust me, okay?" Becca nodded once. "Good."

Noah went to stand but was stopped. Becca reached out and grabbed his hand. Then she stepped closer. Noah wasn't sure what to make of it, so he just waited. Becca kept her feet an awkward distance from him, but then leaned forward at a forty-five-degree angle, and placed her forehead on his chest.

"Thank you for looking after me, Noah."

Noah looked down at the top of her head. He lifted a shaky hand, unsure whether he should embrace her or not. He didn't, though. If Becca truly wanted it, she'd initiate it herself. So, he just patted her arm, going as far as rubbing it. "No problem, kid."

"I'm really scared, Noah," she said, still leaning into him.

"I am too," he said, standing. Her eyes followed him up as she stood straight. He looked around, seeing a large dining room to his right, deeper into the building. "Come on, let's find a place to lie low for a minute."

"What about Mom and Kyle—and Mike?"

Noah didn't have an answer. All he could say was, "Let's hope they found somewhere safe to hide until we meet them."

"Will we?" she asked.

Becca's question caused Noah to pause mid-stride as he went to step away. He faced her again and, once more, knelt. "Becca." She stared into his eyes. "We *will* see them again, okay?"

"Okay," she said. Then she let out a long yawn. "I'm tired."

"I am too." He stood, ventured forward, and spotted exactly what they both needed. "Over there. That looks like a comfy spot to relax."

They weaved their way through an expansive kitchen area, and stepped out into the main dining hall, seeing that most tables still had food on them. This place had been hopping when the world had suddenly changed.

Not only was the dining room's eastern wall of the room made entirely of glass but the place was populated too. A smattering of other survivors greeted Noah and Becca, either with halfhearted waves, or frowns filled with distrust. He didn't blame the latter. Everyone here had been put through the ringer.

Some more than others. He wondered how many of the nine people sitting in the glass dining hall had lost loved ones since the storm had hit.

To their right and left were doorways leading to additional dining rooms. They too contained people. Noah estimated that there were nearly thirty people here with him and Becca. That comforted him, but it also worried him. A few people could coordinate their movements. Thirty people could quickly turn into a panicked mob if one person got out of hand and riled the others up.

Those same people could draw the attention of things like a T.

rex too.

A few of them looked beaten and broken, having endured the new world as Noah and Becca had. But others were dressed nicely and looked no worse for wear. Noah figured it out too. They must've been eating here when everything went down and had smartly decided to stay put.

No one got up to introduce themselves, which was fine with Noah. He wasn't here to make friends. He was here to take a breather and keep Becca safe. He kept his axe propped up on his shoulder, making sure everyone knew he was armed. There was no telling what someone might do if their mental state had deteriorated enough.

The room to his right was narrow and possessed dozens of tables and chairs. The room to his left also contained tables and chairs, but the majority of the space housed a circular bar filled with liquor bottles, though it did look as if a few were missing. Noah couldn't blame anyone for needing a hard drink after witnessing the Cretaceous Period suddenly wink into existence. Had Becca not been with him, Noah would've found the most expensive tequila in the joint and poured himself a healthy glassful.

A long booth made up the western edge of the dining hall. Noah and Becca now stood in a walkway between the back of it and the kitchen. The walkway gave unobstructed access to all three dining rooms. They circumnavigated the booth and fell into the left-hand corner of it. Becca sat close to Noah with her knees tucked into her chest.

Across the room, Noah noticed an older woman sitting next to a girl three or four years younger than Becca. The older woman eyed them, whispered something to who must've been her granddaughter, then stood and walked over to Noah. He didn't make a move to defend Becca. All he did was set his axe on the table, while still gripping its handle tight.

"Hi there," the woman said. "My name is Francine, and that over there is my granddaughter, Alice."

"Hello," Noah said, hearing zero malice in the woman's voice. "I'm Noah. This is Becca."

Francine nodded. "Nice to meet you, though I wish the circumstance was better."

Noah gave her a small smile. "Likewise."

"She your daughter?"

Noah glanced down at Becca who balked at saying anything. He wasn't sure why, but he blurted out, "Yes, well, one day maybe. I'm seeing her mom."

Becca's jaw hit the floor and she looked up at Noah, bewildered.

"That's nice. I'm happy for you," Francine said. "I came over because, well, Alice was thirsty, and earlier I found some juice boxes over in the kitchen. Would Becca want one of them?"

Becca looked away but nodded.

"That would be wonderful," Noah said, "thank you for being so kind."

Francine waved him off. "Don't mention it. Times like this, I think being kind to one another is going to be very important." Her voice softened. "Especially when loved ones have been lost."

Noah glanced over to Alice, the granddaughter. When his eyes met Francine's again, the older woman nodded once.

Dammit, Noah thought. Alice's parents hadn't been as fortunate as their daughter. *At least she still has someone.*

When Francine left, Becca leaned in close to Noah. "Why did

you tell that woman that you're dating my mom?"

Noah shrugged. "It's hard to explain, but a grown man running around with a child that isn't his is even harder to explain. Do you understand?"

Becca nodded quickly. "She might think you stole me."

"Very smart, Becca," Noah said, honestly impressed.

"I'm tired, Noah," Becca said, blinking hard.

Noah spotted Francine coming over with Becca's juice box. "Have a sip of your juice first, then get some shuteye, okay?"

"Okay," Becca replied. "Both sound nice right now."

When Francine stepped over, she showed off something that she had hidden around her back. Noah had immediately thought she had pulled a gun on him, but then he recognized the ice-cold bottle for what it was: a beer.

Noah held up a hand to refuse, but was cut off. "I—"

"Need to relax as much as your Becca does, believe me." She set the bottle and Becca's juice box down on the table. "It's no bourbon, mind you, but it'll still do the job." She gave Noah a wink. "Everyone deserves a chance to relax, Noah. We might not get very many opportunities going forward."

She left with a nod, returning to Alice at the table across the room.

"My mom likes beer...a *lot*."

Noah snorted, unable to hold back his laugh. So he handed Becca her juice box and picked up his beer. He held it out for Becca to *clink* with her cardboard container.

"Cheers," he said.

She happily clinked her drink to his, looking very satisfied with herself. Noah then took a long pull from the bottle, melting into the booth as it made its way down his throat, and to his stomach, where it would then, hopefully, enter his bloodstream and knock off a smidge of the anxiety and fear he was currently drowning in.

Cheers to that too.

But he knew that one beer wasn't going to be strong enough to do the job. Noah was going to need an entire case to negate the dread he was feeling.

17

Sarah, Kyle, and Mike were chased back beneath the trees lining Central Park West. They hung out there, looking for Noah and Becca. The last time they had seen the pair, they had been continuing southeast before disappearing from out of sight.

"They'll be fine," Mike insisted, glancing around, "but we won't be unless we find cover."

"Inside a building this time, please," Kyle added. "No more trees."

Sarah was worried sick, but she needed to trust that Noah would protect Becca. "Okay, yeah." She blinked hard and looked around. "But where?"

Mike turned and saw something he must've liked. "How 'bout there?"

To the southwest of their position was the Holy Trinity Lutheran Church. Sarah wasn't so sure, but Mike was.

"What?" he asked. "When in doubt, one can find sanctuary

in the house of God."

"You religious, or something?" Kyle asked.

Mike shrugged. "I'd say I'm closer to the 'or something,' but my mom and grams always believed it."

"And your dad?" Kyle asked.

Mike looked away and snickered out a small laugh. "Not exactly. His 'Holy Trinity' consisted mostly of Jack, Jim, and Jose."

That made Sarah frown. But the more she learned about Mike Dillon, the more she liked him. He seemed to be a genuinely good guy.

Same as Noah, she thought.

Sarah gazed back at Sheep Meadow, then at her son. With no better plan, she nodded. "Sounds good—the church, I mean."

Mike blew out a breath and said, "Okay, we are going to run across the street and stick as close to the buildings as possible. The flyers can only get so close without clipping a wing and whatnot."

"Lead the way, Detective," Sarah said, patting him on the shoulder.

"We're gonna have to move fast, okay?" Mike said. Sarah and Kyle nodded. "Right, let's do this."

The trio sprinted across Central Park West, then headed south along the sidewalk, doing as Mike had suggested and sticking as close to the front façade of each building they came across. The only time they slowed was when they came to the intersection at West 68th Street. Mike checked west, down the 68th. Sarah did too. She could see a few people hurrying about. One person even opened the front passenger door of a running car.

That's when she noticed the person's face. It was covered by a black bandana.

"Looters—already?" she asked.

Mike sighed. "Looks like it."

"Gonna do anything about it?" Kyle asked.

"Nope," he quickly replied. "I'd like to, but we have bigger fish to fry."

Like not dying, Sarah thought, glancing east, at the park. She tried her best to picture Noah and Becca holed up somewhere safe, but was having trouble seeing anything other than blood.

"You good?" Mike asked, staring at her.

Sarah wiped her eyes and shook her head.

"They'll be okay, Mom," Kyle said. His voice was unusually soft—full of sincerity. "I...trust Noah to keep Becca safe."

Sarah rubbed his arm. "That means a lot, Kyle. Thank you."

He nodded and gave her a small smile.

There's my boy...

"Okay, almost there," Mike said, stepping off the curb. "Only three more blocks to go."

They hurried across West 68th, once more staying glued to the front of the buildings. The sounds of war echoed around them; roars, bellows, and gunfire. Suddenly, a herd of small, bipedal herbivores came sprinting past Sarah, Kyle, and Mike. The animals darted behind them, heading down West 68th. Sarah slowed, watching as the nine dinosaurs headed straight for the looters.

What happened next made her grin. The thief she had seen earlier looked up from inside the open door, spotting the incoming herd. But instead of climbing into the vehicle, he stupidly stepped away and took several, rushed, one-handed potshots at them. And, as expected, the herd panicked. Two of the animals careened into the open door, sending it flinging backward into the looter. He went down, holding his wrist, which, even from where Sarah was standing, she could see it had been bent at an unnatural angle.

Serves you right.

"Sarah?" Mike asked.

The irate driver shouted at his partner, shifted the car into gear, and left—without the injured man. That's where Sarah left them. She joined Mike and Kyle and the trio got moving again.

"What was all that?" Kyle asked.

Sarah smiled but shook her head. "I'll tell you later."

The intersection at West 67th Street went by in a blur. Sarah looked west, down the street, and saw more movement. People ran down the sidewalks, and so did smaller carnivores. The sight gave her the chills. These people weren't looters, they were being hunted. Despite that, Mike did nothing. Sarah did understand why. He, a single police officer, couldn't save everyone. Plus, the game had changed. Individual survival mattered more right now. She was just happy that he was with them.

By the time they crossed West 66th Street, they were winded, and breathing hard. They continued past 55 Central Park West, an apartment building that was featured heavily in a cult eighties movie, but Sarah, someone who was not a huge moviegoer, couldn't recall which one. And, to her, it didn't really matter. Not right now.

"We're here," Mike said, diverting course and heading up the steps of a building situated just to the south of the apartment building in question.

Sarah and Kyle followed behind and just when Mike was

about to knock, the front door opened. An ordinary-looking man wearing a long-sleeved shirt and dusty slacks greeted them. Sarah had expected it to be the pastor.

"Hurry, please," he said, waving them inside.

No one argued with the guy, and they all but dove inside.

Sarah stumbled to a stop just inside the door, bending down with her hands on her knees. "Thank you...very much."

"Anyone in need is welcome here," he said, smiling softly.

She stood upright. "You the pastor?"

The man shook his head. "Music director, actually. Reverend Tim is up front counseling a family at the moment."

"They okay?" Mike asked.

The music director looked away. "They have suffered a great loss. Their son was playing baseball in the park and was lost to a, uh, dinosaur."

Sarah's heart broke for the family. "I know the feeling—or I hope not to." The man gave her a confused look. "My daughter is still out there with a friend of ours. We're hoping to reunite with them shortly."

He smiled again. "And I will pray that you do. Please, sit, rest. Stay for as long as you need. If you need anything, I'm Austin."

"Sarah," she said. "This is my son, Kyle. And this is Mike, another good friend of ours."

"Nice to meet you all."

Sarah smiled softly. "Thanks again, Austin."

"My pleasure." He gave them a nod, then faced the door, peeking through a tall, narrow window. It was clear that Austin was in charge of the door, as well as shepherding people inside.

How appropriate, Sarah thought, looking around.

Mike led them to the central aisle and into the back, left pew.

After a few minutes to calm down and catch their breath, Kyle asked the most appropriate question.

"Think they're fine?"

Mike waved off the question. "You kiddin'? Who better than them to survive out there, right?"

Kyle looked down at his hands as he rubbed his thighs. "Yeah. I...guess you're right."

"Hey, none of this is your fault," Sarah said, wrapping her arm around his shoulder.

"I know. I just..." Kyle sighed and looked at her. "I just wish I hadn't been so hard on her earlier. I said some really nasty stuff to her after she ran off—and I didn't really mean it."

Sarah frowned, but she was glad to hear and see her son's remorse. "I'm sure she knows that."

Kyle's eyes became wet and he looked away from her. "Does she, though? Does she actually understand that sometimes people say things they don't mean?"

"This is about your dad, isn't it?" Sarah asked, sensing a deeper frustration.

"Mark, right?" Mike asked innocently. "What happened to him exactly—if you don't mind me asking?"

Sarah nodded, wiping her eyes. "No, it's okay. He was asked to cover for a coworker whose wife went into labor overnight. Kyle and Becca begged him not to go in. We... We were supposed to have a family outing that day, but—"

"Then he died in that fire you mentioned," Mike finished.

Sarah looked up at the ceiling, holding back more tears. "Yeah, he did."

She heard Mike shift in his seat. When she looked down from the ceiling, she saw that he was now sitting sideways, fully facing her son. "Kyle?" he asked.

"What."

"Do you honestly believe that your dad lied to you that day?"

Kyle looked down at his hands again. "He said he'd be home as soon as he could."

"But did he lie to *you*?"

"No," he replied, tears streaking down his face. "I know he didn't. But it's so much easier being angry at him."

Mike sat back and faced the front of the church. "I know what you mean, bud."

"You do?" Kyle asked.

"Sure do. What I didn't tell you about my divorce was that I had been unconsciously shutting Jasmine out for over a year. I'd go out and drink with the boys, or pick up late shifts, just so I didn't have to go home and face her." He slouched lower. "To those hurt eyes..." He tapped his knees nervously. Sarah could see that this was difficult for him to talk about, which made it that much more authentic. "When I saw her with that lawyer guy, do you know what the first emotion I felt was?"

"I'd be pissed," Kyle replied.

"Yeah," Mike said, grinning, "I'm sure that's what most guys would feel." He looked at Kyle now. "But not me." His eyes flicked over to Sarah as she quietly listened. "I felt regret. I was definitely pissed, but not at her."

"You were madder at yourself than her, huh?" Kyle asked with a look of understanding.

"Yeah. I was *really* mad at myself too. Dark thoughts crept their way into my head." He unfolded his hands. "Luckily, my department shrink is a poker buddy, and he helped me through it all. Believe me, man, going through life alone sucks. You're lucky to have your mom, and your sister."

Kyle turned his head to face Mike. "And your infatuation with redheads?"

Sarah blurted out a laugh that got Austin's attention from the front door. He looked over at them, but she quickly waved him off and apologized with a smile.

Mike leaned in closer to Kyle. "Come on, kid, who doesn't like a redhead?" He nudged Kyle with his elbow, earning a smile out of the teen. "But no, I told myself that if I ever fell in love again, that'd I'd go out of my way to be in it to win it. No more taking life for granted."

Sarah released her grip on Kyle's shoulder and patted Mike's. "You're a good man, Mike Dillon."

Mike leaned back, around Kyle's head, and with a wink said, "So is Noah."

Sarah removed her arm from Kyle's shoulder and looked away, blushing hard. She cleared her throat, searching for something to say. "He, uh... There hasn't been a single person that Becca has confided in more—other than Kyle, maybe—since Mark died. He's perfect for her. That has to count for something, right?"

After a few seconds, it was clear that Kyle had finally processed what had just been said. He sat up and wheeled around on his mother and blurted out, "Wait, do you like Dr. Clark?"

Sarah sank into her seat, feeling her face flush even more. "I, well, you know, stressful times can do a lot to you, and your, um—" It's then she noticed that the pastor was now speaking to the entire congregation. "Shhh, hang on, what did he just say?" Sarah sat forward, refusing to look at Mike *or* Kyle. She blindly waved them off. "We should shut up and listen to what he has to say."

But there, in the corner of her vision, she could see both men smiling wide at her schoolgirl-like behavior.

She rolled her eyes. *Boys.*

Mike lifted his arm and checked his watch. It was then that Sarah realized that she had no idea what time it was. She waited for Mike to say something, but he didn't.

"What's wrong?" she asked, gaining Kyle's attention.

"Bad news," he replied.

The Rakestraws glanced at one another.

"What do you mean?" she asked.

Mike sat forward with his elbows on his knees and twiddled his thumbs. It was obvious that he was trying to choose his words carefully.

"Mike?"

He faced them both. "The sun will start to set in just over an hour."

"What's your point?" Kyle asked.

"I..." Mike started, pausing to collect himself. "I don't think it's safe to be running around Manhattan after dark." Sarah went to stand and berate him, but he snagged her wrist and stopped her. "Hear me out. Please?"

She relaxed, then nodded.

"Look," he continued, "I think it's safe to say that Noah and Becca are intelligent people, right?" The Rakestraws shrugged. "Right. Do you think that *they* think it would be a good idea to go traipsing about New York City at night with some of history's greatest predators back in the mix?"

"I don't even like going out at night on a normal day." The voice had come from behind them. All three of them,

Sarah, Kyle, and Mike turned to find Austin, the music director, looking at them. "Sorry, but I couldn't help but overhear your discussion." He stepped away from the door and continued. "I've been watching this door for hours, and I can tell you, for a fact, that it would be lunacy to go out there after sunset."

Sarah looked back at Mike, who gave her a heartfelt, apologetic smile. "I'm sorry, Sarah, but he's right."

Kyle turned and looked at her. "I trust them, Mom. So should you."

"I...do," she said. "Of course, I do. I'm just worried is all."

"And you have every right to be," Austin said. "I'm worried for them too—for every life on this planet. But I can't do anything, except pray that we find a way to survive."

18

Becca had passed out hours ago. Noah had originally wanted to get moving, but had then realized what time it was. And instead of waking Becca to tell her that they'd be staying put for the night, he just let the girl sleep.

He looked down at his lap, smiling. Somewhere in the middle of the night, Becca's head had found his thigh. Noah had, admittedly, drifted in and out of consciousness. But he had stayed upright, sitting in the same booth they had fallen into the night before. He had also kept his fire axe, his Pulaski axe, on the table in front of him.

Becca was curled up in a ball, facing into the backrest of the booth, away from the world around her. Noah was facing the eastern glass windows. In the night hours he'd been awake, sitting right here with her, he'd seen all manner of creatures pass by—not that he could properly identify them.

Outside the window was a brick patio, and beyond that,

was a row of thick trees designed to give the outdoor-seated, restaurant patrons privacy. Plus, add in the dim lighting, and it made it impossible to see much except shadows and murky, indistinguishable outlines.

He checked the time on his watch and saw that the sun was about to start rising. They needed to get moving and find the others. For the hell of it, he pulled his cell phone out of his pocket, confirming that he still didn't have a signal. But that's not what his eye caught. His lock screen was a picture of him and his father from the day they had discovered *Dreadnoughtus schrani*. It had been the discovery of a lifetime, one that now meant nothing to this new world. Dinosaur bones meant very little when you had living specimens meandering about.

What would you think about all this? he thought.

The internal question had been directed at his dad. Kenneth Clark had been the GOAT, the Greatest of All Time, to Noah. Even some of their colleagues had thought so, but not Constance. She had admired the elder Clark greatly, but was too proud of a scientist in her own right to ever put him on a pedestal like that. Would he think this was all extraordinary, or would he think what had happened was an abomination to history?

Noah had watched several other survivors leave since Becca had fallen asleep, including Francine and Alice. He hadn't wanted them to go, but what could he do, add on two more people to watch out for? Francine had given him a small wave before the two women had left via the side door near the circular bar. At the time, he waited to hear screams as they were cut down by something nasty, but it didn't happen. That gave him hope, yet he still wasn't going to move until morning.

Which is now.

He gently shook Becca's shoulder. "Wakey-wakey," he cooed. Becca shrugged him off and rolled over, mumbling something under her breath.

He tried again, a little harder this time. "Becca, it's time to go." She snapped her eyes open but didn't move otherwise. Noah wasn't sure what to expect, so he eased her into their situation, quickly relaying where they were. "We stayed overnight because I was afraid of going out there at night."

"I don't want to go out there now," she added.

"Yeah, me either," Noah said, gazing out through the glass wall. "But your mom and brother are out there somewhere."

She sat up and yawned. "And...Mr. Mike."

"Yep, him too. We need to help them."

She nodded and rubbed her eyes. "Yes, we do. Mom and Kyle don't know anything about dinosaurs—not like us."

"Think we're the best tag team ever?"

Becca thought long and hard about it, but eventually nodded. "Absolutely." She looked around. "Where's Alice and her grandmother?"

The lightheartedness of their conversation turned dark for a moment. "They left in the middle of the night. There was nothing I could do to stop them."

"That makes me sad."

"Why's that?" he asked.

Becca looked over where the grandmother and granddaughter had been camped out the night before. "Because they're most likely dead now."

The finality of the statement shook Noah. He wanted to reassure her that they were just fine, but he couldn't, because it would've been a blatant lie. He had no way of knowing whether

Francine and Alice were dead, but his gut feeling was telling him it was so. Leaving in the middle of the night—early in the morning, really—had been a bad call, a deadly one.

"I'm sure we'll see them again," he finally choked out, happy Becca hadn't been looking at him when he said it. He knew that the look on his face was very clear that he didn't believe his own words.

Becca didn't believe them anyway. "No...we won't."

She completely understood what was at stake. She understood death better than most preteens, even better than a lot of adults. Everybody had dead relatives, but how many kids have lost their fathers at her age?

Noah picked up his axe from the table and looked it over, taking in the teeth marks left by the *Troodon*.

"Do you like that axe?" Becca asked.

Noah shrugged. "It's served me well so far, yeah."

"I have one hanging in my bedroom."

"You do, why?"

Becca looked up at him, then glanced away. "It's signed by all of my dad's fire buddies."

Once again, for what felt like the thirty-seventh time, Noah's heart broke.

"Come on, kid. How 'bout we go find your mom and brother." He stood and quickly added. "And Mike!"

Noah turned and found Becca sitting there with her mouth agape. She'd been ready to say it but Noah had beaten her to the punch this time. The pair entered the room with the circular bar. It's then that Noah noticed that about half of the people that had been here the day before were gone. But he also noticed a couple of fresh faces. He wondered how many places were like

Tavern on the Green; former hopping businesses that had been transformed into safehouses overnight. Would they ever become what they once were?

Will anything?

Suddenly, a random young man launched to his feet, staring down at his phone. "Holy shit! I got a text through!" Several people, including Noah and Becca turned and faced him. "It's...my mom! She's hurt—nearby too." He looked up and met eyes with Noah. "I have to go."

Noah held up his hands to calm him first. "Hang on a sec, okay?"

"What? Are you crazy?"

"I'm a paleontologist. I've been watching these animals carefully." Now he was speaking to everyone who had gathered. "You can't just go rushing outside. Some of these creatures have acute hearing and sense of smell, not to mention binocular vision. You have to take caution, okay?"

"Caution?" he repeated, laughing at the *ridiculousness* of Noah's statement. "She's hurt—dying. Every minute counts. Like this. I'm wasting my time talking about it."

The younger man hurried for the side door, the same one Francine and Alice had used. Noah couldn't help himself. He followed the guy with Becca gripping his non-axe hand tight. He needed to see what was beyond the doors. The panicked stranger did everything Noah had told him not to. He tossed open the door with a bang and clambered outside into the early-morning sunlight. It had risen enough to cast the grounds surrounding the restaurant into a hazy gloom.

As soon as the young man took two steps, he was tackled to the ground from the side by a pair of one of nature's most feared hunters.

Noah's eyes went wide. "*Velociraptors.*"

Everyone not named Noah or Becca screamed as the foolish young man was torn to bits, ravaged by the dog-sized carnivores. These raptors stood a little taller than Noah's hip and were exactly as he had described them to Mike down in the subway tunnel. They used their razor-sharp teeth and killer hind claws to decimate their prey, the now very dead stranger. Six of the eight people in the room bolted in the opposite direction, but Noah and Becca did not.

Noah yanked Becca to the left, toward the circular bar. She pulled free from Noah's grip and rushed around to the foldable, bartop entry point, the bar flap. Becca ducked beneath it just as Noah planted his hand atop the bar, vaulting over it. He landed in a heap right next to Becca and quickly wrapped his arm around her head, burying it into his chest. She whimpered, but she did not cry out.

"Dammit," Noah muttered, looking around. His only means of defense was his fire axe. It would do in a pinch, but against two raptors...?

He laid his head back, clunking it against the center island of the bar. A vibration shot up and gently rattled the liquor bottles. Noah's eyes darted up. The sight of the booze made him grin. He held up his axe, looking it over. Then his eyes returned up to the bottles. At first, he had thought his axe was his only weapon against the raptors.

Maybe not.

Slowly, Noah released Becca and reached his hand skyward, aiming for a high-proof bourbon. He'd wait to enact his plan, though. Maybe, just maybe, the raptors wouldn't discover them.

The others had made much more noise than he and Becca.

Sniffing, and the clicking of claws on tile, grew louder as the predators entered the building. Then the sounds grew as they neared the bar.

Noah mouthed, "Shit!"

He mentally drew a line, picturing the animals' trajectory as they moved. One was definitely coming straight at them, but the other raptor sounded like it was headed for the main dining room.

Here we go, he thought, lifting the bottle and pouring in a mouthful of bourbon. He did everything he could not to taste it, already feeling a sneering pain in his gums.

Becca looked up at him and silently asked, "What are you doing?"

Noah gave her a wink just as the sniffing drew closer. The raptor was right on the other side of the bar. Noah paled, nearly gagging when he watched a pair of forward claws grip the bartop. They were followed by a blood-soaked snout and a mouth filled with equally bloodied teeth.

The raptor's head cleared the bar, then slowly tilted down at them—receiving Noah's payload: a face full of bourbon. He let loose, spitting it right in the creature's face. The high alcohol content did its job, burning the raptor's eyes. It shrieked, reeling back and whimpering like, well, a wounded animal.

Noah leapt to his feet and tossed up the bar flap as the second raptor came to its packmate's aid. Becca took his hand and the pair sprinted into the dining room. They bypassed the kitchen exit, heading for the other end of the restaurant. Noah looked over his shoulder, happy to see that the other raptor was more interested in what had happened to its friend than to chase them.

They made it to a patio exit in record time. Noah threw open the door, allowing Becca to go first. She turned and instantly screamed. Noah spun, blindly whipping his axe around as he did. It connected with a dense form. But the thing's momentum caused it to continue forward, into Noah, and they both went tumbling outside. They stopped six feet later, lying next to one another.

Noah's shoulder and ribs were killing him. He cringed from the pain, closing his eyes while he waited for the pain to subside. When it did, he opened them and yelped in surprise. The thing that had run him over had been the second raptor, and it now lay, unmoving, in a growing pool of its own blood. Noah's face was less than a foot from its open maw.

He winced at the smell emanating from the animal itself, as well as its agape jaws. "Ugh." He looked down at its chest. "Oh, wow." The head of his axe was buried in the base of the raptor's neck.

Becca appeared next to him. "Nice shot."

"Thanks." Then, a cry from somewhere inside the restaurant reminded them both that there was still another raptor nearby, blinded or not. "Oh, right." Noah sat up, feeling the world spin for a second.

He blinked hard and climbed to his feet, pulling the axe free of his kill as he did. It, and parts of Noah's clothing, were soaked in the carnivore's blood.

"Damn," he said, "that's not good." Then he begrudgingly launched the axe into the trees behind him and wiped his hands off on his jeans.

"What are you doing?" Becca asked.

"Too much blood. That thing will be able to track us if we

keep it."

She inspected his clothes, grimacing. "And all that?"

"Keep an eye out for a fresh shirt, will ya?"

"Okay, but we need that to happen soon, right?"

Noah nodded. "Yep, or *everything*, not just the raptor, will know where to find us."

They hauled butt through the tree line, over a four-foot-tall stone wall, and out onto West 66th Street. Three hundred feet east of Noah and Becca, this road merged with East 65th Street—one of a handful of roads that cut straight through Central Park, connecting one side of Manhattan with the other.

Straight ahead of them to the west, and fifty feet across Central Park West, Noah and Becca spotted a pair of enormous *Edmontosaurus* grazing on a roadside tree. This species of "duck-billed" hadrosaur did not have the same backward growing crest as the *Parasaurolophus*, could grow up 40 feet long, and weighed north of 10,000 pounds.

"*Edmontosaurus annectens*," Becca said in awe. Noah smirked at her as she moved. "What?"

"I believe that is *Edmontosaurus regalis*."

Becca looked at the creatures again, then back up at Noah. "How do you know?"

"Because *regalis* grew much larger than *annectens*," he explained, watching as the larger of the two animals reared back onto its hind legs to reach higher branches. "Based on how big they are, they are most definitely a *regalis*. Though, like a lot of this stuff, it's been debated on for years, so who really knows?"

Becca didn't take the correction poorly, thankfully. She just shrugged and said, "Still, they are beautiful, aren't they?"

"That they are."

The hadrosauridae family was an interesting one. From these two *Edmontosaurus*, to the deceased *Parasaurolophus*, to even the *Iguanodon*, every member of duck-billed family of herbivores possessed a slightly rounded spine and shorter forelimbs. When they moved, they usually did so on all fours, giving them an uncomfortable, hunched appearance. Despite the genus' bone structure, and size, they were quite fast, exceeding speeds of twenty-five miles per hour with relative ease.

Noah watched the larger *Edmontosaurus'* hind legs flex and drive its weight higher. Its base was incredibly strong, that much was clear. It made sense too. Hadrosaurs didn't sprint on all fours, they did so by lifting themselves back onto their hind legs, and putting use to those powerful muscles.

A cry from behind them got Noah and Becca moving faster. They hurried south, along the eastern edge of Central Park West. Directly across the street from them was 55 Central Park West, Dana Barrett's apartment building from the original *Ghostbusters* film.

"Spook Central," Noah mumbled.

"What?" Becca asked.

He shook his head, looking around. "Nothing. Keep an eye out for the others. I doubt they went far." But he saw no one. He checked his phone again, just in case, but saw that it didn't have a signal. "Come on, guys, where are you?"

19

Sarah got up and began pacing back and forth behind the last pew half an hour ago. The sun was just now showing itself through the church's east-facing, front windows. If they were going to leave and go look for Becca and Noah, now was the time to do so.

"Anything I can help with?" Austin the music director asked. Sarah stopped and looked his way, unsure if he was asking about helping with her soul or her search for the others.

She decided that the question had not been a spiritual one, though it would've been comforting to know that it was, but instead, a simple offer of assistance. "My daughter," Sarah said joining him at the door, "she's wearing overalls and has strawberry-blonde hair. The man she's with, Noah, he's tall, athletic—and wearing jeans and a baseball cap. Have you seen anyone who matches those descriptions?"

Austin stroked his stubbly chin, thinking hard. "No, I'm

sorry," he replied, glancing back outside, "I—well, would you look at that?" Sarah glanced over at Kyle and Mike. They both stood. Austin smiled and stepped aside. "Have a look for yourself." Sarah dove at the window, feeling her heart soar when she spotted Noah leading Becca south, along the eastern sidewalk of Central Park West. "It looks as if your prayers have been answered."

Sarah leaned forward, kissed the man on the cheek, then rushed outside, screaming, "Becca, Noah!"

They stopped and turned as Sarah burst forth and descended the front steps of the church. She immediately took a beeline across the road, overwhelmed by emotion. She couldn't help it. Seeing Becca and Noah alive after such a horrifying night had sent her to the moon. But, for some reason, the others weren't as excited to see her. In fact, Noah shouted at her.

"No, wait!" he yelled, looking *above* Sarah.

Suddenly, something massive snatched her shoulders and began to lift her off the ground. Sarah was being tossed around so violently that she couldn't look up to see what it was. But whatever had grabbed her, it was a flyer, and it buffeted the road as it lifted her clean off the ground.

"Help!" she shouted, gripping the animal's clawed feet. She was already six feet off the ground and rising.

Ten feet—fifteen, twenty. Now, as she clutched the creature's scaly feet, she hoped that it *wouldn't* let go—not yet, anyway. Up and up she went, feeling several of its clawed toes puncture her flesh. She grimaced but held on, hearing the cries of Noah, Kyle, Becca, and Mike from below.

As the animal stabilized, she could finally get a look at it. She knew from Becca that it was some sort of pterosaur, but she had no idea which one. She recalled the flock of *Pteranodon* that had chased them into Sheep Meadow. This one was so much bigger than they were. Its feathers were deep blue and purple, but also stained with God-knows-what; blood, urine, feces? Sarah figured it was all of the above. She looked down. The others were quickly becoming specks to her. She must've been eighty feet off the ground and *still* climbing!

As the flyer gained altitude, it edged closer and closer to the twelve-story apartment building to the south of the church, across West 65th Street. They continued over the building, just as the pterosaur's right claw lost its hold. Sarah squeaked, dangling over 125 feet above ground, millimeters from death. There was nothing that could save her if it lost its grip with its other foot. Sarah held onto its left foot with both hands, willing the animal to *not* let go. She looked around, frantically searching for a way out.

And, like inside the church, her prayers were answered.

The pterosaur stalled above the apartment building. Directly beneath Sarah's feet, thirty feet beneath them in fact, was the roof of a glass structure. She looked up, then back down at the glass roof, seeing blue beneath it. Sarah's eye lit up and she began to pound on the pterosaur's toes.

"Let go of me, bird!"

Her efforts were answered with a squeeze of its foot. The pain was excruciating, not to mention whatever virus she may have just contracted due to the animal's obvious lack of hygiene. Still, she needed to keep trying. This time, she balled up first and slugged the animal in the gut, hitting it repeatedly.

"Let go, you damned...dirty...bird!"

On *bird*, the pterosaur let go.

Sarah screamed as she free fell, before smashing through a pane of glass, and plunging into the apartment's rooftop pool. In all, the fall had measured fifty feet from bird to water.

The air from Sarah's lungs had been expelled when she hit the roof, and she hadn't been given the opportunity to refill her lungs before going under. Her body instinctively inhaled, sucking in water instead of oxygen.

Sarah's feet struck the bottom of the pool, and she immediately pushed off. When she broke the surface, she vomited out the water she had inhaled. She just stood there, in five feet of water with just her head and neck protruding from it, breathing hard. Blood seeped out of her wounds, diluting into the pool water around her. The entire scene looked very grim to say the least.

"What the hell did you do to my pool?"

Sarah caught her air and turned to find an older black woman sitting on a lounge chair, book in hand. Sarah was confused. Had this lady just been sitting here, enjoying a good read, while the world went to hell?

"Sorry?" Sarah replied, unsure of what else to say.

The woman sneered at the state of the water, but got up, slipped into a pair of flip-flops, and limped over to the pool's edge. "But seriously, are you okay?"

Sarah shook her head. "No, not really."

The woman stepped over to Sarah's right. She looked and saw that the stranger was heading for the steps. Sarah slowly walked over to them, thankful that the water was taking most of her weight.

"C'mon, girl, get movin'," the lady urged. "We don't want that thing to come back, do we?"

Sarah shook her head and winced, feeling pressure in her neck. "No, we definitely don't want that." She looked up. "Believe me. Oh, and my name is Sarah."

"Isn't that nice..."

Sarah rolled her eyes and gingerly scaled the stairs without any help from the woman. She had no intention of entering the water. But once Sarah was close enough, the woman offered her a hand, steadying Sarah as she fully exited the water.

The woman frowned at the state of the pool. "Betcha that asshole property manager is gonna make the tenants pay for this mess."

Once again, Sarah replied with an apology. "Sorry."

"You'd better be!" She threw a towel over Sarah's shoulders. "Now, c'mon. Let's go take a look at you." She looked up at the newly created entry point. "See, this is why I don't like birds."

Sarah didn't know what to make of the very outspoken, boisterous woman.

At least she wasn't alone, and bleeding out in a pool.

20

What else could Noah do other than shout and stare in awe at the power of the winged beast? It was a magnificent creature to behold. Something that big that could still somehow fly!

"What the hell is that thing?" Mike asked, pushing Kyle and Becca beneath the trees to the east of the road. Noah had not joined them—not yet. Even after the animal had dropped Sarah.

"Noah, come on, man!" Mike shouted, finally getting his attention.

He turned and hurried over. "*Thanatosdrakon*, the 'dragon of death.' Second largest flying reptile in recorded history."

"Second largest?" Kyle asked, voice shaky. "Wait, so there's something bigger out there still?"

"Possibly, yeah. An even bigger pterosaur from down in Texas."

"He's talking about *Quetzalcoatlus*," Becca explained, eyes wide, staring at the sky. "Forty-foot wingspan, stood as tall as a giraffe when on land. Even its skull was seven feet long. *Thanatosdrakon* is smaller everywhere, including carrying a wingspan of thirty feet, though still very impressive." She removed her eyes from the sky and found Noah. "I'm scared, and I want my mom."

Noah nodded, then glanced at Mike. His eyes said it all. Like Noah, Mike wasn't sure Sarah had survived.

"Then let's head up to the roof and find her," Noah said.

They gave the sky above the street a long look, then took off across it, heading straight for the apartment building's front door.

"A *T. rex* is one thing," Noah said as they moved, "but it can't fly."

Mike instinctively kept his head down as they weaved through immobile cars. "Man, I hate birds. Nothing but assholes with wings."

Noah hit the bottom of the steps leading up to the building and looked up. "On any other day, I would've said that you're overreacting, but not now."

Off to the left of the apartment building's entrance was another door, a glass one. This one sported a red cross on it. Noah had to remember that the vast majority of buildings in New York City possessed businesses on the first floors, not residences. This building contained the same—a pharmacy, in this case.

Noah paused on the bottom step as Mike, Kyle, and Becca continued climbing.

"What are you doing?" Mike asked. "That dragon-bird could come back."

Noah motioned to the door. Mike held out his hand, then

pointed at the nearby awning. They slid beneath it, while he joined Noah on the sidewalk, pistol in one hand.

"She could be hurt," Noah said softly, glancing up at the kids.

"I'm sure she is," Mike whispered. "Or worse..."

Noah looked past Mike and found Kyle and Becca staring at them, waiting for them to get moving again.

"We need to try."

Mike nodded. "I know. Thinking of getting some meds?"

"Yeah, we might need them later, regardless of what happened to Sarah."

"Don't be long," Mike said. "We really need to keep moving. Getting bogged down again won't help our cause."

Noah faced the kids. "Mike's going to lead you up to your mom—" he held up his hand and stopped both Kyle and Becca from saying something, "while I go next door and grab some medicine for her, okay? She could be badly injured."

That sobered them up a little. Kyle and Becca nodded, keeping any verbal reply to zero.

Noah grabbed Mike's shoulder and squeezed. "Be careful."

Mike looked up and down Central Park West. "I'm more worried about you."

"Same," Noah said, blowing out a long breath. He looked up at the kids. "Go. Help your mom. I'll see you soon."

Noah waited for Mike to lead the Rakestraws inside. He replayed what had happened to Sarah, watching her get snatched up right before his eyes. The *Thanatosdrakon* had come in from out of nowhere. The stealth the animal had put on display had been second-to-none. Given its size, Noah thought he would've heard something—anything at all.

He headed further to the south, coming to the pharmacy's

front door fifty feet later. Unlike the apartment building's entrance, there were no stairs here. Noah quickly shoved his way inside, hearing the classic chime of a bell. He looked up and found that the origin of the sound was connected to the doorframe. The sight made him smile slightly. He was also happy that the door had not been locked, though he was confident that he could've smashed through the glass had the need called for it.

It was clear that this was a privately owned venture and not of the corporate variety. The shop was small and only contained two centrally located shelving units. Each stretched twenty feet to Noah's left. The door was in the front right corner, and its positioning gave him an uninterrupted view of the pharmacy counter. Noah headed right for it. Luckily, camping and hiking with his parents had taught him a thing or two about first aid, as had a general interest in the subject. Plus, add in that he could sometimes be on dig site for days on end, sometimes weeks, and it was always a good idea to know the basics.

"Anyone here?" he called out, confirming that he was, indeed, alone. The owners had left in a hurry, understandably so.

Satisfied that he wasn't going to get shot by the proprietor for shoplifting, he vaulted over the counter and got to work finding what he thought he might need. He focused mostly on painkillers, antibiotics, and anti-inflammatory medicine—the good stuff too, the kind you needed a prescription to acquire.

Or an end-times scenario, Noah thought, shaking his head. He was stealing drugs, after all.

The last thing Noah grabbed was a handful of disposable syringes before tossing everything into the largest paper bag he could find. Just to be safe, Noah doubled layered the bag with another, then tightly rolled down the top. Instead of vaulting back over the counter, he gently sat on it, then lifted his legs and spun, hearing the chime of the front door as he did. One-hundred and eighty degrees later, he discovered a newcomer standing between him and his exit.

"Hey there, pal," he said, talking to the *Stygimoloch* as if it were a dog.

The bipedal herbivore was one of the cuter dinosaurs from the Cretaceous Period, in Noah's opinion. It was around ten-feet-long, stood at chest level, and weighed as much as Noah did. Like its relative the *Pachycephalosaurus*, it also possessed a domed skull made of solid bone. But this species, *Stygimoloch spinifer*, the "horned demon from the Styx," also sported several demonic-looking horns around its hard head, as well as a beaked mouth. Noah wasn't sure about the species' temperament, and honestly, who could be sure? It was truly impossible to know which variety of animal acted like what. Noah had always just assumed that every animal from the prehistoric era was aggressive to some degree.

"And so are you, huh?" Noah asked it as it lowered its head and snorted. "Aw, crap..."

The curious horned demon pivoted forward and launched itself right at Noah. He quickly stood, ready to leap for it once it got close enough. Unfortunately, he slipped on a random piece of paper that had been left on the countertop. The delay cost him as the living missile struck.

The counter exploded from the force of the impact, then crumpled beneath Noah's weight. Thankfully, he didn't fall in front of the animal. Instead, he fell chest-first on top of it—which, let's face it, wasn't much better.

As soon as he landed, the *Stygimoloch* threw its head back, bucking Noah off, sending him flipping feet in to the air. The Raggedy Andy doll that was Noah landed hard atop the nearest shelving unit, still five feet off the floor. Now he was lying on his back, bent over the shelving in a way that made him come face-to-face with the animal.

"Can't we be friends?" he asked it nicely.

The upside-down *Stygimoloch* snorted, lowered his head and dove at his face. Noah sat up enough for the animal to miss him...but not the shelving unit. It folded, then tipped toward the front of the store, taking Noah with it. He held onto the bag of meds, surprised that he hadn't let go of it, and went for, yet another, ride. This one ended a little less poorly than the other. Noah landed first, then had the shelving unit, and its contents, come crashing down on top of him. He wasn't completely buried though. The unit had stopped a foot above him.

The *Stygimoloch* was out of sight, but Noah could hear it stomping around and snorting, looking for its missing enemy. Noah couldn't blame the thing for attacking him. It was scared, alone, and unsure of what Noah was. Just like how this was the first time any human had seen a dinosaur, it was also the first time a dinosaur had seen a human. Trust was gained within the animal kingdom, not a given.

Noah tipped his head back, watching as the creature's feet continued toward the front door. He was curious how it was going to get out since the door had shut behind it. It simply bellowed and smashed right through. Noah laid his head back and breathed, then went about removing the items that had fallen on him from his chest.

He picked up one of several thin, rectangular boxes, read

160

the label, and rolled his eyes. They were boxes of magnum-sized condoms. Noah was lucky that no one had been here with him to see him like this, especially Mike, because Noah was covered in the things.

He pictured the Manhattan skyline and sighed. "Always a good time in New York City..."

21

Kyle and Becca followed Mike up the stairs of the apartment building. They had checked the elevator first, and had gratefully found it operational. But Mike had still opted to use the stairs. Kyle understood why. It was the same here as it had been in the museum. What happened if something was standing just outside the doors when they opened?

Yeah, no thanks, Kyle thought, gripping Becca's hand tighter.

They were five stairs behind Mike the entire time, giving the NYPD detective room to work and maneuver. Kyle would've liked to have been closer to him, but he was afraid of what Becca might do if Mike was forced to pull the trigger. Loud noises spooked Becca sometimes, and Kyle wasn't about to go chasing after her, not again.

He groaned. Who was he kidding? Of course he'd run after her again. Kyle didn't want anything bad to happen to her, but he also didn't want his mother to find out that it could've been prevented had he tried. Disappointing his mom had become routine the last few years, not that he enjoyed the feeling it gave him. He also hated the look she gave him when he did, inevitably, screw up.

They were nearly to the roof, when Mike slowed. Kyle looked around and found a floor map.

Eighth floor, got it.

"What is it?" Kyle asked, hearing a muffled sound emanating from behind a door down the hall to his right.

Mike stepped into the hallway and aimed his pistol in that direction. Kyle leaned out and looked back the other way, down the left-hand hall. A door had been blown outward from the inside. He stared at it for a second, trying to comprehend what had happened. There were no scorch marks, so it hadn't been an explosive. Then, he put it together. An animal had blipped into existence *inside* someone's apartment—on the eighth floor!

"Holy crap," he mumbled. He squinted and thought, *Where are you now?*

He snapped his head around when he heard the sound from earlier again. It was definitely a person—someone screaming—a woman. Mike inched closer to the door as the commotion continued. The woman yelled again, this time rambling off enough words for Kyle to know it was familiar.

"That sounds like Mom!"

Mike nodded, then faced the door. He gently tried the knob, but found it locked. Then Kyle watched him lean in and check to see if the deadbolt was engaged. Mike must've liked what he saw, because he leveled his gun at the doorknob, fired a single round into it, then kicked at the decimated door. On the second impact, it violently swung open and smashed into the interior wall with a bang, dislodging a picture frame from it.

"Police!" Mike shouted before stepping inside. "I need you to remain where you are and raise your hands! I am coming in!"

He gave Kyle and Becca a quick look then stepped through. The Rakestraws followed him inside, staying right on his butt.

"Shut the door and lock it," Mike instructed, stopping and looking back at Kyle.

Kyle nodded, shut the door, and flipped the deadbolt into place. The handle was done for, but the deadbolt had survived just fine.

They continued inside, stepping lightly.

Kyle wanted to call out to his mother, but he didn't. He didn't want to cause something bad to happen. He'd let Mike do his thing, uninterrupted. He exited the entrance hallway first. From what Kyle could see, the apartment was quaint, but nicely decorated, featuring two closed doors, bedrooms perhaps, and a kitchenette with what he assumed had all the typical equipment; fridge, microwave, stove, oven.

Suddenly, one of the doors opened. Kyle couldn't see who had opened it with Mike blocking his view.

"Thank God," Mike said, "we weren't sure if you had made—"

Mike spun and leveled his gun at someone, but he did not fire. Actually, he blanked for a moment.

"Mike, don't!" the voice belonged to Kyle's mother.

Mike looked away from the unseen person. Kyle figured it was the apartment's owner. The distraction of Sarah being alive was all the person needed to advance. A woman stepped forward and swatted Mike's gun away with her bare hand. Her other hand came around and smashed a cast iron frying pan into the side of his head.

Mike turned into a wet noddle and collapsed in on himself.

22

Before Noah left the mom-and-pop drug store, he scoured the place for gauze and bandages, finding them mixed in with everything else that had been destroyed by the *Stygimoloch*. He had slithered out of hiding, bag of meds in hand, and waited. He currently stared at the door just in case the ruckus between him and the rowdy herbivore had been noticed. But after thirty seconds, he decided enough was enough.

Noah stepped through the decimated front door and hustled outside, crunching over glass as he moved. He bolted left, toward the apartment building entrance. He didn't stop until he entered, and when he did, he stumbled to a stop at the sound of a muffled gunshot. Noah looked up, picturing Mike battling with someone, or something, nasty. He also pictured Kyle and Becca huddling in a corner and watching the whole thing, wondering if they were next to die.

Noah launched himself at the stairs and pounded up them

at a steady pace. He wanted to run up them but there was no way his body could handle it right now. Plus, what happened when he became winded, out of breath and needed in a fight? Noah needed to conserve himself as much as he could. Still, even moving at seventy percent, he quickly lost his breath. But he refused to slow as he wheezed for air.

He checked the doors near each floor's landing, but found nothing out of the ordinary, nor did he hear any screams—any voices at all. His plan was to make his way up to the roof first, then work his way down from there at a slower pace if he didn't find anything on his way up.

When he came to the eighth floor, he spotted debris on the hallway carpet, discovering its origin in the form of a busted door. It was clear that Mike had shot out the doorlock. Noah quickly stepped up to it and pushed, but it didn't budge because someone had locked it from the inside with the still-intact deadbolt.

So, Noah did the only thing he could think of doing.

He knocked.

"*Who the hell is it?*" a gruff, female voice shouted from the other side.

Noah leaned close to the hole in the door and said, "I'm Noah Clark—Dr. Noah Clark. I believe your guests are friends of mine."

The deadbolt snapped open and the door was tossed away from the frame. Noah was still bent at the hips when a furious woman in a flower dress and flip-flops stepped up to him. He swallowed and stood tall, towering over her by a good eight inches. Her eyes were alight with rage, and her face was bursting with annoyance.

"Uh, hi," he said.

The woman's hands found her hips. "You don't look like no doctor." Attitude poured out of her.

"Rough day?" he asked, trying to calm her down.

Instead, she just stood there, glaring at him.

Noah stuck out his hand. "Noah Clark, I'm a paleontologist—dinosaurs mostly." He hoped that announcing his profession as an expert in fossils, particularly dinosaurs, would settle her down some.

"Oh, so you're one of them fakey doctors, huh?" she asked, deflating his attempts. She gave him the biggest eye roll he had ever seen and stepped aside. "Well, c'mon, the party is in full swing."

Party? he thought.

"Um, thanks."

She stomped away from him as he stepped inside. "And shut the damn door!"

The first thing Noah saw was that Mike had been laid out, though he was beginning to move some. The second thing he saw was Sarah sitting on a plush couch alongside Kyle and Becca. She was safe, but she looked awful. Noah shut the door and locked it, then hurried over to Mike, setting down the bag of meds. The cop groaned and blinked his eyes open. They settled on Noah.

"You good?" Noah asked.

"I don't know, how do I look?" Mike carefully propped himself up on his elbows. He motioned to the home's owner and said, "This witch hit me with a damn frying pan. A frying pan, Noah! Who does that?"

She stepped forward, pan in hand. "Someone that doesn't

wanna get shot, that's who!"

"I wasn't going to shoot you," Mike explained, holding a hand up to Noah. He took it and helped Mike to his feet, holding him in place until the man could prove that he wasn't going to fall over.

"And how the hell was I supposed to know that?" she asked loudly. Noah had to lean away from her as she spoke.

"Because of me shouting, 'Police!'" Mike replied. He winced when he touched his head. His fingers came away with blood, but luckily it wasn't a lot. It looked like the knock had barely broken the skin. "Besides," he continued, "it sounded like you were torturing Sarah!"

"She was," Sarah said, glaring at the woman.

Sarah stood, showing off her shirtless upper body. Sarah still wore a sports bra, however. Noah looked over her injuries, but he also couldn't help but notice what good shape Sarah was in. Her wounds didn't look all that bad, but they were numerous. Noah imagined the pterosaur opening and closing its feet to reset its grip on her as it pumped its wings and climbed higher. It would've dug its clawed toes in, over and over again.

"Oh, quit your complaining," the woman said. "I was just trying to clean your wounds is all."

"You bathed me in rubbing alcohol!"

The woman threw her hands up then set the frying pan down on the kitchen counter. She faced Noah. "See, this is what I get for trying to help people." She opened the top door of her fridge and pulled out a frozen bag of peas. "And you, Mr. Policeman, put this on your head." She lobbed the bag to Mike with a scowl.

Mike caught it, then gently placed it on the side of his head, glaring at the woman the entire time.

Noah turned and held out his hand again. "Thank you for your help, Miss…"

"Regina Davis," she replied, taking his hand and shaking it. "My friends call me Gina. And don't go making no 'Gina Davis' jokes, 'cause I've heard 'em all." She locked eyes with Mike and laid on some more sass. "This one can call me Ms. Davis."

The corner of Noah's mouth turned upward. "Well, thanks again…Gina."

"Yes, well, you're welcome," she said, calming down some.

"You know," Mike said, "you remind me of my aunt." He glanced at Noah. "Lovely woman."

Gina turned on Mike. "And you remind me of my pain-in-the-ass, good-for-nothing nephew."

This time, Noah shared a smile with Sarah. They were both getting a kick out of the exchange.

Noah cleared his throat. "We really appreciate you looking after Sarah."

"You're welcome again—and by the way—it was *nobody's* pleasure." Gina looked back and forth between Noah and Sarah, then boisterously asked, "She your wife?"

As if on cue, both Noah and Sarah blurted out, "No!"

"Mmhmm, I see." She looked at the bag down on the floor. "That from the drugstore downstairs?"

"It is," Noah said, reaching down for the bag.

"Smart man. I can see why she likes you."

Noah's fingers wrapped around the bag just as Gina had muttered the words. He slowly turned his head and looked at Sarah, but she was too embarrassed to look his way. So, he unfolded himself and stood tall.

"That's…good to know."

Gina placed her hand on her stomach. "Now, if you'll excuse me, all this excitement has gone straight to my colon."

With that, Noah, Mike, and the Rakestraws were alone.

At last.

"She's...interesting," Kyle said.

Noah shrugged. "Some people just call it how it is."

"She really does remind me of my aunt," Mike said, glancing at Noah. "She's a witch too."

Noah stepped over to Sarah and dug into the bag. "Can I?"

She nodded and turned so Noah could get a better look at her wounds. Now he stood behind her. His eyes darted back and forth from one injury to the next.

"Let me," Mike said, holding out his hand.

"You have medical training for stuff like this?" Sarah asked.

Mike shrugged then shook his head. "Not for flying dinosaur attacks, no, but I know the basics. We get retrained on medical pretty regularly."

"*Thanatosdrakon* isn't a dinosaur, it's a flying reptile from the order of *Pterosauria*," Becca explained.

Mike looked at her, then Noah. "Sure thing, kid, thanks for clearing that up..." He tipped his chin at a nearby window. "I've seen some wild stuff out there—before the, uh, dinosaurs, I mean," he snapped his head around at Becca, "*and* the flying reptiles."

Becca sat back and looked away.

"Okay, then..." Mike took Noah's place and leaned in to take a look at Sarah's shoulders. "Nothing too serious, from what I can tell. Super irritated, though."

"You can thank Gina's alcohol bath for that," Sarah said.

Mike snorted. "Yeah, I'm not doing that... There's a couple

of puncture wounds that could use stitches, but they should be okay with enough gauze and bandages—for now." He stood and leaned around Sarah so she could see him. "Gonna bruise like hell, though. Just as sore too."

"You got lucky, Mom," Kyle said.

She nodded. "I know. Believe me, when I looked down and realized how high we were going, I grabbed that prick's feet and held on for dear life."

"And the fall?" Noah asked.

"Oh," she replied, looking sheepish, "that was all me. I saw an opening and started gut punching it."

Mike stepped all the way around so he could look Sarah in the eyes. "You punched an animal in the stomach—one that was carrying you over a hundred feet in the air?"

Sarah shrugged. "Well, yeah."

"Amazing," Noah said, getting Sarah's attention. "When we saw it let go, we—"

"I almost died," Becca said, diving into her mother's lap.

Kyle smiled softly and patted her hand.

"What about you?" Sarah asked Noah.

"I mean, I didn't 'almost die,' but yeah, I was really scared for you." He glanced at Kyle and Becca. "For them too."

Sarah laughed. "How do you think I felt?"

"Right," Mike said, getting to it. "This is going to take a lot of antiseptic, gauze, and bandages. And we need to keep an eye on it, just in case it becomes infected."

"Think there are any hospitals still in operation?" Noah asked, looking outside from where he stood.

"Probably," Mike replied, "but they must be overrun with hurt people right now. Best thing we can do is get out of the city and find a local clinic, or something."

"So, is Lincoln Tunnel still the play?" Kyle asked. His words caused Becca to sit up. She was also curious.

Noah took off his hat, rustled his hair, then threw it back on. "I guess so, yeah. Worst case, we can just walk to New Jersey."

Kyle and Becca scooched closer to their mother.

"How far is it?" Kyle asked.

"Not too far," Mike replied. "Less than a mile from one side of the tunnel to the other. Shouldn't be hard...unless—"

"Unless?" Sarah asked.

Mike glanced over at Noah.

"Unless," Noah replied, "we have a repeat of what happened in the subway."

23

Once Mike was finished getting Sarah patched and shot up with a healthy dose of painkillers, antibiotics, and anti-inflammatories, the group got moving. Their goodbyes with Gina were short and *not* sweet. The woman preferred her privacy and solitude, that much was for sure.

They took their time descending the stairs back to ground level. Noah would've liked to have hurried along more, but they needed to allow Sarah's drug cocktail to fully kick in. Until then, she'd be more of the same: a hunched, grimacing wreck. Noah guided her along, despite her telling him several times that she was fine. Still, he didn't release her arm, walking in stride with her as they rounded the last landing. Now, all they had was a single string of steps and the door.

"Let me take a peek," Mike said, gripping his gun hard.

Everyone else stayed put on the landing between floors, waiting for him to signal them to either stay put or join him.

But instead, he just waggled his hand. It was the universal sign of "unsure."

Noah gave Sarah a look then descended the steps, leaving the Rakestraws behind. He joined Mike at the front door and immediately saw what Mike was looking at. The grounds—and skies—teemed with life. Most of the land animals were herbivores, though, so that was a positive, unless you counted Noah's encounter with the *Stygimoloch*. This was why Mike was unsure of what to do next.

The flyers were much smaller than *Pteranodon* and *Thanatosdrakon*. Noah couldn't tell what they were because of the distance, but they looked absolutely tiny.

"Think we're okay?" Mike asked, never taking his eyes off the outside world.

"Not at all," Noah replied. The two men met glances. "But what choice do we have? We need to get out of the city. Sarah needs proper medical attention." He patted Mike's shoulder. "No offense."

Mike snorted. "None taken. I did what I could." He nodded. "Alright, let's get going, I guess."

Noah waved the Rakestraws forward. Kyle helped his mom. Becca did too, but mostly as moral support. As they walked, Becca held Sarah's hand, while Kyle kept one of his buried beneath her left armpit.

"I told you, I'm feeling better," Sarah said.

"Yeah, I don't buy that for a minute," Kyle countered. "You look awful."

Sarah shook her head. "Thanks."

"Well, you do," Becca added with a shrug.

Mike grinned. "Kids can be honest-as-hell sometimes, huh?"

"Definitely," Sarah replied. "But it's better than the alternative."

"Ain't that the truth," Mike said. "Kids, be as brutally honest with your mom as possible, okay?"

Sarah held up her hand. "Whoa, whoa, whoa... I didn't say that."

Noah smiled, then tipped his head toward the door. "Ready?"

Mike nodded, but said, "Nope, but how 'bout we do it anyway?"

As they had done countless times by now, they kept close to the front façade of the buildings as they exited and headed south along Central Park West. A handful of bellows could be heard with a reply of a mighty roar. Noah stammered but didn't stop. He looked around, knowing it was the *T. rex* from earlier.

"We need to get off this road," he said. "Away from the park."

"On it," Mike said. "We'll make a right here."

And they did. The group came to the next intersection at West 64th Street and headed toward the water, the Hudson River. They kept to a fast walk for Sarah's sake, but also for everyone else's. They were all tired. Running needed to be a last resort.

They passed Lincoln Plaza and quickly crossed Broadway and then Columbus Avenue. Directly in front of them was Lincoln Center Plaza where many renowned ballet and opera performances had happened over the years. They headed for the center of it all, the open-air, Josie Robertson Plaza. Behind it was the Metropolitan Opera House. To the left was the David H. Koch Theater, home of the New York City Ballet.

This Koch guy is everywhere, Noah thought, recalling the

name of the dinosaur wing in the museum. Koch's name could be seen in the Smithsonian in Washington D.C. too, sponsoring the museum hall of fossils.

"We saw the Nutcracker there once," Becca said, breaking Noah out of his thoughts.

"You did?" Noah asked. "How was it?"

She glanced up at him. "Awful."

He smiled. Becca made him smile a lot. She was something else. Then, his smile faded as he noticed the bodies. The entrance to the opera house sat on the western edge of the plaza—the eastern side of the building itself. The only reason Noah cared was because it was clear that something had made it inside. Several of its doors sat ajar, propped open by the dead.

The other thing that Noah saw was that the further they moved away from the park, the more the city returned to life. People moved about. Some even drove where they could. The buildings broke apart the landscape nicely. It was also the first time Noah had ever thought of being in a huge, overdeveloped city as "nice."

Plenty of hiding spots, though, he thought, looking around.

They cut south, toward West 62nd Street. As they hurried along, they came upon the west side, the ballet on their left. A side door inched open and an older man peeked out. He spotted Noah and the others, but paid them no real attention. He was surveying the battlefield. Noah watched him disappear inside before returning with six young women dressed in tights and leotards; dancers. Mike gave them a wave, showing off his now-empty gun hand.

Must've holstered it. Noah didn't blame him, either. Running around New York City, while brandishing a firearm—cop or not—was never a good idea.

West 62nd was a mess. There were car wrecks as far as Noah could see. Mike led them across the street and between the Fordham University School of Law and McKeon Hall. There were more people here. Most were alive, though some were not. Noah pegged the young adults as students. A few were armed with an assortment of improvised weapons like baseball bats, golf clubs, and even a good, old-fashioned two-by-four. The latter even had a couple of nails driven through the end.

"Someone's a gamer," Mike said, seeing the classic apocalyptic weapon.

"Cheap but effective," Noah said. "Can't blame him for trying it out."

They continued across a central common area, threaded themselves between two other buildings, and popped out at West 60th Street. Here, there were hardly any wrecks.

"Think we can find a car?" Kyle asked, saying what Noah had been thinking.

Just then, a motorcycle whizzed by, heading south. The rider was quickly overrun by a flock of small, flying predators. Noah counted at least a dozen of them.

Noah watched as they swooped in and pecked at the biker's unprotected hands and head, forcing him off the road where he careened headfirst into the back of a panel van. Everyone winced at the impact.

"What the hell are those things?" Mike asked.

"I believe that's the smallest pterosaur ever found in North America, *Piksi barbarulna*," Noah replied. "Three-foot wingspan, weighing in at a whopping *two* pounds."

"What's its name mean?" Sarah asked.

"Strange elbowed chicken," Becca quickly replied with zero humor in her voice. Everyone looked at her, even Noah. She shrank away from the attention. "What? I didn't name it... *Piksi* is Blackfoot for 'chicken.' And that man should've been wearing a helmet."

"Wait, 'Blackfoot?'" Mike asked. "Like the Native American tribe?"

Becca nodded. "Uh-huh. Its remains were first found on a Blackfoot reservation—in Montana."

Mike shivered where he stood. "Birds..."

"I take back what I said earlier," Kyle said. "I don't want to find a car."

Noah agreed. "Yeah, we're much quieter if we stay on foot. We can also escape indoors a lot easier too."

With the carnivorous *chickens* gone, they continued west, pushing further and further away from Central Park, the museum, and Noah's *Dreadnoughtus*. He still couldn't believe that it was the last time he'd ever see it. Noah was confident in that too. He had no reason to ever return to New York City. It had been the only reason he was here in the first place.

It, like Constance and so many others, was gone forever.

"How far are we now?" Becca asked.

"Not far—about a mile straight down 10th Avenue," Mike replied. "It's the next street west of us."

As Mike had said, the next street west of them was, in fact, 10th Avenue. Traffic here naturally flowed north since most of the city's roads were of the one-way variety.

Not that it matters for walkers.

They decided to keep to the eastern side of 10th as they marched toward their destination. The sounds of chaos still echoed around them, but none of it was present for them to see. People hurried in and out of apartment buildings and businesses, even a few bicyclists pedaled up and down the street. Every single person they came across had the same look on their face. They were all scared.

The streets were coming and going in a blur. Noah had forgotten how narrow the blocks were here. From above, all of New York City south of Harlem looked like cookie cut, thin rectangles with the north and south running streets acting as the shorter sides.

They made it six more streets, down to West 54th, when the screech of a large flyer startled everyone. Noah didn't look to see what it was. He surveyed the area and found an abandoned charter bus further ahead.

"There. Go."

The five survivors ran for it, leaping inside as the creature descended upon them. Mike was the last inside. He turned and tripped backward onto the entrance stairs. The accident had saved his life. A monstrous winged beast barely missed him with its hind feet. Their taloned tips closed only inches from Mike's chest. The shadow the animal created sent chills up and down Noah's body as he dragged Mike inside then shut the door.

Mike just lay on the floor, panting.

"You good?" Noah asked.

Mike nodded. "Yeah. That...was close."

But Noah wasn't looking at Mike anymore. He was too transfixed on the winged behemoth as it landed thirty feet in front of the bus. Noah stepped closer to the windshield and peered through at it, lost in the majesty and horror.

"It's here."

"What is?" Mike asked from the floor.

Noah looked down at him with wide eyes. "*Quetzalcoatlus,* the 'feathered serpent,' king of the skies."

24

It took Mike a moment to understand what Noah was saying. The group had briefly talked about *Quetzalcoatlus* when the *Thanatosdrakon* had first appeared and taken Sarah for a ride up to Gina's place. Noah had hoped they wouldn't come across the animal, because if there was one animal he truly feared, it was this one.

As it landed, it folded its wings and leaned forward on the appendages' fingers to use as front limbs. It shambled toward the bus, lowering its head and inspecting it. Noah had no doubt that it could see them inside and was wondering how it could pry them free.

"Whoa," Mike said, climbing to his feet. He slowed when he spotted the creature. "You weren't kidding about it being as tall as a giraffe, were you?"

Noah shook his head. "No, but I wish I was."

Its wings were a dark tan color and looked thicker than Noah could've imagined. They reminded him more of a bat's wings than anything else. Its underbelly was covered in grungy, gray feathers that morphed into an attractive teal color as they traced up to its long neck.

From there, the feathers changed color again, becoming a dark blue by the time they got to the top of its head, as well as the pronounced crest that grew between its eyes. Unlike the crest of a *Pteranodon*, which grew backward, essentially elongating the skull, the crest of the *Quetzalcoatlus* grew skyward from the creature's forehead, resembling the dorsal fin of a shark, though turned backward.

It opened its impossibly long, toothless beak and cawed at them. The sound punched Noah in the chest, even here, inside the bus. It leaned in closer and gently tapped the windshield with the tip of its beak. Noah stepped away, unsure of how aggressively it was going to pursue them.

"Can't you shoot it?" Sarah asked.

Mike shrugged. "Well, yeah, but do we want to yet?"

Noah didn't. Yes, their lives were more important to him than its life was, but he didn't want to see it die just because a cosmic storm forced it here.

"I'm okay with it," Kyle said.

Mike waved him off as the animal tapped on the glass again, this time with enough force to crack it.

"Crap," Noah said, grabbing Mike and leaping away as the mammoth flyer reared back and drove its beak straight through.

Noah and Mike hit the deck as the Rakestraws hurried deeper into the bus. The two men were showered in glass. Luckily, both had rolled onto their stomachs and tucked their chins in, avoiding any of it from slashing at their faces. A few pieces did nick Noah's neck and ear, though, opening small, superficial wounds.

As it tried to squeeze its head inside, Noah and Mike army crawled to the others. Sarah and Kyle helped them up.

"Aren't we, you know, too big for it to eat?" Kyle asked.

"That didn't seem to mean much to the one that grabbed me," Sarah replied. "This one is even bigger too."

Noah got up and backed away some more as the *Quetzalcoatlus* cawed at them again. The noise made his ears ring, much like how the rex's roar did.

"No, he's right," Noah said, shaking his head. "This type of behavior doesn't make sense, even if it's just a response to the event."

"It's because of me," Becca said.

Noah glanced down at her, then back to the animal. It cawed again, then glared right at Becca.

"Oh, no," he said, looking up at Sarah. "She's right."

Sarah protectively stepped in front of her daughter, cutting off the creature's line of sight. "Yeah, good luck with that, asshole."

Sarah's defiance was noble, but it didn't fix anything. The flyer was lost in a rage-filled bloodlust and it wasn't backing down. They either needed to kill it, or at least, drive it away.

But how?

Noah looked around and spotted the answer...back at the front of the bus. There, strapped in place beside the bus driver's seat, was a fire extinguisher.

"That'll do the job," he said.

"What will?" Sarah asked, seeing it a second later. "Are you out of your mind? Mike, shoot it."

Mike drew his pistol, but he did so slowly, unwillingly.

"Let me try this first," Noah said. He pointed at the *Quetzalcoatlus* as it tried to jam its head in further. "Its movements are limited."

So far, it had gotten half of its eight-foot-long neck inside, plus its seven-foot-long head. But because of the tightness of the interior of the bus, as well as the rows of seats, it couldn't look down. If he could crawl beneath it...

"This is so stupid," he said, getting down on all fours. Then he lowered himself to his belly and got moving.

"Please, be careful," Sarah said.

"That's the plan," he said, not stopping.

Soon he was directly beneath the animal's beak. It tried to reach him, but it couldn't. Noah looked up for a moment and made eye contact with it as it rolled its head sideways to see him better. It let loose a guttural barking noise, then cawed again. The animal was livid that it couldn't reach him. It thrashed, but couldn't tilt its beak low enough to impale him. So, Noah did his best to not pay it any more attention and scurried forward until he reached the front dashboard area. Debris fell on him as the *Quetzalcoatlus* tore the bus apart.

Is it crazed? Did something snap in its brain chemistry to make it so bloodthirsty?

Noah had no idea, but it could've definitely been the reason. There was no scientific explanation on this one. There wouldn't be an expert popping up on television—if they were even still broadcasting—to tell the planet what happened and how, not yet, anyway. For now, humanity was left to figure it out on their own. In a world run by chaos, there was only one rule: survive at all costs. And when the rest of mankind figured that out, things were going to get dicey. Metropolitan cities were bound to turn into proper war zones.

Noah reached for the strap holding the fire extinguisher in place. Not wasting any more time, he quickly unbuckled it, pulled the pin, then rolled onto his back. He wanted to give it the *Scarface* treatment and yell, "Say hello to my little friend!" but that would've been childish. So instead, he only thought it, and let her rip, just as the beast angled the left side of its face down to look at him.

A cloud of white fire retardant exploded from the end of the short, handheld hose, striking the monstrous pterosaur in the face. It immediately swung its head straight up, striking the ceiling with its immense beak. Noah closed his eyes and refused to breathe as he kept the propellant coming. When, and only when, he heard the animal cry out and sounds of it backing off, did he release the trigger paddle.

He opened his left eye, the only one not covered in the stuff. The creature was gone. He could hear it shrieking and rustling about outside somewhere, though. Slowly, Noah let out his held air and rolled on his hands and knees, facing the floor.

"Stay there," Mike said, kneeling beside him. "Try not to breathe. I found some bottled water, I'm going to splash some on your face, okay?"

Noah nodded, and calmed. Mike splashed Noah's face several times, rinsing it clean enough for Noah to open his right eye. Mike helped him to his feet and they took in the scene.

The *Quetzalcoatlus* was slathered in the stuff, looking absolutely ridiculous. Noah glanced down at his own body, seeing much of the same. The teal and blue parts of its feathers were mostly white now. It screamed and shook its head like a giraffe-sized dog, trying to rid itself of the noxious substance. Noah almost felt sorry for it—almost. Finally, it left, but not before giving the bus, as well as its occupants, one last angry caw.

Mike placed his hand on Noah's shoulder and squeezed. "I'm kinda disappointed that you didn't go with 'Why the long face?'"

Noah grinned. "I almost gave it the *Scarface*, to be honest."

"Ooo, good one. That would've been epic. Very *True Lies*—Arnold."

"*You're fired*," Noah said, slipping into a terrible Austrian accent.

"Seriously?" Noah and Mike turned to find Sarah staring at them with her hands on her hips. "You two are dumb, you know that, right?"

Kyle looked down at his feet.

"What's wrong, kid?" Mike asked.

He glanced up at his mother, then over at Noah and Mike. "I, you know, thought it was funny..."

Both men smiled wide.

Sarah just sighed, shut her eyes, and rubbed her forehead with her hands.

"Look, we're alive, aren't we?" Mike said, stepping away from Noah. He held out his hand toward the door. "Now, if we could, I'd love to leave before Ms. Frizzle returns."

Sarah nearly wailed. "Really? You... Now it's *The Magic School Bus*?"

"But it's a charter bus," Becca said, confused.

Noah, Mike, and even Kyle couldn't hold back as they burst into laughter. Sarah and Becca did not, but for two very different reasons. Becca didn't understand what was so funny. But Sarah wanted to strangle all three "boys" at once.

Man, it feels good to laugh, Noah thought.

"Here," Sarah said, holding up a random t-shirt. She shrugged. "The people aboard left in a hurry. Found a couple bags in the back."

Noah accepted the clothing piece and looked it over. It was much too small for him to wear comfortably, but that didn't mean it wasn't still useful. He went about wiping himself down, using it as a towel. First was his face and neck, then his clothes. The minor cuts on his neck had taken in a healthy dose of the fire retardant, which stung mightily. He didn't get to remove all of it, but at least the front side of him no longer looked like a battle-hardened Frosty the Snowman.

"*Woof*," he said, sniffing his arm and cringing. "That's gonna take some getting used to."

"Yeah, man, you stink," Mike said, grinning. "But don't we all at this point?"

No one argued. They all needed a hot shower and a change of clothes. Even a cold shower would suffice, at this point.

"What about under the bus?" Kyle suggested. "I bet there's more suitcases and bags below us."

"Kyle, I..." Sarah started.

Noah reached out and clutched her arm gently. "It won't hurt to check. This smell isn't good for anyone. It's bound to attract some unwanted attention." He glanced down at her tattered, bloodied shirt. "You could use a clean shirt too."

She looked down at her right shoulder and bit her lip. "Yeah, okay. I guess it won't hurt to look."

Noah and Mike offered to do the job. Well, mostly Noah. Mike kept watch for their bird friend, but it looked like it had left them behind for good since taking its noxious chemical bath.

Noah popped the outside cargo doors and riffled through a few bags. He didn't check everything in them. All he was looking for were clothes that were clean and suited him and the others for the time being.

He and Mike climbed back aboard the bus and dumped half a dozen duffel bags and suitcases on the floor.

"We're in luck," Noah said. "Looks like there were a couple of families on board. Found clothes for everyone, even Kyle and Becca."

"I'm fine," Becca quickly said, stepping away.

Sarah wrapped her arm around Becca and squeezed a little. "I know it's strange, but you really should change."

Becca glanced at Noah, who nodded. "Fine. Shirt and underwear only. I'm keeping my overalls."

Sarah rolled her eyes. "Deal. Come on. Ladies will change in the back." She stabbed a finger at Noah, then Mike. "No peeking, you two."

A smirk formed on Noah's face. "I'd never dream of it..."

"Ugh, c'mon, man," Kyle groaned, "I'm standing right here."

Slightly embarrassed, Noah snapped his head around. He knelt and pulled out a gray, long-sleeved thermal. *Good enough.*

He stood and faced the front of the bus. Then he slipped off his grimy flannel shirt.

"Good God, Noah," Kyle said. "What happened to you?"

The scars on Noah's shoulder and back were old news to him, but they were always a shock to those who had never seen them before. He looked over his ruined shoulder, seeing Sarah looking at him from the back. She had just pulled her head through her shirt's collar, but had yet to expose herself more. She held it in front of her chest and slowly rejoined the guys.

"Mountain lion," Noah replied, reliving the attack in his head. He felt his skin breakout in goosebumps. "Still gives me nightmares."

"When did it happen?" Sarah asked.

Noah twisted his upper body around a little to see her better. "When I was twelve. We went camping on the outskirts of the Antlers Formation. It's a well-known fossil site in Oklahoma, well-known to those who care to know about it."

"I know about it," Becca said, chiming in.

Noah glanced back at her and nodded. "I figured you would, Becca."

"So, it just up and attacked you?" Mike asked.

Noah shrugged. "Wrong place, wrong time. I was small for my age and the cat must've thought I was an easy meal."

"How'd you escape?" Becca asked, still standing in the rear of the bus.

Noah snorted. "I monkeyed up a tree and screamed my guts out until my dad found me. He always carried a rifle when we camped. I tried to jump down to him, but the mountain lion got to me first."

"While you were in the tree?" Kyle asked.

Noah shook his head. "As I jumped. It caught me by the shoulder in midair with its fangs. I hung there for a second before Dad put two rounds in the cat's chest." Noah slipped on the fresh shirt. "I don't remember hitting the ground. Woke up in the ER covered in blood and in more pain than... It hurt a lot."

"Ho-ly shit," Mike said. "That's...insane, Noah. You do know that, right?"

Noah nodded, then softly chuckled. "More insane than time traveling dinosaurs?"

"No way!" Mike blurted out. "*Nothing* will ever be more insane than that."

25

Sarah tugged at her new shirt as she walked. It was a hair tighter than she usually preferred. Though she still kept herself in good shape, Sarah, the forty-year-old, stressed-out widow, did *not* find herself attractive, or worthy of being ogled. A few of her friends within her support group—other firefighter wives—had said quite the opposite when a random man had hit on her one night.

Once a month, their group went out for dinner or just drinks. They all got dolled-up a little too. Everyone except Sarah. She never wore a skirt or dress, preferring a pair of comfortable jeans and a basic t-shirt. She was as "plain Jane" as it got most days. After she had nearly laughed in the guy's face, she turned to her friends and asked what that was all about.

"Duh, it's because you're a MILF, Sarah," Dani had replied, blurting out her reply through loose, alcohol-laced lips. "Seriously, you need to take advantage of the years you have left."

"She's right," Nina added. "Look, we all loved Mark, but you need to get back on that horse, and it starts with facing the facts."

"And those are?"

Dani leaned in and playfully licked her lips. "That you're a hot piece of ass."

Sarah stepped off the curb, jarring her knee. She also jarred her mind out of the memory. The athletic-cut shirt accentuated the parts of her body that it was supposed to very well. But man, did she feel awkward. She found herself glancing over at Noah often to see if he was looking at her. But she never caught him in the act. If he had checked her out, he'd been sly about it.

"Listen to yourself," she said, shaking her head.

"Are you okay?"

The question startled her. "Ah!" It was Noah. "Oh, wow, didn't see you there."

He looked around. "I've been next to you for five streets, Sarah. I almost had to go diving for you just now." His eyebrow rose a little. "You sure you're okay?"

"Yeah, I'm good," she said, feeling her cheeks flush.

Why are you so perfect? she thought.

The schoolgirl crush was in full effect and Sarah knew it. She'd done everything possible to reject the advancements of men since Mark had died. Even now, thinking about another man as more than just a human being out in the world felt weird. It didn't feel wrong, just strange.

And of all times to think it.

But what she had told her son was true. The stress of what was happening, coupled with Noah agreeing to help them for no other reason than because it was the right thing to do, had really opened her eyes—not his rugged good looks, his charm, his...physique. It was Noah's unwavering loyalty to Sarah and her kids that she admired the most. He'd taken to Kyle immediately, and his work with Becca was astonishing. Even he and Mike had quickly become friends, though Sarah knew that it was a lot easier for guys to get along and find commonality.

The only thing Sarah had in common with her friends was that their husbands worked together.

Did work together... Was that the only reason she still hung out with them?

"How much further is it?" Kyle asked, looking as exhausted as Sarah felt.

"Ten more streets," Mike replied. "The entrance to Lincoln Tunnel is straight down West 39th."

"*Ten* more streets?" Kyle asked. His chin was down on his chest.

Mike grabbed his shoulder. "Hey, man, it's not as bad as it sounds. It's barely half a mile away."

That seemed to perk Kyle up some. "Oh, alright. Yeah, that's not too bad."

Becca had said very little at all, per usual. As she had said she would do, Becca had changed her underwear and shirt. They had found a young girl's belongings on the bus. Both garments were a tad loose, but they were close enough. Kyle and Mike had also changed their shirts, finding solid colors from the same person. Kyle liked his clothes baggy, so the extra-large shirt was perfect.

They had even found deodorant. Sarah and Becca had shared one, while Kyle, Noah, and Mike had also shared one. Kyle had refused to use it at first until Mike wiped it off on his discarded shirt.

"C'mon, kid," Mike had said, holding it out. "Noah and I were teenagers once, and we used to get pretty ripe at that age, right?"

Noah could only shrug in agreement.

"I'm hungry," Becca said, gazing up at Sarah as they walked.

"I am too," Kyle added.

Sarah looked at Noah and Mike. Neither man said anything, which to her, meant that they were too.

"Do you mind?" Sarah asked. This was hard enough on her kids. She knew that filling their bellies could only help.

"There's a CVS on the corner of West 42nd," Mike replied. "Once we get there, we'll take five minutes and grab a few things before heading for the tunnel."

"Waters too," Noah said.

"That too," Mike said. "We honestly need a backpack."

As they crossed West 48th Street, Kyle slowed and pointed across the street. "There's one."

Sarah looked where he was pointing and staggered to a stop. A body lay face down, across the street, in the western crosswalk. Nearby it was a mangled bicycle. It didn't take a rocket scientist to figure out what had happened. Someone had hit the cyclist with their car, then left the scene.

"I'll check it out," Mike said. "You guys stay put."

Sarah nodded and turned to find two cars butted up against each other as the result of a classic T-bone. "Over there," she said, motioning to it.

"Yeah, that works," Mike said. "Tuck yourselves into the wreck. I'll be right back." He looked at Noah. "Keep an eye on them."

"Of course."

Noah and the Rakestraws stepped in close to the pinned vehicles then got down on one knee. They watched Mike as he checked his surroundings, then he quickly dashed across the street to the body. He didn't waste any time, either. He immediately stripped the deceased cyclist of the pack, threw it around his own shoulders, and sprinted back to the others.

"Come on," he said. "We'll go through it once we're indoors."

Sarah nodded and got to her feet. A gunshot to the east, behind them, drew everyone's attention. They all turned and watched in horror as one man gunned down another.

"Oh, no," Sarah said, covering her mouth with her hands.

"Looks like the crazies are coming out of the woodwork," Mike said.

Noah looked around them. "Which means we need to hurry."

"It sure does," Mike said, stepping away.

This time, they didn't speedwalk down 10th Avenue. The five survivors ran. Halfway to the CVS, the run slowed to a steady jog. Everyone was spent and on edge. Still, Sarah was confident that they had put good distance between themselves and the gunman back at West 48th.

"Woulda been nice to be back in Oklahoma right now, huh?" Mike asked Noah.

"I wouldn't be as worried about everything, if that's what you mean," he replied.

Sarah looked away.

"What?" Noah asked.

She sighed and gazed up at him. "And we'd be dead if you were."

"You don't know that," he said. "You still have Mike, right?"

"Yeah, but—"

Mike leaned around Noah. "But what?"

Sarah held up her hand. "No offense, Mike, but you'd probably be dead without Noah too."

"I, well, I..." He looked away. "Shit... You're probably right."

"Me being here didn't help Connie, any," Noah countered.

Sarah reached out and clutched Noah's hand, uncaring what it looked like. "Don't do that to yourself, Noah. It was terrible what happened to her, but it wasn't because of anything you did." She reflexively squeezed his hand tighter.

She noticed that Mike and her kids were slowing, but she was still paying full attention to Noah. He was also zoned in on her.

"Ahem," Mike said, clearing his throat. Sarah and Noah turned their heads and looked at him. "We're, uh, here."

Sarah glanced down at hers and Noah's hands. They were still clutched. She quickly yanked hers free of his grip. With rosy cheeks, and stares from both her kids, Sarah marched Kyle and Becca across the street, and to the CVS. She didn't care whether Noah or Mike were following her. She hadn't embarrassed herself like that in a long time.

"Hey, Mom?" Kyle asked.

She let out a long breath. "What is it?"

"It's okay," he replied. The sincerity in the two words struck home hard.

She stopped just outside the store's doors and looked them over. Both kids met her eyes.

"Noah is really great," Becca added, going as far as giving her a small smile.

Kyle smiled too. "We want you to be happy, Mom."

Sarah hugged them, engulfing them with both her arms. "I love you guys."

"We love you too, Mom," Kyle said.

Sarah released them and wiped her eyes. She chuckled softly as she did. "Is it strange that I'm kind of happy right now?"

"Yeah, it is," Mike replied. Sarah spun to find him and Noah standing only a few feet away. "Like *psycho* strange."

Noah just stood there, with his hands in his pockets, looking anywhere except at Sarah. He looked as uncomfortable as anyone could. So, Sarah decided to give the man something to chew on. It would also act as a proper thank you. She stood tall, faced him, leaned in, and kissed him on the cheek.

"Thanks, for everything," she said, grinning at his reaction.

"Uh, you're welcome?" he said, glancing at her kids, then to Mike, and then back to Sarah. "My pleasure."

"I'm sure it is," Mike said. "Now, we ready to do a little shopping before getting the hell out of Dodge?"

Becca grabbed her gut. "Please!"

"Right," Noah said, "let's get to it."

"Yeah, but remember, in and out," Mike reminded.

They all shuffled inside to find the place deserted, as expected. But unlike a few of the places they'd seen, CVS had been ransacked and looted.

"Damn," Mike said, drawing his pistol and looking around. "We were definitely not the first ones here." He turned and faced everyone. "See what you can find and meet back here in five minutes."

Sarah, Kyle, Becca, and Noah all nodded and got to work.

While Sarah and her kids went to the snack aisle, Noah headed for the row of refrigerators. She remembered him mentioning needing water. Sarah watched her kids grab whatever they could find, and damn the calories, food dyes, and preservatives. Sarah snagged two bags of pizza-flavored Combos.

She didn't eat like this often, but when she did, Combos was it for her.

And you, she thought, snatching a bag of bold Chex Mix.

Kyle smartly grabbed as many bags of beef jerky as he could. It had been his go-to snack since Sarah could remember—since he had enough teeth to enjoy it. Then she remembered why he loved it so much. It had been Mark's favorite work snack. They used to buy it by the case when he was alive.

Sarah glanced back over at Noah. He spun, holding five enormous bottles of water in his arms. When they met stares, they smiled at one another. He gave her a quick nod, then got back to shopping.

"How are we on meds?" Mike asked from somewhere out of sight.

Sarah had an assortment of packaged pills in her pockets. She rolled her shoulders, only slightly feeling uncomfortable.

"We should be okay!" she replied. "But grab whatever you think we'll need. We have a backpack now, right?" Her eyes lit up. "Did you ever dig through it?"

"No, but I will in a second!"

26

Six minutes later, they regrouped at the front desk and dumped what they had collected on its surface. The variety of stuff made Noah nauseous, but it was all necessary. They had five people to feed, so it made sense that a smorgasbord like this one existed.

Mike set his snacks down, as well as a re-upped supply of medicine. Then he slipped out of his pilfered backpack and sat it next to their goods. He unzipped it and looked inside. His face fell and his mouth opened wide. When he looked up at the others, his expression was blank.

"What is it?" Noah asked.

Mike reached inside and removed three stacks of twenty-dollar bills—thousands of dollars. Then, three more stacks. He stopped at fifteen stacks.

Fifteen grand—cash, Noah thought, blowing out a long breath.

"What the hell?" Sarah said.

Next came an absurd assortment of beautiful jewelry.

"Wow," Becca said, picking up a diamond necklace.

"Hey, Noah?" Mike asked.

Noah leaned in closer. "Yeah?"

"This is for you."

The last item Mike pulled out of the bag was a handgun.

Sarah, Kyle, and Becca all took a step back.

"Relax, guys, it has a thumb safety—and it's on," Mike explained. That seemed to calm them, and they rejoined Noah and Mike.

Noah accepted the offered firearm, recognizing it as a nine-millimeter M&P 2.0. He'd shot one before, but like most people in the world, he'd always been a Glock fan when it came to pistols. The holster it came with wasn't the greatest, but it would have to do. He preferred something a little sturdier than just a pocket of thick meshy material and a crappy belt clip.

Beggars can't be choosers, he thought, ejecting the magazine and looking it over. The pistol wasn't brand new but it was still in good shape. It went into the front of his pants with little thought. "Carrying" wasn't anything new to him.

"Who the hell was this guy?" he asked, peeking inside the bag, confirming that it was empty.

"A criminal, most likely," Mike replied. "Looks like he was on his way out of the city when he tried to play *Frogger*."

Sarah sneered at the comparison.

Kyle and Becca looked at one another funny.

"Oh, come on, you don't know what *Frogger* is?" Mike asked, beside himself.

Instead of saying anything, Kyle locked in on the stacks of money and happily began flipping through them. "And to think, no one stopped to check his bag before us."

"Yeah, I know," Mike said, voice trailing off.

"Something the matter?" Noah asked, feeling a little on edge about it himself.

Mike waved him off, and put on a brave face. "No. Nothing, but we need to go."

And they did.

Noah didn't like being holed up in a single location for too long right now, especially with the "crazies" coming out as Mike had said earlier.

And especially with a small fortune in stolen property.

"What do we do with it all?" Sarah asked.

Kyle started to say something, but Mike held up his hand and stopped him.

"Look, I know I'm the cop here, but I say we take it with us." He gave every member of the group his attention before continuing. "We don't know what we'll need in the coming days. Banks could be shut down for a long time. This," he pointed at the pile, "might be our only ticket to survival."

Noah let out a long breath. "I don't like it, but I agree."

"Sarah?" Mike asked.

She nodded. "Yeah, but I'm with Noah on this. I don't like it."

"Me neither," Mike said. "Believe me, I don't like it one bit."

Noah and Mike loaded the backpack up, putting the loot in first. Then went their food and drinks, and their medical supplies. If this was the new world, then Noah and his ragtag bunch were starting it off with a bang.

Unless Mike runs off with it?

He didn't think so, though. Mike could've left them high and dry hours ago, but he hadn't. He'd been armed the entire time too, so it's not like Noah or the Rakestraws could've fought back. Mike was in it until the end. He, like Noah, didn't have anyone to go home to. And Sarah had everything with her. They were all in it until the end—together.

"But what's the end?" Noah mumbled.

"What?" Sarah asked, gently touching his arm.

He smiled and looked at her hand, then up at her eyes. "Nothing. Everything's fine."

"Ugh," Mike jabbed, slipping into the backpack and heading for the door.

"I agree," Kyle said, following him.

But Becca stepped closer to Noah. "I like it."

"Thanks, kiddo," he said, patting the top of her head. "Appreciate that." Then Becca headed off with Mike and Kyle.

He watched Becca leave then met Sarah's eyes again. They said the same thing. She was thankful for Noah.

"You ready?" he asked.

"Absolutely," she replied. "Are you?"

He nodded. "Yeah, let's get the hell out of here."

"What about this?" Sarah asked, looking at her hand. It was still touching his arm.

Noah hesitated for a second, then laid his own hand atop hers. "I promise we'll talk about it more when we're safe, okay?"

She grinned. "So, never?"

"You two coming, or what?" Mike's annoyed tone got them both moving for the door. "I swear, sometimes I feel like I'm babysitting four kids instead of two."

"Can it, Dillon," Sarah said sharply.

Noah gave her an impressed nod.

Mike grinned. "Onward?"

"Yes, sir," Noah said, stepping outside and adjusting his belt, needing to loosen it a bit. Carrying a gun, essentially, added to your waistline. He was naturally in between pants size, so that wasn't a problem since he always wore half a size too big.

He eyed the northern end of the street, in the direction of where they had seen one man shoot another in cold blood. Noah had no plan on getting shot in the back today. Eviscerated by a dinosaur...? Still, no, but that was honestly more likely at this point in time.

The entrance to Lincoln Tunnel was up ahead, three streets to the south of their current position. They put the brief respite inside the CVS to good use and put on some speed, jogging their way across West 41st and 40th streets. They only slowed when they came upon West 39th because of the sea of wrecks. Car after car had collided into one another as they had attempted to squeeze into the two-lane tunnel.

But—they were in luck! Most of the wrecks had occurred fifty feet in front of the entrance. Noah spotted a handful of sideways, jammed up vehicles that had obviously been the cause of the bottleneck. But beyond the blockade the way was mostly clear, including the Lincoln Tunnel's two lanes.

"'Bout time we've had some luck," Mike said.

They zigged and zagged through the maze of inert cars and trucks, heading straight for the tunnel. Noah didn't care if they were forced to walk to New Jersey. They'd made it here and that's what mattered most.

A gruff-sounding roar made Noah's skin go cold.

He'd heard the rex several times by now. This sound belonged to a super predator, but it did *not* belong to the Tyrant Lizard

King. It was slightly higher-pitched than the rex's and a touch grittier sounding. They turned and watched as a dark-red and brown beast appeared from the south. It was massive, though not as heavy as the aforementioned *T. rex*. This species was just as tall, though longer and leaner. Its skull was a bit more elongated and narrower, and its teeth were serrated, like the blade of a steak knife.

"The 'shark-toothed lizard from the Sahara,' *Carcharodontosaurus saharicus*," Noah said softly, eyes bugging out of his head. "More athletic than a rex could ever be."

"Wonderful," Mike said, looking around.

"I take back what I said earlier," Kyle said, "I *really* want to find a car now."

Noah did too. With the front of the tunnel clear, using a car made the most sense now. He spun and found a silver Prius within the wrecks, only it wasn't completely pinned in place. The owner looked to have panicked, gotten out, and made a run for it after he or she backed over a foursome of orange road cones.

"Over there—the Prius!" Noah said, rushing to it.

Mike did too. "A Prius?"

Noah nodded. "Yeah, it's electric—silent."

Mike didn't argue, and neither did anyone else.

"Sarah," Noah said, "get in and get it ready. Everyone else, grab a cone!"

Everyone did, even Becca. They all zoomed around, diving beneath the car, or digging the debris out from within the wheel wells. When they were finished, the *Carcharodontosaurus* noticed them. It faced the tunnel entrance, snarled, then stomped its way to them. Their one saving grace was the miasma of wrecks. That slowed the beast down enough for them to pile inside the vehicle and pull away. Mike dove into the back seat with Kyle and Becca, while Noah sat up front with Sarah.

"Sorry," she said, ramming into the car in front of her. She gave the Prius more gas—or power—and shoved the other vehicle forward enough for the Prius to clear its front bumper. Then she cranked the wheel to the right and got them moving.

"Floor it!" Mike shouted.

The apex carnivore was upon them. It snapped at the rear of the car, catching the trunk lid in its jaws. For a moment, there was a tug-of-war battle. Luckily, the lid ripped free, now belonging to the Saharan *Tyrannosaurus rex*. Noah spun around in his seat as they entered the tunnel to watch the *Carcharodontosaurus* fling the trunk lid away, then roar at them as they left it behind.

"Think it'll follow us?" Kyle asked, looking behind them.

"God, I hope not," Sarah replied.

The two lanes were mostly clear for the first quarter of a mile. Sarah was able to keep them moving by swerving back and forth over the median. The median possessed hundreds of flexible delineator posts. The plastic-wrapped posts were used to mark lanes and were more of a nuisance in Noah's opinion than anything else. A driver could easily run them over, bending them back until they popped back up...or the posts would simply explode and cover the road in bits of plastic.

"They sure make a racket, huh?" Sarah said, wincing as she clobbered another one.

"Just keep moving," Noah said flatly, staring in his side mirror.

He could see her glancing back and forth at him in his peripheral vision. "You okay?" she asked.

"Not until we get to New Jersey."

Mike let out a tired laugh. "Never thought I'd hear someone say that..."

Suddenly, the tunnel began to shake. Noah gripped the overhead handle hard. The Hudson River flowed directly over them. If the tunnel's structural integrity failed, it could fall apart and flood in an instant.

"What is it?" Kyle asked.

"I don't know," Sarah said, peering through the windshield.

Noah didn't either, though he could see shapes up ahead. Lincoln Tunnel was still mostly lit, but like other areas, some lights were out. Sarah continued forward, but eventually slowed as she leaned closer to the windshield.

"Is that...?" she asked.

"Go back!" Noah shouted. He spun and faced her. "Now—put it in reverse!"

"What's wrong?" Mike asked, leaning forward.

Noah turned and said, "Stampede."

21

Now, everyone shouted at Sarah to drive—and do so faster. The problem was that she didn't have enough room to turn them around and had to perform their escape while in reverse. She scraped cars as she drove, even grinding against the tunnel walls a few times. She didn't wreck, though. With what was coming, wrecking the Prius would be a death sentence.

So is what's waiting for us at the entrance, Noah thought, praying the *Carcharodontosaurus* had lost interest and left.

"They're getting closer!" Mike shouted, leaning forward and pointing toward the windshield.

Noah gave the tunnel entrance one last look, then faced forward, dreading what he saw. Cars were being periodically tossed aside as if they weighed nothing.

A minivan was hurled against the northern tunnel wall.

A four-door sedan followed, crashing into the southern wall. Once it was out of the way, Noah finally got a good look at the creatures causing the mayhem.

It was a second herd of *Triceratops*. The bull that led them was enormous, bigger than the one he and Becca had seen squaring off against the *T. rex* in Sheep Meadow. It snorted as it galloped forward, looking very much like a leathery, oversized American bison.

Except that the Triceratops weighs ten-times more...

The 24,000-pound snow plow kept its head low and simply flicked it sideways when it came upon another tiny annoyance—a car. Noah was in awe of the animal's power, unable to truly comprehend it. What he was also struggling with, and trying to grasp, was that the bull was heavier than even a rex, and by a few thousand pounds. It was 10,000 pounds heavier than *Carcharodontosaurus* too. Noah had always known that *Triceratops* could get this big, but he had never actually believed it.

Until now.

Kyle and Becca screamed, and Sarah slammed on the brakes. Noah bounced around for a second, looking around. They had stopped ten feet outside of the tunnel.

"Why did you stop?" he asked.

Sarah looked in the overhead mirror. "That."

Noah twisted around and saw it. The *Carcharodontosaurus* was still here. It had been facing in the other direction, but had quickly twisted around its upper body to greet them. Noah snapped his head around, back to the west, just as another vehicle went flying into the tunnel's southern wall. The herd—the stampede—was closing in fast.

"What do we do?" Sarah asked.

Noah flicked his eyes down to the side mirror, then back into the tunnel, trying to come up with a plan.

"Noah?"

He held up a hand, then faced Sarah. He knew exactly what he had to do. "We join them."

Sarah, Mike, Kyle, and even Becca, all said, "What?" Their collected outburst caused Noah to flinch.

"Sarah turns us around and pulls off to the side as far as she can, then we wait for the herd to pass us by—they'll pulverize everything in front of them—"

"Including the wrecks," Sarah finished, understanding. "They'll clear the way—keep that shark-tooth monstrosity busy too."

"Exactly!"

Sarah quickly performed a rough three-point turn, bonking the wall behind them as she did. It didn't matter, just as long as the car didn't get trashed. She pulled them up against the northern wall of the entrance ramp. It was wider here than inside the tunnel.

The rumbling emanating from within Lincoln Tunnel was unnerving to say the least. The Prius shook as the herbivores drew nearer. The *Carcharodontosaurus* became agitated by it. Noah watched it lower its head and widen its stance, exactly the same way the *Moros intrepidus* had. It was preparing for a fight, and thankfully, wasn't even looking at the meaty morsels inside the mobile sardine can. While the humans were the easier prey, Noah and the others were not the most dangerous threat.

The thundering footfalls of the *Triceratops* nearly shook Noah's fillings free as they exited Lincoln Tunnel. The bull bellowed into the air, announcing this herd's arrival to New York City, just like a ship coming to port. The *Carcharodontosaurus* answered the call with one of its own, lifting its head and roaring straight into the air. And as Noah had hoped, the stampede did not stop.

Nine *Triceratops*, including three calves, continued forward, obliterating everything in front of them. Even the smaller females got into the action, lowering their horned heads, and shoveling cars out of the way.

Smaller... Right. The "cows" were still enormous, pushing somewhere around 15,000 pounds.

"Go, stay close," Noah instructed. Sarah just stared at him. "As close as you can..."

She grumbled something under her breath but did as Noah wanted. She threw the Prius into drive and released the brake. Then she gave the car more power and picked up speed. The way was clear, thanks to the relentless herbivores. But then, chaos exploded as the super predator went after one of the calves. It snapped at it, earning a shove from one of the other *Triceratops,* presumably its mother. She lowered her head and got her stout horns beneath the tall carnivore, tossing it aside with a quick jerk of its neck.

The *Carcharodontosaurus* flopped onto its side, crushing a car, roaring in anger as it tried to regain its footing. It scrambled to its feet only to find that the female had moved off. Now, it was just the carnivore, the massive bull...and the Prius.

"Oh, crap," Noah said, looking around.

The herd had stopped further ahead. Now, while the bull squared off against the predator, the others huddled behind it, forming a protective circle around the calves. The Prius sat in front of the remaining herd but behind the bull. Now, the only way out of this mess in a car was behind the carnivore and back into Lincoln Tunnel.

It might be clear enough to drive straight through, Noah thought.

He was about to tell the others when the two brutes collided. The *Triceratops* was in a rampage as it backed the *Carcharodontosaurus* toward the tunnel entrance. This was where some herbivores had the advantage. Predators were better with their teeth and claws, but some prey, like *Triceratops*, *Ankylosaurus*, and *Stegosaurus* had been given some pretty amazing ways to defend themselves, or in this case, go on the offensive. Then there were the titanic sauropods. Nothing could take them down except Father Time or a fluke illness.

The carnivore was quick, though. Despite its size, it slipped out to the right, away from the bull's brow horns and went for its neck. But that's where *Triceratops'* other evolutionary gift came into play. Not only did its eight-foot-long skull possess a pair of killer, lance-like horns, but it also possessed the perfect defense against a killer bite from an attacking carnivore.

The animal's bony frill kept the *Carcharodontosaurus'* jaws at bay. All it took was a simple turn of its meaty neck and the predator's teeth were deflected away with ease. The defensive maneuver threw the carnivore off balance, giving the bull enough time to shift its stance and square itself toward its foe. The *Triceratops* charged again, this time driving the carnivore back toward the Prius.

"Uh-oh," Mike said, swinging around and looking at Noah. "This is gonna be bad."

But before Sarah could get them moving, the super predator's tail slammed down on the vehicle's roof, caving it in some. It grated backward across the top of the car as the creature backpedaled toward them, coming within a foot of either stepping on the Prius, or sitting on it. Neither were preferred.

The *Carcharodontosaurus* snapped its jaws shut on one of the bull's brow horns. The bite wasn't strong enough to crack it, but it did give the predator enough leverage to push back. It dug its wide, powerful feet into the road and pushed, much to the rage of the bull *Triceratops*. The herbivore snorted and bellowed like mad as it was slowly pushed further and further away from the rest of the herd.

Noah had completely forgotten about them. He looked to his right and found that a few of the cows had stepped forward, coming dangerously close to the Prius. If they decided to get in on the action, the miniscule automobile would get flattened.

The carnivore's tail ground against the roof as it continued forward. Then it was gone.

"Get us out of here," Noah said softly.

"Where?" Sarah asked.

Noah looked around, locking eyes with the closest cow. "Anywhere!"

It charged.

Sarah threw the Prius into reverse and stomped on the gas. They shot backward, between two other cars. They heard the sounds of screeching metal mixed with the call of the charging female. Once the Prius popped free, they were clear of the wrecks. Sarah didn't stop there, though. She continued in reverse until they were on West 40th Street and out of range of the battle, and the entrance to their exit.

The sounds of war continued for a minute longer, then there was an ear-piercing shriek. Noah couldn't tell which animal had been injured, but he knew the sound. He'd heard it many times back home in Oklahoma. The sound of a distressed animal was a common sound when you lived on a farm, as his grandfather had; a dog's whimpered cry, a pig in distress, a horse with a bum leg.

They waited two more minutes, watching a now bloodied bull lead the herd into the city. It was cut up here and there, but its own injuries weren't what had gotten Noah's attention. Its brow horns were slathered in fresh blood, as were the horns of the cow that had joined in.

"They killed it?" Kyle asked from the back seat.

"Looks like it, yeah," Noah said. "Or they hurt it bad enough that it finally gave up and backed off."

Kyle patted Noah's shoulder. "Herbivores can be badasses sometimes, huh?"

Noah looked over his shoulder and smiled. "Yeah, they can, especially *Triceratops*."

The group sat in silence for a moment as they watched the herd disappear around a corner. Noah closed his eyes, willing his pulse to let up. His mind, and his heart, were going a million miles a minute.

"Well," Mike said, "that was stupid."

"Says the guy who came up with the plan," Kyle jabbed.

Mike tried to face Kyle, but they were too squished into the back seat for him to do so. So, he just jammed a finger in Kyle's face and gritted his teeth. But nothing came out.

"Just...watch it, kid."

And there, taking the brunt of it, was Becca. She was smushed against the driver's side, passenger door, sitting in silence, staring out her window.

"You okay, Becca?" Noah asked.

She quickly nodded. "That was amazing."

Sarah groaned and flopped her forehead against the steering wheel. "Sure, Bec, that's one way of putting it."

Noah softly rubbed Sarah's arm. "You did great, by the way."

"Yeah, thanks," she said, still slumped forward. She leaned back and let out a long breath. "So, where do we go from here?"

Noah relayed his thoughts about the tunnel being cleared by the herd.

"I hate it, but it's worth a shot," Mike said.

"Yeah, it can't hurt to take a look, at least," Sarah said.

She edged them around the corner enough that they could see the Lincoln Tunnel entrance again. Noah was confused at first. The *Carcharodontosaurus* was gone. There was no body, living or otherwise.

That's when he spotted the blood trail.

"It entered the tunnel," Noah said.

Mike sat back. "Well, there goes that idea. Ain't no way we're going in there with that thing."

"What if it's dead?" Kyle asked.

"Its body would surely block the road," Becca replied. "*Carcharodontosaurus saharicus* weighed 14,000 pounds and was 40-feet-long. We'd never be able to move it out of the way."

"She's right," Noah said, glancing back at her and nodding his approval of her assessment. "And our guy was easily that size. Either we catch up to an injured and pissed super predator, or we find its corpse blocking the way."

"Neither option helps us," Sarah said.

Noah sighed. "No, they don't."

"What about Holland Tunnel?" Mike asked. "It's only two miles south of us."

"No," Noah quickly replied. "No more tunnels. And backtracking north, up to Washington Bridge, isn't an option, either."

Mike folded his arms across his chest, unintentionally making himself wider in the process. Kyle *and* Becca pushed him, making him roll his shoulders in, narrowing them. Then, his eyes perked up.

"What about a ferry? There's one that services Staten Island on the southern tip of the island."

Noah thought it over, then posed the question to the others. "Any objections?" No one argued against it. "Right, ferry it is."

"And the car?" Sarah asked.

"It's silent, right? We'll use it until we can't."

Kyle shifted in his seat. "So, we're escaping on the water?"

"Yeah," Noah replied, looking over his shoulder.

The teen sat back and stared out his window as Sarah got them moving. "Yeah, sure, okay." Noah could tell Kyle was just trying to convince himself that it would work. He faced Noah again. "I mean, how bad can the water be right now, right?" Then Kyle returned his attention to the world outside his window.

Before Noah turned around, he shared a quick look with Becca. Like him, she knew just how bad the water could be.

Really bad, Noah thought, hoping they weren't about to go from really bad to worse.

"Try the coast," Mike offered. "12th Avenue is wide, might not be packed."

Noah knew what Mike was talking about. 12th Avenue grew to an impressive eight lanes in width in some parts, even wider if you counted the occasional turn lane. The other side of the island possessed something similar to 12th, FDR Drive, though that was an elevated highway of sorts, not a coastal road in the classic sense. And to Noah's knowledge, both roads ran along their respective riverbanks, all the way down to a place called "The Battery." The waterfront park was a tourist hotspot that provided visitors a beautiful view of the Statue of Liberty.

"The Battery..." Noah said, focusing his thoughts. "Where's the ferry terminal in relation to it?"

"Literally right next door," Mike replied. "The Battery butts up against the 12th, though down there it's called West Street." He waved away any questions. "It's New York, the road names are complicated sometimes. The ferry terminal also butts up to the FDR. Both roads merge directly beneath the park and the ferry terminal to become the Battery Park Underpass. 12th—West Street—will take us the entire way."

Sarah glanced back at him. "If it's navigable."

"Yeah, if it's navigable," Mike agreed.

She turned them west, toward the Hudson River. "I guess there's only one way to find out."

28

As Mike had suggested, Sarah turned them onto the coastal road of 12th Avenue, pointing them south. The highway was the largest she'd seen since thus far. Most New York City roads were tight, only two, maybe three lanes wide, and they were almost all one way. 12th Avenue was eight lanes wide in totality, half of them traveling north, and the other half traveling south.

The highway had traditional medians, like she was used to seeing on the interstate. No grassy expanses to pull off onto or use as a way to make an illegal U-turn, not that Sarah had ever done the latter.

Well, maybe once, she thought.

The median was raised above ground level in a way that made it look like a long planter. It was nice in a way, breaking up the over-developed city a little, and adding a touch of green to the gray. Unfortunately, the greenery made it that much more difficult to maneuver. Sarah couldn't switch from the northbound lane to the southbound lane, not unless they came to an intersection, or if there was a wide enough crosswalk that fit the Prius. Luckily, because of how busy the city was, the builders had allowed for just that. Dozens of roads emptied into 12th, and with each intersection, there was a pair of aforementioned crosswalks at their disposal too.

Sarah kept them moving, slowly, keeping to around ten miles per hour. She and Noah chatted back and forth about where to go next. The traffic was lighter than expected, not like it had been back at the Lincoln Tunnel entrance ramp. It was clear that exiting the city was going to be a pain in the butt, but navigating the areas between those exits seemed to be mostly possible.

"Damn," Sarah said, coming to an impasse. Several cars were wedged into one another and there wasn't a way through. She sat up higher in her seat and looked across the raised median, to the northbound side of 12th. "See anything over there?"

"Maybe?" Mike said from the back seat.

Noah pointed a little further to the north. "No, it's blocked too." He looked around. "Where are we anyway?"

Mike looked around for a second, stopping as he looked back to the northeast. "Charles Street."

"How do you know?" Sarah asked. "I can't see a sign from here."

"There's a wine store on the corner of Charles and West Street—er, 12th Avenue. West and 12th merged a mile back, by the way. Either way, I can see the shop's front doors from here."

Sarah turned and looked at him. "A wine store?"

"And?" Mike asked, defensively.

She shrugged and faced forward. "Nothing, just didn't take you for a wino."

"Why, 'cause I'm black?"

Sarah choked on her air, then snapped her head back around to find Mike grinning. "Damn you, Mike Dillon."

"Sorry, couldn't help myself. Honestly, I used to be a big beer guy," he explained, "then as I started getting back into shape, I discovered some pretty decent wines. Even went to a couple classes to learn about it more. Some of it's rotten, but not all."

"And our way through?" Noah asked.

Mike shook his head. "I don't see anything."

"How much further do we have?" Sarah asked.

"'Bout two miles," Mike replied. Both kids groaned. "Hey, don't look at me. I didn't build the damn place!"

Noah put down his window, half climbed through it, and sat on the door frame, propping himself up higher. He plopped back inside a few moments later.

"Anything?" Sarah asked.

He nodded. "Yeah, actually. The wreck is pretty light. I bet Mike and I could shove a couple of them out of the way." He looked over his shoulder. "You game?"

Mike shrugged. "Not unless I want to walk the rest of the way—which I don't."

Noah looked at Sarah. "Right, we'll be back in a jiffy. You guys sit tight."

"You don't have to tell me twice," Kyle said, shrinking away when both men stared at him.

"Or you could get out and help?" Mike countered.

Kyle leaned away from him. "No, I'm fine. I'll just get in your way."

Mike stretched his arms wider, pushing against Kyle *and* Becca. "You already are."

"Be careful," Sarah said, biting her lip and meeting Noah's eyes.

Noah gave her a wink, then opened his door. Kyle opened his and let Mike out without getting out himself. Mike grumbled as he was forced to climb over the teen, nearly falling headfirst onto the road as a result.

"Thanks," he said, slamming the door hard.

Sarah winced, and by the looks of it, so did Mike and Noah. Mike didn't mean to make so much noise, he was just understandably and rightfully, frustrated.

"Kyle," Sarah said, twisting around to look at him, "take it easy on Mike, will ya? You do realize that he's trying to save your life?"

Her son folded his arms tightly into his chest, then sighed. "Yeah, okay... Is this what it's like to have an annoying older brother?"

"Yes," Becca quickly replied. "It's exactly how it is."

Sarah couldn't hide her smile. Kyle just tightened his arms and leaned away from both women, gazing out his window. Sarah wasn't going to push him any further. Becca had already nailed the coffin shut.

With authority, she thought. *Sorry, Kyle, but you walked right into that one.*

She turned her attention to Noah and Mike, watching as they alternated steering and pushing the vehicles. Some of them were drivable, having been abandoned with keys still inside, though that was rare. Sarah knew exactly how they were doing it too, moving parked cars when there was no key. Her car had died in her garage one day, and when she'd tried to move it, so that a family friend could get a better look under the hood, he had showed her a little trick: the shift lock release. He had quickly popped a small panel near the car's shifter, jammed a screwdriver inside, then depressed the brake with his foot, and shifted her car into neutral.

Noah and Mike clearly knew that already, because they were making short work of the wrecks. One by one, they moved four cars out of the way, allowing Sarah to pull the Prius forward in the left-hand lane. She stopped next to two very exhausted men. Noah had his hands on his knees, catching his air. Mike was leaning back on the hood of an expensive-looking Mercedes.

She lowered the passenger window. "You guys okay?"

Noah waved her off. "Fine, just give us a minute."

She tipped her head into the car. "How about you take your minute in here, you know, away from the teeth and wings?"

Mike and Noah looked at one another, then quickly climbed inside. This time, Mike shoved Kyle into the middle seat, squishing him against Becca.

"Hey!" Becca yelled.

"Wait—ow!" Kyle argued.

Now Mike had the entire rear-passenger side to himself, gloating as he adjusted the recline of his body. "Oh, yeah, much better."

"Comfy?" Kyle asked. The simple question was laced with venom.

"Very, thanks for asking," Mike replied cheerfully. He gave Kyle a playful elbow. "You're okay, kid."

Sarah carried them forward. The only sound now was the subtle whine of the Prius' electric motor. She came to the next intersection and used the opening to cross into oncoming traffic. She passed a three-car fender bender. There, between the second and third cars, pinned between their bumpers, was a crushed dinosaur of some kind.

"That's one way to do it," Mike said from behind.

Sarah nodded. "Sure is." Then she sped up, not sticking around long enough for Noah or Becca to identify the creature.

They traveled against traffic for another half mile, before Noah and Mike were forced to push another pair of cars out of the way. But the guys got it done in minutes, then returned to the car, gassed again. Mike lifted his pack, dug through it, and handed Noah one of the large water bottles they had taken from the CVS. From out of the corner of her eye, Sarah watched Noah greedily guzzle down half of it.

While they drank, Sarah glanced back and forth at the river to their right. They had passed several piers as they drove. On any other day, they'd be packed with boats, but not now. The only ones they had seen were half-sunk, or drifting too far off the coast to access.

Before Noah screwed the cap back on his water, he held it out to Sarah. "Drink."

"No, I'm fine," Sarah said, shaking her head. "You should drink more."

This time, he shook his head. "No, *drink*." His other hand now hovered over the steering wheel.

"Fine," she said, giving in. She really was thirsty.

Sarah downed half of what was left, wanting nothing more than to sit back and enjoy the feeling of it entering her body. She knew she was borderline dehydrated, but she wanted to conserve their rations for as long as they could.

She handed it back to Noah, then retook the wheel. "Thank you."

Their hands rubbed against one another's as the bottle was passed.

"No problem," he replied. "We need you healthy too, Sarah. This isn't just about Mike and me—or your kids."

She nodded, blinking her eyes. "Don't suppose you have any coffee back there, do you, Mike?"

"Yeah, I do...sorta," he replied, plucking a tall purple can out of the bag. "Snagged a few of these on our way out."

Noah retrieved the drink, eyes wide, "Oh, man. God bless you, Detective."

It was a purple Monster energy drink.

Mike plucked a second one from his bag and passed it forward. But it was Sarah who rejected it. "No," she said. "I can never drink an entire one, but Noah and I can share." She glanced at him, getting a small nod out of the man.

"Yeah, sure. That works."

Sarah heard a huff from the back, and she knew exactly who it had been and what *he* was reacting to. Sarah and Noah weren't exactly hiding their feelings from one another right now. Or rather, it was Sarah who'd been super obvious.

Noah cracked the drink open, startling Sarah. She nearly sideswiped a delivery truck because of it.

"Whoa!" Mike yelped, glaring at her in her overhead mirror. "Really? Pull over and let Ray Charles drive, huh?"

She watched him crack open his own energy drink and when he put it to his lips, Sarah jerked the wheel. Her actions caused Mike to pour the drink down his chest rather than in his mouth. Between her smirk and Kyle's snorted laugh, Mike was about done with the Rakestraws.

"Really, Sarah?"

She shrugged. "Don't comment on my driving, okay?"

He sighed and took a swig, then said, "Yes, ma'am. Just keep us on the road, and I'll shut my mouth."

"Deal," Sarah said, holding out her hand. The can found it, thanks to Noah, and she took a healthy pull. "Ah, just what the doctor ordered."

"Actually, Mom, those things are terrible for you," Becca said. "No doctor would ever prescribe them."

Noah smiled, which made Sarah's heart sore. If they made it out of the city alive, she was definitely going to see what else was behind it. Was there a future with Noah Clark, or were they just caught up in the moment? Either way, Sarah needed to know—she wanted to know.

For better or worse.

Half a mile later, she crept by an abandoned stretch limo. All of its doors were open, as was the sunroof from what Sarah could see. Traffic was such that she had to squeeze past at an uncomfortably slow speed. When she was halfway down its length, an animal, a carnivore of some kind, popped its head up through the sunroof and looked right at them. It was munching away on something and was slathered in fresh blood.

"Oh. My. God," Sarah said, giving the electric car more power. She heard her son dry heave in the back. "You okay?"

"Yeah, he's fine," Mike replied. "Just shook up a bit."

Sarah looked in her mirror, seeing Kyle sitting with his eyes closed. "I'm...fine..."

They rode in silence for a bit, changing from driving against traffic to with traffic twice. The scene up ahead made Sarah brake and stop.

"Well, damn."

Her comment was apt. The cars in front of them were just like a *dam*, holding back the flow of cars in this case. And even from inside the Prius, Sarah could see that this accident went on for some distance. She glanced at Noah. He popped open his door and climbed out. She and Mike also opened their doors and got out to confirm what they already knew to be true.

"Looks like this is the end of the line," Noah said.

"Sure does," Sarah said. She looked east, down... "Murray Street," she announced, finding the sign for it. "Should we head back into the city and look for a way through?"

Noah looked around again, squinting, thinking hard. Then he looked up at the sky, specifically the sun. They'd been at it for hours now, since Sarah had rushed outside and been abducted from above. The only time they had stopped was to treat her wounds and to re-up on supplies at CVS. Sarah hadn't realized how late it was getting.

"It'll be getting dark soon," she said softly.

"I was thinking the same thing," Noah said. "We have a couple of hours, at most."

"So, wait, we're staying the night again?" Becca asked from inside the car. She sounded none-too-pleased.

Sarah looked at Noah again before replying. "Looks like it, yeah."

Even if the sun wasn't about to set, they could all use a break from the action. The energy drink was helping to clear her head, but there was no way it was going to keep her from sleeping. She was too frazzled and tired.

If I can sleep.

She rolled her shoulder and cringed. Her painkillers were wearing off.

"Hey, Mike?"

"What's up?"

She looked over at him. "Gonna need something for the pain soon."

He nodded. "Okay, I got you." He pulled his backpack out of the car. "How 'bout we do it while on the move?"

"That's fine," she said, leaning back into the car. She looked at her kids. "Come on, guys."

Kyle and Becca moaned but did as they were told.

"Know anywhere we can hole up for the night?" Noah asked.

Mike looked around, then up. "Yep, sure do."

29

They hurried along the eastern sidewalk of West Street. The accident was dozens of cars deep, and on both sides of the road. They stepped onto Barclay Street, now just one more intersection away from what was, in Noah's opinion, the crown jewel of New York City, One World Trade Center.

Built on the original site of 6 World Trade Center, a much smaller, seven-story structure, One World Trade Center was currently one of the tallest skyscrapers on the planet and a beacon of freedom, which was fitting because of its nickname, "Freedom Tower." To the south of it was the original site of the North and South Tower. The pair had been a key piece of the famous New York City skyline, specifically that of Lower Manhattan. But then, on September 11th, 2001, the unthinkable happened.

The seemingly immortal structures, weakened by a combination of explosions, jet fuel, and fire, fell.

Noah had been in college when it happened. It was the year he had quit football to focus on his paleontological studies. It was the day the entire country, and much of the world, stood still as two airliners were flown into the towers. Many died because of the Islamic terrorist attacks that occurred here in New York, but also in other parts of the country. A third plane hit the Pentagon, killing 125. Yet another crashed in a rural section of Pennsylvania after the hijackers were rushed and forced to crash the aircraft early, accounting for 40 more casualties. The coordinated strike led to the deaths of 2,977 innocent lives in total, with thousands more injured.

To this day, it was the single deadliest terrorist attack ever carried out on American soil.

Now, a tranquil public square sat on the site of the Twin Towers, Ground Zero. Noah had visited it the last time he'd been in the city, and it had given him the chills. It gave him the chills just thinking about it now.

The group slowed as the doors to One World Trade Center opened. Five office workers, three women and two men, cautiously stepped outside onto the same sidewalk as Noah and the others. Mike pushed them to the front corner of the building, choosing not to openly greet them.

"What are you doing?" Sarah hissed.

"I saw movement further ahead."

Noah faced him. "Describe it."

"I can't, I didn't get a good enough look," Mike replied. "But there were several of them over near the memorial grounds."

And now we have another group of people to contend with, Noah thought.

Suddenly, one of the women wailed.

Noah, and everyone else, leaned around the corner and watched a pack of small predators come darting across the street and at the newcomers. The office workers pushed each other back inside as one dinosaur, a carnivore Noah and the others had already met, made it across the street.

"More *Troodon*," Noah muttered, watching with fascination.

The last time they had come across one, it had been alone and acting independently of a pack. Here, there were five of them, and they squawked and jabbered at one another, unable to figure out how to make it through the door. But then, the largest of them stepped forward. The others backed off. This was clearly the alpha of the group, a big female probably. She casually walked up to the door, sniffed the handle, then poked at it. There was no doubt it could smell the person who had just touched it.

She also saw how the door had opened.

This was where the *Troodon*, and its oversized brain, shined. The alpha gently closed its teeth around the handle and pulled. As it pulled, one of the males slipped its snout inside and pushed from the other side. The other three males charged indoors, then the fourth male let go and joined them. The alpha did too, but she stood in between the door and the frame and looked around before following her pack.

"Unbelievable," Noah said, leaning back into cover. "That was *unbelievable.*"

Sarah didn't think so based on her body language. She just stood there, hugging herself. "Should we help them?"

The innocent question purged Noah from his stupor, as did Mike's reply.

"No." The detective took in the group. "We'll just have to hope they got away."

Noah could see how much it hurt him to say that, but he was also right. One *Troodon* was difficult enough to fight. Five, including the large female, would be impossible, even with both of them being armed. Plus, the skyscraper had an infinite number of hiding spots. Noah prayed that the office workers had found one of them quickly.

Instead of continuing past the skyscraper's front doors, Mike led them across West Street. They stayed low, behind the dotted wrecks, and used the western sidewalk to wrap around the back of the memorial to the south of Freedom Tower, Ground Zero itself. They came in from the southwest, from the crosswalk at the intersection of West and Liberty.

Directly across the street from the memorial was a remarkably constructed Greek Orthodox church. Noah had never seen anything like it. The designer had obviously been influenced by hard angles and geometric shapes when coming up with the blueprint of the all-white building.

Well, it definitely stands out. That's for sure.

"So far, so good," Sarah muttered, gaining Noah's attention, "because we haven't alerted the pack to our presence."

He grinned. "I knew what you meant."

"Then why are you smiling?"

"No reason," he said, looking away.

"Oh, there's a reason..." Mike led them beneath the canopy of the treed square, kneeling next to the South Tower Pool.

Noah didn't take the bait, he just knelt and listened. The 200-foot-wide, square memorial pool was something to behold in person—both of them were. They were designed to be thirty-foot-deep waterfalls. Water ran down the length of all four dark granite walls before emptying into a central void. The roar of the waterfalls was powerful enough to even drown out the ambience of the surrounding city.

"Where exactly are we going?" Kyle asked.

"The museum," Mike replied. "It's perfect."

Noah glanced at Sarah, who shrugged. She had no idea why, either.

Mike must've sensed their confusion, because he gave the grounds a look before facing them all. "It's a public building."

"And?" Sarah asked.

"*And* I don't feel like getting shot when trying to kick in the front door of someone's home."

Noah removed his hat and scratched his head. "He has a point. We're bound to find more survivors there too. Strength in numbers—unless moving through the city."

"Exactly," Mike said. "I'd rather have fifty people around when I'm trying to get some shuteye."

The light went on in Kyle's head. "Oh, gotcha. There's a better chance that someone sees or hears something in a place filled with other people."

"Bingo," Mike said, tipping his head toward the museum. "Come on."

They stayed low, aimed north, and ran forward, keeping close to the South Tower Pool. The National September 11 Memorial & Museum sat between the immense pools. The group hooked east, toward Greenwich Street, passing beneath even more of the trees. Then they turned left, heading north alongside the road. They quickly passed through a gate with a sign reading "Group Check-in."

Well, we are a group...

They continued a little further before making it to the

ticket counter, and more importantly, the front doors. The entire façade was constructed of thick, reflective glass, giving the museum a very modern look. A single vertical bar running longways made up the door's handle. Mike gripped it and pulled, allowing everyone to enter before he did. Noah stepped inside but didn't go far. He waited for Mike to join them, not taking any chances. They'd been in this together from the start, and nothing was going to change that.

Who am I kidding?

Noah knew he couldn't do anything to change what had happened to Constance, and could he really do anything to save Mike if the same thing were to happen to him? Sure, he was armed, but could he really pull his gun and shoot whatever, beast *or* man, to stop Mike, or anyone else from dying? Noah wasn't ex-military or even a cop. He was plenty proficient with firearms, but not in any meaningful way outside of hunting deer or home defense. He couldn't clear a room properly or aim three inches to the right of someone's head just to hit the bad guy rushing up behind them.

"Hey, you doing alright?"

He blinked to find Sarah standing next to him. She was gently rubbing the back of his arm now. He glanced down at her, then over at Mike as the other man stepped in.

"Having a lot of self-doubt right now." He stared outside, waiting for some gargantuan carnivore to come bashing through. "Did you know that I almost joined the military after 9/11? I didn't, though. I knew there was no way I could hack it when the time came. My dad talked me into staying home and focusing on school."

Sarah faced him, now gripping his arm tightly. "Noah, don't

do that to yourself."

"Why not? I'm not cut out for this, Sarah."

She stepped closer, only a foot from him now. "Noah."

"Yeah?"

She buried her eyes into his. "I trust you. My kids trust you." The corner of her mouth curled upward ever-so-slightly. "Let that be enough, please?" He opened his mouth, but didn't get the chance to say anything. "We need you, Noah." She leaned in and kissed him softly on the lips. "I need you."

Then she was gone.

Noah stared blankly at a nearby wall. When he followed after her, he found her by her son and daughter, both of whom looked very uncomfortable, especially Kyle. Becca didn't look as embarrassed. Her reaction wasn't any different than other people who witnessed public displays of affection. She didn't hate what she'd seen, she just wished she hadn't seen it at all.

"You old dog," Mike whispered, patting his shoulder. "Congrats, my friend. She's a keeper for sure."

"If we make it out of here."

Mike nudged him. "Not only do I promise to do whatever I can to keep you guys out of harm's way, but I also promise to make it so you get to see the light at the end of this particular tunnel."

Noah sighed and shook his head. "Thanks, bud. How 'bout we start with finding somewhere to camp for the night, then we can focus on my love life."

"What did you say?" Sarah asked.

Apparently, Noah had said the last part a little too loud.

"Nothing!" Mike quickly barked. "He...was just telling me about the *gloves* he used to wear when playing football. It's a

234

small manufacturer called 'Glove Life.'"

Sarah looked at them both, then rolled her eyes and turned away.

Noah held up his fist and Mike quickly bumped it. "Nice save."

"No prob. Oh, and Noah?"

"Yeah?"

Mike leaned in closer. "Take it from me, don't waste it, okay? This really is a 'now-or-never' moment for you guys."

30

Now, Noah had another reason to make it out of the city. At first, their mission was to escape and survive. After his and Sarah's moment, he added "find out where this will go" to the list. Noah had no intention of generating feelings for Sarah when they had initially run into one another—quite literally too. He poked his busted lip with his tongue, happy that it didn't sting anymore. It had quickly crusted over as it had begun to heal.

But for now, he needed to focus on the present, not the "what if" of tomorrow.

What a lot of people didn't know was that most of the 9/11 museum was actually underground, constructed within the sub-basement of the original World Trade Center, specifically the North Tower. The first and only other time Noah had visited he had taken a guided tour, discovering that the museum was built an astonishing seventy feet beneath street level.

He and the others descended the same ramps that Noah

had used years back. Large digital panels replayed interviews of people from around the world, recounting the attack, including where they were when it had happened, how they felt learning of it, and how the attack had changed them. The "We Remember" installation really set the tone for what to expect when you made it to the bottom.

An emotional rollercoaster, Noah thought. Two of his classmates and one teammate had lost relatives in the attack.

"Looks like we have full power," Mike said. "Fantastic news."

"Why so cheery?" Kyle asked.

Mike glanced back at him from the front of the group. "Do you want to be seven stories beneath the surface with no lights on—in a place memorializing the death of thousands of people?"

"Point taken," Kyle said. "I've never liked graveyards for that reason."

"This isn't a graveyard," Sarah said. "It's just a museum."

Noah shook his head. "No, it's a reminder."

"Of what?" she asked, looking at him while she walked.

He met her eyes. "Of our mortality." He faced forward. "Of how easily it can be taken from us if we aren't careful."

"Is that why funerals are called a 'celebration of life' nowadays?" Kyle asked.

"We had one for Dad," Becca added. "It was awful."

Noah shrugged. "I guess so. For a lot of people, it's easier to focus on the things the deceased accomplished when they were alive versus focusing on their death." Kyle and Becca looked up at Noah. "We had one for my dad too." He removed his eyes from the kids and let out a long breath. "And yeah, it sucked."

At the bottom of the switchbacking entry ramp was an observation platform giving visitors a great vantage of Memorial

Hall, and an enormous wall made of blue mosaic tiles, as well as the words "*No day shall erase you from the memory of time.*"

"Virgil, right?" Noah asked.

Mike nodded. "Yeah, very powerful, all things considered. Did you know there are remains of bodies interred behind it?"

Noah did, but he had forgotten about it until now.

"Wait, really?" Kyle asked, looking at his mother. "How come I didn't know that?"

"Because I went out of my way not to tell you."

"It's not as cool as you might think," Mike explained. "First of all, it's not a public place. Only the families of those who couldn't be identified can access it as a way to pay their respects. As I'm sure you know, some bodies were too damaged to be identified." They stopped at the railing and looked out over Memorial Hall. "It's operated by the medical examiner's office."

"For upkeep?" Kyle asked.

Mike shrugged. "Yes, but also because they're still hard at work analyzing DNA and whatnot."

"Oh," Kyle said, cocking his head to the side a little, "yeah, that's still pretty cool."

From there, you could descend even deeper, either using a nearby staircase, escalator, or an elevator. And since they still had power, the group decided to use the escalator.

"This is my favorite part," Mike said, stepping onto the escalator.

"They have these in malls too, you know?" Kyle said.

Mike looked back at him and rolled his eyes. "Not the escalator—that." Noah followed his outstretched finger, and found that he was pointing over at the Survivor Stairs, stairs that served as an exit during the attack on the North Tower. "To me, they represent 'hope.'"

"We could all use a little of that right now," Sarah said.

"Not just us, either," Noah added, looking deeper into the museum. "Everyone."

There, at the bottom of the escalator, was the wall of blue tiles, but there were also dozens of people scattered around the place. Noah's group quieted as they entered.

"There's gotta be fifty people down here," Sarah said softly.

"More," Noah said. "Remember, this is only half of it. We still have Foundation Hall, as well as a bunch of nooks and crannies. Could be well over a hundred of us."

"Still feel comforted by a crowd?" Kyle asked Mike.

Mike looked back at Kyle, then higher at Noah as they continued down. "Not anymore..."

Noah was last to exit the escalator. A group of four was twenty feet in front of it, huddled against the wall. The man gave him a nod, then returned his attention to what must've been his family; his wife, a young boy, and a girl who couldn't have been more than two. Noah returned the man's greeting with a small nod of his own. It was clear that the stranger thought that the Rakestraws were his family.

They headed around to the left and beneath the escalator and entry ramp. They passed a bevy of artifacts left over from the attack, including a smashed fire truck belonging to Ladder Company 3. The entire crew of eleven firefighters had died while trying to evacuate people from the upper floors of the North Tower.

Kyle, in particular, gave the engine the most attention, and it was pretty clear why.

"Thinking of your dad?" Mike asked quietly.

Kyle wiped tears from his eyes. "All the time."

Mike and Kyle hadn't exactly gotten along thus far, but it was a nice touch when Mike placed his hand on Kyle's shoulder and stood there with him for a moment. Noah turned and faced Sarah and Becca. Sarah had tears streaming down her face as she too stared at the ruined fire truck. Becca also cried, but she wasn't looking at the truck. She was looking off to the side, but was no doubt lost in some memory of her fallen father.

"I'm really sorry for your loss," Noah said.

Sarah smiled, but didn't wipe her tears away. "I know, thank you."

"We shouldn't have come here," Noah said. "This was a mistake to make you guys relive what happened to Mark."

"No," Kyle said, turning away from the truck. "It's...it's okay. We need to feel this way." He looked at Noah. "We need to remember him."

Noah gave the teen a curt nod, one of respect. It was something most adults couldn't say, let alone a sixteen-year-old kid.

They pushed further into the museum. The next room really put things in perspective. The Foundation Hall was exactly what its name implied. They were now inside the foundation of the North Tower. The sixty-foot-tall ceilings were what really pulled you in. The group was now deep underground, yet the ceiling was, somehow, so far away.

The main attraction were pieces of the tower's slurry wall. They stretched from floor-to-ceiling, again, showing off the magnitude and scale of the place. In essence, the slurry wall had been the center of the retaining wall that kept water from seeping into the tower's bedrock foundation. Within the slurry wall itself, were over fifty steel tiebacks. Those "anchors" helped attach the slurry wall to the bedrock behind it.

Noah could never wrap his head around the architecture and engineering of places like this. It blew his mind. Studying dinosaurs and their remains had always seemed so trivial, so juvenile, when compared to stuff like this. The thought processing it took to achieve something like this was beyond impressive.

"Still gives me goosebumps," Mike said. "The immensity of this place, you know?"

Noah did.

"Over there," Sarah said, pointing toward the opposite side of the hall. "I see a couple of benches not being used."

"I see them," Mike said. "Can't wait to park it for the night."

"Same," Noah said. "Then we can go over our plan for the morning."

They stayed close and threaded their way through loners, couples, and families, like the foursome Noah had seen earlier. But there were also groups of what looked like friends, possibly coworkers from the surrounding buildings.

Noah caught snippets of conversation as he followed the others across Foundation Hall. Most of what he heard was regarding the event; what it really was or why it had happened. A few people believed it was God's wrath. Others were convinced that it was signs from another world—aliens. But Noah knew the truth. It was simply that Earth had been in the wrong place at the wrong time.

Shit luck, he thought. *Really shitty luck.*

They found a place near a beat-up, blue chiller motor. It had been part of the North Tower's air conditioning, and had been recovered then put on display here. The Rakestraws sat against the wall while Noah and Mike picked up an unused bench and carried it over. They set it down six feet in front of Sarah and her kids, then Noah and Mike sat on top of it. Everyone stayed silent, taking a much-needed rest.

Noah watched Kyle's eyes dart around the room. As he continued his stationary tour, he said, "This place is the reason Dad became a firefighter."

"The museum?" Mike asked.

Kyle shook his head and focused on the two men sitting across from him. "The attack. Dad grew up on Staten Island—was living there when the towers went down. He was in high school at the time. A couple years later, he graduated and took the fireman's exam and joined FDNY."

"That was very honorable of him to do," Noah said, reflecting on what he had said to Sarah about not having it in him to do the same thing back in 2001. He glanced at her, but she was too busy paying attention to Kyle to see it.

"Yeah, it was..." Kyle said, looking at his mom. "I miss him a lot." Sarah wrapped her arms around her kids and squeezed.

"So do we, Kyle," she said. "Everyone that knew him does."

Mike threaded his fingers together and leaned forward on his knees. "I'm sorry I didn't. Sounds like a standup guy."

Sarah released Kyle and Becca so she could wipe her eyes. "He was. Mark was one of those people that was exceptional at everything he did, but all he wanted to do was help others." She settled down a little, then slouched into the wall some more. "Why did you become a cop, Mike?"

"A little of the same," he replied. "I'm third generation cop, first in New York, though. Dad and Grandad pushed me to join the force even before I knew I wanted to. But once I understood the job—really understood it—I fell in love with it."

"But not now?" Noah asked, hearing a touch of disappointment in his voice.

"It's become a game over the years. Politics has ruined it for a lot of us that just want to make a difference. Too much red tape and corruption nowadays."

"Where were you during 9/11?" Kyle asked Noah.

"I had just retired from football."

Mike faced him. "Oh, yeah, that's right. You mentioned that before, but we never got into it more. Where did you play?"

"Played wide receiver for Coach Stoops at Oklahoma."

"No, shit?" Mike said, a little too loudly. Several people paused their own conversations to look at them. Mike curled into himself a bit before continuing. He looked up at Noah's University of Oklahoma hat and shook his head. "The hat makes sense now."

"I was a top recruit too," Noah said. "Was even on the 2000 national championship team."

"Wow, really?" Mike glowed right now. "You got to play in the national title game?"

Noah looked away. "No, actually, I didn't. Had my bell rung the game before. Missed the title game because of prolonged concussion symptoms."

"Oh, dang. Sorry to hear that."

Noah shrugged. "After the season was over, I went home and thought long and hard about my future. The concussion scared me big time. So, I talked it over with my folks, and we decided that the best move was to step away from the game."

"Is that when you decided to study paleontology full-time?"

Becca asked.

"It is, though I've always been interested in it thanks to my dad."

Mike sat back, almost looking visibly ill. "I can't believe you gave up a chance at the NFL to dig up bones…"

"I sure did."

"Any regrets?" Sarah asked.

Noah looked around. "Besides now?" Sarah could only roll her eyes. "No, it was the right decision. A couple years later, we found the *Dreadnoughtus* down in Argentina, so I'd say it worked out okay."

Mike held up his hand, raising one finger at a time as he ticked off his next words. "Mauled by a mountain lion as a kid—grows up to be a high-level NCAA recruit—then becomes a big-shot paleontologist. Talk about your origin stories!"

"He's right," Kyle agreed. "I doubt anyone in Hollywood could come up with something like that."

Noah looked away, but smiled softly. "Sure, yeah. Hey, maybe they'll make a movie about my life someday."

Or write a book.

"You mean, if they ever make another movie again," Kyle muttered. Everyone just stared at him. He threw his hands up and said, "What? I bet half of Hollywood is dead already."

"There he is!" Mike announced. "Mr. Glass-Half-Empty has returned!"

31

It took everyone some time to settle in. The prospects of sleeping on the hard, unforgiving floor of the museum wasn't what kept Noah up late into the night. He'd done similar when out in the field, or roughing it after deciding to camp for the night during a long hike without the proper gear. No, what kept him up was the possibility of being ambushed by a pack of hyper-aggressive predators while his guard was down.

But exhaustion had finally beaten him into submission. And he slept, dreaming of tomorrow, of what was to come. He dreamt of surviving, not of dying. He also dreamt of six months from now. What would life be like? Would anything truly change? Was Hollywood dead, as Kyle had suggested? Would the nightly news still broadcast? Were schools open? Was his school open? Did the grocery store still get shipments of milk and eggs?

The loud *hoot* of an excited creature startled him awake, but he didn't move. Noah just opened his eyes and placed his hand atop his lower abdomen—atop his concealed pistol. A second and third voice answered the first one. Then two more voices. A group—of men—had just entered the museum, and they didn't exactly sound all that worried that they'd wake the people camping out here.

"What the hell…" Mike moaned, groggy.

Noah sat up on his elbows next to Mike. Before settling down for the night, they had put themselves between the other people sleeping around them and Sarah, Kyle, and Becca. The Rakestraws were also rousing, as were most, if not all, of the survivors. The footsteps of the newcomers could be heard as they descended deeper into the stillness of the museum. Then, one of them peeked over the edge of the observation platform that overlooked Foundation Hall, where most of the survivors were.

Noah watched the guy look out over the sea of people. Another man joined him. They quietly conversed with one another before disappearing. Noah tracked their footfalls to the next ramp and then the escalator down to the bottom level. Mike gave Noah a quick look, then climbed to his feet. Noah did too, and the pair headed over to meet the newcomers halfway.

"Not tonight," Mike said, stomping furiously.

"Troublemakers?" Noah asked.

Mike shook his head. "Doesn't matter. But we can't let them try, either way. Needs to be nipped in the ass—*now*."

Noah agreed. Everyone's safety was on the line if these guys decided to get rowdy.

"Think they'll really cause us a problem?"

"When you've done what I've done for as long as I've done it, you come to believe that some people just really love to cause trouble."

Noah scratched his chin. "Uh, I'm usually too busy to cause trouble."

"You were also raised right. I can tell just by talking to you."

"Also true," Noah said. "Mom and Dad didn't put up with anything."

Mike nodded. "Neither did my folks." He snorted. "And forget about Grandad, he would've whooped my ass just for thinking about something nasty."

They made it back to the fire truck when five men came into view in front of the wall of blue mosaic tiles. They gabbed at one another, throwing around unnecessary profanity and slang words that Noah couldn't decipher. A lot of it was in Spanish too. Noah knew enough of the language to get by, but that was the limit of his ability with it.

"Looks like gang members. *Los Diablos de la 42* if I had to guess. They've been active around Times Square of late."

"And they're here?"

Mike shrugged. "Could be looking for a place to crash too?" He stopped thirty feet from the strangers and called out, "Gentlemen, really?"

The five youths spun, looking very unhappy to be interrupted. And they were young. Noah placed the youngest at fifteen or sixteen. The oldest member, the one at the center of the group, couldn't have been more than twenty.

"Who are you?" the *older* one asked.

"Look, it's the middle of the night," Mike replied, ignoring the question. "We've all had a long couple of days."

The leader stepped away from the others. "Who died and made you the boss?"

Noah folded his arms across his chest. "A lot of people have died, *boss*."

"And yeah, I'd say this makes me in charge," Mike said, producing his badge. "NYPD. Unless, you don't think I still have the authority to arrest you?"

The leader snorted. "For what?"

"Disturbing the peace," Mike replied, pocketing his badge. "You guys are more than welcome to camp out here for the night. As you can see, there is plenty of space. But—"

"But what?" the leader interrupted, stepping even closer. Then the other four gang members did too.

Mike didn't back down. "But you *will* keep it down."

"And if we don't?"

Footsteps behind Noah announced the arrival of Sarah, as well as a few other people Noah hadn't met. This was quickly growing into a potential conflict. Noah knew he needed to help Mike out. Threatening these people with the law wasn't going to cut it. It was already clear to him that they didn't take the law seriously.

Noah took a step closer. "Then *I* will personally toss your asses outside. After that, we'll lock the doors and start placing bets on which predator eats you first."

That shut them up.

"You better listen to him," Sarah said, stepping up next to Noah, "he knows what he's talking about."

Mike must've gotten the gist of what Noah was doing, because he jumped in. "Tell me something, Noah, what was that big red one that attacked back at Lincoln Tunnel?"

"*Carcharodontosaurus*," he replied. "Mean son of a bitch. Shark-like teeth and as big as a *T. rex*—only more athletic and faster. Absolutely terrifying." He stepped closer again, staring at the gang leader. "Or how about the flying monstrosity with the forty-foot-wingspan that stood as tall as a giraffe?" He looked the other man up and down, guessing he was somewhere around five-five. "Could easily swallow you whole."

The leader glanced at his people, then back to Noah. "They got that big?"

"Sure did, *boss*," Noah replied. "*Quetzalcoatlus*, the largest flying animal in history—also a relentless hunter." Noah looked over his shoulder at Mike. "Man, did that thing have it out for us, or what?"

Mike and Sarah stepped forward, stopping once they were in line with Noah.

Mike slapped him on the shoulder and said, "Especially after you sprayed it in the face with a fire extinguisher."

"Yeah, I probably painted a target on my back with that one." Noah looked around, then up at the rampway. "In fact, I wouldn't be surprised if it tracked us here and is waiting for us to leave."

Noah had these guys hook, line, and sinker. He could say anything about the animal and they'd believe it. So he did.

"It can sense body heat, so good luck hiding from it. The only way to keep one from plucking you from the ground is to hide—and to be very quiet."

Sarah pulled her shirt collar aside to show off her bandages. "I didn't get away in time."

The leader's eyes went wide. "You... You guys are crazy!"

"Believe me, they are," a familiar voice said.

The three adults turned to find Kyle and Becca standing further back, along with a dozen other people. The random citizens all looked pissed for being woken up.

"Sometimes," Kyle continued, "I think about feeding myself to the dinosaurs just so I don't have to hear them talk anymore."

Noah clenched his jaw to keep from laughing. So did Mike, based on his facial expression.

Mike stood taller. "So, gentlemen, what's it gonna be? Are you going to keep it down, or are *we* going to have a problem?"

The *we* meant everyone here, not just Mike and the others.

The gang leader looked past Noah, Sarah, and Mike, fully comprehending that they were outnumbered.

"Well?" Noah pushed.

The gang leader mumbled something to his people, then glanced at Mike before turning his eyes down to the floor. "Yes, apologies. We'll...keep it down."

"Thank you," Mike said.

"And remember, we're in this together," Noah added. "The world has changed. So must we."

The next time Noah woke up, it was hours later. He confirmed as much by checking his watch. It was 6:37 in the morning. He was used to getting up early, but not in these conditions. Noah didn't exactly go to bed early on average, but he was usually in the comfort of his own home and mentally ready to do so.

He groaned and rolled onto his hands and knees, using the bench they had moved to climb to his feet. Kyle and Becca were still asleep, but Mike and Sarah were not. They were standing a few feet away, quietly talking to one another. When they noticed Noah, they turned and faced him.

"Mornin', sunshine," Mike said. Like Sarah, he sported heavy bags under his eyes. Noah figured he had them as well.

"Anything from our guests?" Noah asked.

Mike shook his head. "Gone. Already checked on them."

"They must've left in the middle of the night," Sarah said.

"Good riddance," Noah said, yawning. "Dodged a bullet with that."

Sarah snorted out a laugh. "Literally, based on what Mike said about them."

Noah and Mike had been armed during the confrontation, though neither of them had made that fact known to the opposing force. A situation like last night's was exactly why Noah was against openly carrying a firearm, even when a state law allowed it. The guys from last night would've seen Noah's exposed pistol and immediately labeled him as a threat that needed to be taken out. The same could be said for anyone else. Bad guys wanted their *job* to be easy, so it only made sense to target anyone that had the ability to stand up against them.

Mike had already endangered himself by announcing his profession. That alone could've ignited the conversation into something spicier. Luckily, it hadn't. And it was clear to Noah that the gang members hadn't been outwardly seeking conflict. They had just been extremely rude.

Plus, getting into a gunfight deep within a museum didn't seem like a viable option. There were no easily accessible exits and there were too many innocent bystanders. Add in that Noah had never fired a gun at another human being before... Any sort of a violent outburst from the gang would've ended in bloodshed, though Noah wasn't sure whose blood it would've been.

Could he really aim a gun at someone and pull the trigger?

He glanced at Sarah and Mike, then Kyle and Becca. The answer became crystal clear during this time of reflection.

The answer was *yes*. If push came to shove, he would protect those he cared about. And right now, he cared about the Rakestraws, as well as Mike. The thought of killing someone chilled his spine. He knew, first-hand, that force rarely caused peace. He had broken up his fair share of scrums on the football field. Most of those had been started because of ego. Talking it out would've solved ninety-nine percent of them.

Mike had already broken several laws in his fight to survive, and had last night's altercation gotten out of control, he would've had to have broken more, that Noah was certain of. Their fight wasn't just for their lives, but it was also for their morality.

Could Noah really shoot and kill another human being?

Was Mike willing to continue to go against everything he stood for when he had sworn to protect and serve?

Even Sarah was battling with herself, stressed to the max over her children's safety. Could she hold on a little longer before the weight of it all caught up to her?

Noah's gut told him *yes*, but he had always been a romantic when it came to a person's inner strength. Some people wanted to be strong hero-types, but simply weren't cut out for it.

32

Sarah, Kyle, and Becca followed Mike and Noah up the ramp, toward the museum's designated exit in the southwest corner of the surface-level floor. They had decided to go this way instead of backtracking to their original entry point since they needed to keep moving south. Now, they wouldn't have to wrap around the entire museum to do so. They did it while still in hiding, so to speak.

The exit led them into the heart of Ground Zero, between both Memorial Pools. Sarah couldn't hear the pounding of the waterfalls from inside the museum, but she knew she would once they opened the doors.

Like at the entrance, the museum's walls comprised of solid glass, giving the five survivors a solid look at what awaited them. So far, it looked as if Ground Zero was completely deserted. Sarah didn't see anything twitch other than the leaves in the trees that dotted the area.

"We clear?" she asked, holding hands with Kyle and Becca. Her son had become more and more comfortable with her touch since the event had happened. He had reverted into a child who needed his mommy, which was alright by Sarah.

"Looks like it," Noah replied.

He stayed with the Rakestraws as Mike inched closer to the doors. Twenty feet later, he gripped the solid vertical door bar and pushed. He cracked it open, then immediately shut it. Sarah was about to ask why he had hesitated, but then she smelled it.

"There's a fire," Mike announced, looking back at them. "A big one."

Kyle gave the most obvious observation. "But dinosaurs don't start fires—not on purpose."

"Exactly," Mike said.

"The men from last night," Sarah suggested.

Mike nodded. "Could be, yeah. Would it shock you to learn that once they left the museum, they went on with their hooliganry?"

"No," Noah said, "and I never thought I'd ever hear someone use 'hooliganry' in a sentence."

Mike gripped the door handle again. "Well, I'm full of surprises."

"What if they're out there waiting for us?" Becca asked, leaning into Sarah.

"We won't let anything happen to you, Bec," Sarah replied, looking over at Noah, then Mike. "Right?"

Noah and Mike looked at one another, then both drew their pistol.

"No, we won't," Noah said.

Mike pushed open the door, holding it for Noah and the

Rakestraws. He followed them outside, then took up the lead again. The smoke was heavier to the south, but the trees made it impossible to locate the source.

"This is actually good," Noah said. "We'll be harder to track because of the smoke." Then his shoulders fell a little. "Until we're out of the smoke. Then our clothes will make it easier."

"I remember when my parents would go out to dinner," Sarah explained, "before the national smoking ban in restaurants. I could smell them both from across the house depending on which place they ended up."

Noah nodded. "Yeah, but at least we'll be outside. The trail won't be as concentrated, like it is indoors."

"Nothing we can do about it," Mike said. "Regardless of how much of an ashtray we smell like, we need to get to the ferry terminal ASAP. I'm not spending another night on this rock."

"You won't get an argument out of me," Sarah said.

"Same," Noah said. "Mike, get us moving."

The New York cop nodded and did just that. "We'll backtrack to Liberty Street and cross there, then head south down West Street."

"That'll take us to Battery Park, right?" Sarah asked.

"Yep. The ferry terminal is on the other side of the park." Mike faced them. "*But* we gotta get there first."

"Then what are we doing standing around burning daylight?" Kyle asked.

Mike's right eyebrow crawled up his forehead. He slowly lifted his hand and extended his finger at Kyle's face. "You...are correct." He dropped his hand and turned. "Let's get moving."

Kyle gave Sarah a quick look that was accompanied with a small smile. He and Mike were starting to get along better, from what she could tell, not that they had been at each other's throats or anything.

They did as Mike had suggested and backtracked through the grounds. They skimmed past the South Tower Pool, exactly as they had the day before. They slowed as they got closer to Liberty Street. The smoke was so much heavier now. Sarah was forced to pull her shirt collar over her nose. Her sinuses had never liked heavy smoke. Campfires were amazing, just not to her eyes and nose.

"What's across the street?" Noah asked.

"I don't remember," Sarah replied, "we rarely come this far south when we're in the city."

Mike stopped beneath the last tree on the property, looking up at the remains of a brutal fire. Sarah and Noah joined him, leaving her kids for a moment to take it in.

"Oh, no..." Sarah said, voice trailing off.

The Greek Orthodox church from yesterday was no more. The once gleaming white building was now nothing more than a charred husk. Based on the extent of the damage, it had been burning throughout the night, and with the city in shambles, including its emergency services, it had been left to burn itself out. There were still a few smaller flames, but it was mostly just a smoking, roofless husk. Weakened by the fire damage, the roof had collapsed in on itself.

"Damn," Mike said.

Sarah glanced at both men. "We still thinking it was the guys from last night?"

Noah sighed. "I hope not, but I guess it's possible they did this—even before running into us."

Sarah knew that, if it were them, Noah and Mike would

feel some responsibility for it. Short of killing them, what could they have done differently? They kept five gang members from harming anyone inside the museum. At the time, it had been the most pressing matter, the immediate danger. What happened after that couldn't have been stopped unless Noah and Mike had followed them outside, which would've been an incredibly stupid thing to do.

"We traded one wrong for another," Mike said defeated.

"Did you ever go there?" Kyle asked from behind.

Mike shook his head. "No, never been inside. But it was a church, a place that was supposed to be safe, somewhere people could go when in need."

"Like the one you guys hid in?" Becca asked softly.

Mike faced them. "Exactly."

Sarah held up her hands in a calming gesture. "We still don't know it was intentional. There are many reasons why a building can burn down, Mike."

"If it was them... *That* will really piss me off."

"This isn't your *or* Noah's fault, either," Sarah said.

"She's right," Kyle added. "You protected a lot of people last night."

"And we have condemned more to death in the process." Sarah left Noah's side and stepped up to Mike. She leaned in and wrapped her arms around him. He didn't return the embrace. He just stood there and accepted it. "You're a hero, Mike. You've done more than anyone could've asked."

When she stepped away, she was surprised to see tears in his eyes. Sarah hadn't taken the time to think about what was going on inside Mike's head. He had always seemed so in control, but it was plain to see that everything was deeply disturbing him.

"Thanks," he said, sniffing back tears.

But it was Kyle who reset the mood, not Sarah or Noah.

Her son held out his hand to Mike. He didn't take it right away, but when he did Kyle squeezed hard. "Thank you."

Mike smiled softly. "Yeah, kid, uh, no problem."

When they released grips, Mike's shoulders shifted back, into a display of confidence. He sucked in a deep breath then blew it out until his lungs were empty. He already looked back in control.

"Right."

Noah nodded. "Right."

Mike turned and faced the smoldering church again. "And thank you all for understanding. Once we left the museum, and I saw what my city has turned into, it…"

"We get it, Mike," Sarah said. "We're all struggling with what's happened. Just don't bottle it up anymore, okay?"

Noah patted him on the back. "Yeah, bud, we need you in tiptop shape."

They followed the sidewalk east to the corner of Liberty and Greenwich then dashed across the intersection, heading south. They were now moving along the eastern edge of the church. The smoke was substantially thinner. From here, Sarah could see the breeze carrying the smoke north toward the museum.

They stayed on Greenwich Street for two blocks before being forced to hang a right onto Carlisle. A two-on-four battle royale was taking place between two separate groups of carnivores. Sarah could see a larger body in the group, possibly that of a thick-bodied herbivore. Shrieks and cries, funneled down the tight confines of the skyscraper-lined road. The two-dino team consisted of a pair of fairly large predators, though not nearly as big as a *T. rex*, or even the shark-toothed beast from the Lincoln Tunnel entrance.

What the hell was it called? Sarah had no idea. She couldn't keep up with Becca, let alone Becca *and* Noah.

Mike and Noah led the way, both still gripping their guns as they moved. Sarah hustled along behind them, all while gripping one of each of her kid's hands. Mike climbed through a destroyed construction site fence, cutting the corner at Carlisle and Washington. The fivesome ran southwest through the site, popping out on Washington and continuing right along to the south. They zoomed past a newer-looking Holiday Inn, now jogging next to a line of additional construction sites. Washington Street was filled with them from what Sarah could see.

A feral cry stumbled everyone to a stop. They spun to find one of the two larger carnivores from the battle royale coming up behind them. The stout theropod was gray except around its eyes and down its spine. Those areas were speckled with a dull, red color.

"Damn, it must've smelled us!" Mike said.

"Yeah, probably," Noah said.

Mike raised his pistol, intent on stopping the behemoth with force instead of simply running.

"Aim center mass," Mike said. "Put as many into it as you can until it drops."

Noah sighed, but lifted his gun anyway. Sarah knew he didn't want to kill the creature, but what choice did they have? All they'd done is run and hide.

Noah looked at Sarah and said, "Get behind us." His words contained a healthy dose of bravado. Once the Rakestraws stepped aside, he squeezed the trigger, striking the carnivore in the meat of the shoulder. The beast flinched, but didn't go down. Mike sent a round low, into the animal's midsection. That hurt it, causing it to slow. But again, it didn't stop.

Sarah pulled Kyle and Becca back some, distancing themselves from the fight more than before. She had faith that Noah and Mike would save them, but she still had her kids to worry about. However close she'd grown to the two men, Kyle and Becca's safety mattered more.

Noah's next round hit the predator near the base of its neck. Mike also hit it in the same roundabout area. The carnivore stumbled, toppled forward, and landed on its chest. It slid to a stop, whimpering from the wounds. Noah looked back at Sarah for a moment. It was clear that he wasn't sure what to do next. She watched him raise his pistol, then return his attention to the dying carnivore. Noah was struggling, no doubt questioning his actions; whether he should put the animal out of its misery or just let another animal come along and do it for them.

Mike didn't share the sentiment. He marched right up to it, leveled his gun at its head, and pulled the trigger twice, executing it then and there. Once it was dead, everyone took a second to regain themselves. The predator's demise obviously bothered Noah, but to Sarah he looked more angry than sad.

That's because he is angry, she thought, returning to Noah's side.

"It's always been one of my favorite carnivores," Noah said. His voice was barely audible.

"What is it?" Sarah asked.

He stared at the deceased animal and said, "*Majungasaurus.* When I was a kid, the name made me laugh." And that's all he said. It was obvious that he didn't want to talk about it further.

But that didn't stop Becca.

"Its name means 'Mahajanga Lizard,' after the Mahajanga region of its home country of Madagascar. It was the island-nation's apex predator at the time. Twenty-five-feet long, but with a stocky body and a short snout. Those unique features distinguished it against the other, more vanilla bipedal theropods."

A call echoed around them, announcing that a second *Majungasaurus* was nearby.

"That's our cue," Mike said, grabbing Noah's arm and pulling him.

As they hurried south, Sarah kept an eye on Noah. He was still in shock over having to shoot the creature. He loved these animals in the same way a conservationist loved a rhino or an elephant. They, dinosaurs, were his life, and when he'd finally been able to see one in the flesh, he'd been forced to hurt one only days later.

33

They crept back toward West Street by turning west down Rector Street. They made a left at the next intersection, officially on the homestretch to Battery Park and Whitehall Terminal. They hoped to hitch a ride on a ferry to Staten Island, if there even was one there. Noah prayed the service was still running, maybe by the National Guard or the Coast Guard, as a means to evacuate people from the city.

They kept to the eastern sidewalk as they trudged south, passing in front of, yet another, tunnel entrance.

Hugh L. Carey Tunnel, Noah thought, reading the name on the sign to himself. Like the Lincoln and Holland Tunnels, the Carey Tunnel also carried travelers beneath the water, but instead of depositing them in New Jersey, you'd exit in Brooklyn.

"This is it. Only one block to go until we get to the park," Mike announced.

"Thank God," Sarah groaned, rolling her shoulder.

Noah gave her a worried look. "You okay?"

"Yeah," she replied, "the cuts are just really itchy."

"Means they're healing," Mike said.

Sarah rolled her eyes. "Really, I had no idea?"

The buildings ended, leaving Noah and the others with a 200-foot-wide gap of empty space between them and the trees of Battery Park.

"We take it at a dead sprint," Mike said.

"Good choice of words," Kyle said.

Noah wasn't paying attention to their banter. His eyes were on the skies. They'd seen less and less flying reptiles as they had moved away from Central Park. It made sense in a way. The tight streets and tall buildings would make it difficult to maneuver, especially for the bigger ones. But now, there was nothing. There were no tall buildings in sight, not unless you squinted and looked deep into the Brooklyn skyline, or over at the eastern shoreline of New Jersey.

There were several flyers in sight, but none were directly over them. Noah spotted a few smaller pterosaurs circling above the park, but closer to the water. He also spotted one big one flying high above the Hudson River to the west.

"Ready?" Noah asked. "Sky looks clear, for now."

Mike gave him a nod and the group took off, putting on as much speed as they could. They dodged a handful of abandoned cars as they slinked through traffic. Noah led them this time, glancing up as he pushed on. He came to a bus, then darted to the right, toward the front of it.

"Ugh," he heard Kyle say between breaths, "no more buses."

Noah agreed, but kept his attention on their surroundings. The bus had slammed into the back of a small two-door coupe, crumpling it some. The gap between the vehicles was narrow, but he decided to use it anyway. It slowed them down, but it was the most direct route to the park. He turned sideways and sidestepped to the left with his back flat against the equally flat front of the bus.

The windshield shattered above his head, showering him with glass. The maw of a large theropod carnivore burst through, as did its surprisingly long forelimbs. It also sported a little feathering along the top of its head and down its back. Noah waited to be mauled, but it didn't happen. The dinosaur thrashed in place.

It was stuck.

He finished his heart-stopping trek, then waved the others forward. "Stay low. It can't reach you."

Sarah didn't look so sure, but she went next, ducking as low as she could as the animal screamed at her, doing everything it could to squeeze through. She gripped Becca's hand and half-dragged her daughter along too. Kyle needed a good shove from Mike to get moving, and when he did, he practically crawled on all fours to get to the other side. Mike didn't look so sure, either. Nevertheless, he got low and slipped beneath the snapping jaws and raking claws of the beast.

"How the hell did that happen?" Mike asked, breathing hard, backpedaling away as he watched it. The carnivore turned its head and let loose a carnal roar in reply.

Noah shrugged. "There's no way it could've squeezed inside. *Dryptosaurus* was too big, hence it being stuck."

Kyle's eyes opened wide. "It blipped into the bus!"

"Yeah, that's gotta be it," Mike said. "Talk about your bad luck, huh?"

Noah glanced at him. "Tell that to the people who were on the bus..."

Mike sneered at the thought. "Oh, right."

They left the irate *Dryptosaurus* alone. Its vengeful calls were bound to attract the attention of another predator. Noah relaxed some when they stepped beneath the first tree inside Battery Park. The cover would keep them out of harm's way from above, but they were still nowhere near safe. Keeping to the trees, they continued south then began to swing east, following the natural shape of the shoreline. Battery Park was technically on the southwestern corner of the city, whereas the ferry terminal sat on its exact southern tip.

The waterfront park had seen its share of bloodshed. Scavengers, both modern and prehistoric, picked at the remains of several bodies. The manicured lawns were stained red and a handful of trees had been uprooted by something immense. Noah pictured a brawl between apex carnivores or perhaps something like what they had seen between the *Carcharodontosaurus* and the herd of *Triceratops*; brutes on either side of the food chain duking it out.

The remains of several small herbivores were present too, and they were likewise being stripped by scavengers from both eras of time. Noah blanked at the sight of a black vulture fighting over food with a small pterosaur.

This was the world now.

"What do you think the rest of the country looks like?" Sarah asked.

Noah had been thinking about that too.

"Well," he replied, "if what Mike said about people being traded is true—which I think it is," he quickly added as Mike looked at him, "then I think it's safe to say that urban cities got the worst of it because of their dense population."

"Your 'cabin in the mountains' is looking better and better," Mike said.

"Does that mean we're leaving New York for good?" Becca asked.

Sarah slowed but did not stop. None of them had really talked about their home situations—the future of them. They were trying to get out of the city, plain and simple. But what happened after that? Could any of them go home?

Noah's situation was a little different back in Oklahoma. Yes, he worked in a bigger city, but he lived in suburbia, on a solid piece of property. The area was still heavily populated, but it was nothing like the boroughs that made up New York City. He wondered what a place like Hong Kong or Beijing looked like now—or other densely populated cities like those over in India. How many millions of people have died since the event took place?

The one saving grace of being in a place like New York City was the buildings themselves. As Noah and his group could testify, they provided their own kind of much-needed protection. If you could slowly move toward one of the city's many exits, you could get out by piggybacking into, and out of, buildings.

Be quiet, don't go out at night, and avoid Central Park, Noah thought, mentally listing what he believed was the best strategy to use. A large structure came into view through the trees. *But what about the water?*

The Staten Island ferry terminal was an impressive building in its own right. The high-glass walls stood out against the blank canvass of concrete beneath it, as well as the water beyond it. The words "Staten Island Ferry" had been built into the entrance, like a proper theme park entrance. Other people hustled around—in and out of the terminal, or just passing by it.

"I thought there'd be more," Sarah said, likewise watching the people.

"Yeah, same," Noah said.

This worried him deeply. If the ferries were still running, shouldn't there be lines of people waiting for the next boat to arrive? He pictured it being like any post-apocalyptic movie made in the last three decades, or a classic disaster movie. But no, there was hardly anyone here.

Mike threw open the door and stumbled in to see what they had been dreading.

There was no ferry.

Even from the front door, Noah could see the water on the other side. The dock was empty.

"Haven't seen one in almost twelve hours." Noah turned to find an older man sitting off to the side. "I missed it by minutes."

"You've been waiting for another one?" Noah asked.

He nodded. "Sure have, but none have come."

"And you're still here?" Sarah asked.

"Where else am I going to go? I have a bad hip and a bum knee. I'm not going anywhere fast, so I might as well wait."

Kyle stepped up close to his mother. "What if it doesn't come?"

The older man stared out through the front doors, toward the city. "Hmmm... I have faith that one will." He faced the group again. "Just don't ask me when."

Deflated, they left the stranger to himself and stepped over to the eastern windows. They all parked it on the floor, unable to go on any further at the moment. They had no other plan except the ferry. They needed to take a moment and figure out what to do next.

What can we do?

Becca was the only one that didn't sit. She just stood, between Noah and Sarah, looking through the window. Noah rubbed his face hard with both hands, trying desperately to reinvigorate himself, to snap himself out of the depressed lull he'd quickly fallen into.

Sarah reached around Becca's ankles and rubbed Noah's thigh. He dropped his hands down to his lap, gripping her hand with one of his. She smiled softly at his touch. Noah smiled back, but then his expression darkened, and he looked away. It was looking less and less likely that he'd be able to see where this went.

"What about that?" Becca asked.

Noah and Sarah looked straight up to find Becca pushing her finger into the glass.

No, not the glass. She's pointing at something outside.

Noah climbed to his feet first, turning and seeing it. "That's it!"

"What is?" Mike asked, getting up. Sarah and Kyle did too.

"That," Noah replied, tipping his chin to the east. Their ticket to freedom was another of the city's iconic landmarks. It stretched across the East River—to freedom. "The Brooklyn Bridge."

34

They exited the ferry terminal and immediately worked their way east along South Street, a road that followed beside the much larger FDR Drive. The latter rose subtly until it leveled off forty feet above the ground. The issue wasn't going to be the distance to the Brooklyn Bridge, it was only three-quarters of a mile away. The issue was that, because of the sheer magnitude of the traffic that used the bridge on a day-to-day basis, the entrance to the Brooklyn Bridge was another third of a mile inland.

As they jogged east, they kept a watchful eye for dangers lurking, but also useable cars, and even boats. Like the Hudson River, there were plenty of piers on this side of Battery Park, along the East River. Noah was hoping for a boat at this point. He dreaded having to head back into the city for any reason at all, even to leave.

Then you had the mile-long-distance of the bridge itself, plus the incline. Noah's back and feet ached just thinking about it. He also wondered about what would happen on the bridge, what creatures could they run into with few places to hide, especially from an aerial attack.

Further ahead was a helicopter tour agency, as well as its pier filled with several helipads. Unfortunately, like a lot of the city, it too was abandoned. Noah even spotted a few wrecks. Three aircraft were crumpled in place on their helipads. He was curious if any had crashed into the water.

"Think regular joes tried to fly them?" Mike asked, seeing it too.

"Could be, or maybe they were knocked out of the air by something?"

He glanced at Noah. "The bird from the bus?"

"It's possible, or at least something large enough to cause a tour chopper to crash."

To their left, and directly across the street from the pier with the crashed helicopters, was the New York Vietnam Veterans Memorial Plaza Square. Noah angled himself toward it and slowed. The treed grounds provided much-needed shade, but also something else of value: cover. He stopped and leaned against a tree, catching his breath.

"Two minutes," he said, getting nods all around.

They walked east, beneath the canopy of green as they caught their breath. Running the entire distance from the ferry terminal, across the bridge, and into Brooklyn, was going to be impossible. They needed to take it easy and keep their pace steady. Passing out from exhaustion or hurting oneself wasn't going to help anyone.

Bird calls picked up deeper into the war memorial, causing Noah to flinch and pull his gun free. But he quickly realized they were just the squawks of two vultures fighting over some scraps. He holstered his pistol, shook off the jolt he'd felt, and got moving again.

There was a lack of cover being on the shore. It bothered Noah greatly.

"Use the road," he said. "Stay between the cars. Use them to shield you if you see something."

"Copy that," Mike said, looking around. Then he looked up. "I hate having nothing protecting us from above."

The elevated FDR highway did, technically, offer them some protection from above, but not much. Had it been lower to the ground, it would've been perfect. There was still plenty of room for something to swoop in and attack them.

As South Street and the FDR began to turn north, Noah got a glimpse of a cargo tanker that had run aground. Its nose was buried into the right lane of FDR Drive. Mike headed to it and so did the others. It was such a strange sight to behold that they all needed a closer look.

Noah spotted another pier two hundred feet further past the wrecked tanker. From what he could see, it looked like another ferry terminal. "Think they tried an emergency docking, or whatever it's called?" Noah wasn't a sailor. He wasn't overly fond of open water, in fact. It had always scared him, even now as a grown man.

"That's my guess," Mike said, "though Pier 11 is really just a ferry terminal. I doubt it's equipped to handle such a monster-of-a-boat. Wonder what spooked 'em into coming here?"

The group came in from the south of the tanker, craning their heads back as they looked up and up at the bow railing. The wind coming off the water was sharp and it assaulted Noah's face and ears, making it difficult to hear anything other than the wind itself. But then, he thought he heard voices. That confused him. Why would people still be on board after two days?

Suddenly, those same voices grew louder. Then Noah witnessed the unthinkable. People began to leap from the ship to the FDR. Each one shouted in fright as they did. Several more must've not been able to make it to the front of the ship, because he watched, stunned, as three sailors came into view along the port side and launched themselves over the railing.

The third man was slower than the others and it cost him his life.

A creature with a pair of devil horns protruding above each eyebrow, feeble, useless forearms, and a short, pug-like face appeared behind him. It used its jaws to snag the airborne man by the left shoulder. The sailor cried out and was pulled back onto the deck of the tanker where he was, presumably, slaughtered.

The *Carnotaurus* was one of many accomplished predators from South America, specifically Argentina. That area had been ripe with toothy carnivores of all sizes, like the twenty-five-foot-long *Carnotaurus*, the 'meat-eating bull.' But it was also home to the largest land animals to ever exist, the titanosaur sauropods, including Noah's *Dreadnoughtus*. No other region, in Noah's opinion, sported as diverse a biome than it.

"I think I've seen enough," Sarah said, backing away.

"Same," Kyle said, turning around.

Mike patted him on the back. "You okay, kid?"

Kyle placed his hands on his knees and started to

hyperventilate. "Yeah, sure, I'm—"

He gagged, then vomited.

Mike jumped away, but quickly rejoined Kyle, rubbing his back. "Whoa there, tiger, you're okay. Uncle Mike is here."

"*Uncle Mike?*" Noah and Sarah both said.

Mike shrugged. "What? I think the last couple of days has qualified me as much, don't you?"

Noah looked at Sarah for an answer. She just shrugged and said, "Uncle Mike, it is."

"Too much..." Kyle choked out, regaining his air. "Too much death. I... I..."

Sarah stepped over to Kyle's other side and took over from Mike. "Hey, it's alright. It's hard on all of us."

Kyle nodded, then spat the last traces of his vomit on the ground. He wiped tears from his eyes as he stood upright.

"Hey," Noah said, getting Kyle's attention, "you are going to make it, alright?"

The absolution in Noah's voice forced everyone's eyes on him. "We haven't come this far to not make it, right?"

He happily received nods all around, even from Becca, who was still the only one staring up at the tanker. She then turned and looked at Noah with her jaw clinched tightly. He knew that look by now. She was about to explode unless she got to talk about the animal that she'd just seen.

Noah knelt in front of her and gripped both her shoulders, making sure she was looking at him. "Becca, I need you to let it go. I know you want to talk about that thing, but we need to push it aside and get the hell out of here. Can you do that for me?"

Becca's mouth flopped open, then she snapped it shut, and

looked at her mother. Sarah nodded.

"Fine, but only because my brother can't hold his lunch."

Noah just about died laughing. And based on the garbled noises from Sarah and Mike, so had they.

"Thanks, Bec," Kyle said, sighing, "I love you too."

Becca snorted, sounding exactly like her mother, then slugged Kyle in the arm. "Come on, Kyle, don't be such a square."

Mike glanced at Sarah then Noah. "Square?" he repeated. "What is it, the 1950s?"

Noah shook his head, then remembered the other men that had jumped from the ship into the East River. He rushed to the railing and looked over the edge and found...nothing. No one else seemed to notice, and he kept it that way. But something had pulled the two sailors under, and he doubted that it was a bass or a flounder.

Maybe another Elasmosaurus?

Although he, admittedly, didn't focus on marine reptiles as much as land animals, he knew of a few that had roamed the waters of the Cretaceous Period. He and Becca had seen one when they'd been at Sheep Meadow. The plesiosaur species had been blipped onto land instead of sea. But what other marine reptiles had been dropped in or around New York City? What killed those men?

A quarter of a mile to the north of Pier 11, and the wrecked tanker, were Piers 15, 16, and 17. Piers 15 and 17 were event venues, and Pier 16 was a maritime museum that included a few decommissioned ships.

They now kept beneath the FDR, using its supplied cover as they continued their push to the northeast, toward the Brooklyn Bridge.

"We're going to have to start heading inland soon," Sarah suggested, jogging along.

Mike nodded and slowed to a fast walk, panting. "I know." He looked around, then pointed at a sign for Fulton Street. "There. We can follow that to Pearl."

"Whatever you say," Noah said. "You're the tour guide, not me."

Fulton Street was a pedestrian-only road lined with restaurants, bars, and other small businesses. It was part of a greater commerce district called "The Seaport." Mobility here was easy thanks to the lack of vehicle traffic. Noah caught a look inside the busted-out window of a restaurant. The dining room was a disaster. Beneath the flickering lights, and within a sea of overturned tables, were bodies. Something had gotten inside, fulfilling the age-old idiom of a "fox in a henhouse."

"Looks like something similar happened across the way," Mike said in a hushed tone. "See?"

Noah looked away from the brutality and discovered that another business, this time a flashy bar, had also been ransacked by an animal. Noah spotted a body lying face down within the doorway. The corpse was propping it open like a cadaver-sized doorstop. Noah recalled seeing the same thing at the opera house.

"There too," Sarah said, pointing to another business across Fulton Street. The hair salon had also seen its share of death.

"What did all this?" Kyle asked.

"No idea," Noah said, "and I don't plan on us finding out."

Kyle nodded and swallowed down a large lungful of air. "Yeah, that would be ideal."

Noah had seen so many potential culprits since the fog had

lifted, from *Moros intrepidus* to *Velociraptor* to *Troodon*, but there were still many more that they had *not* seen that could've caused so much concentrated death. To him, whatever it was had rampaged through Fulton Street, killing dozens—and that was just in the businesses that Noah and the others had spotted. He slowed as he passed a "mall map" of the Seaport shopping district. There were fifty-plus businesses listed.

What about the others? He looked around, visualizing the other streets pictured on the map. *How many people died just in this one area?*

35

Pearl Street cut diagonally to the northeast and continued under the architectural marvel that was the Brooklyn Bridge. In the grand scheme of bridge building, Noah knew that this bridge wasn't all that extraordinary. But walking beneath it now, it loomed over him. He felt its crushing weight, but followed Mike anyway.

"The bridge's Pearl Street exit will be quickest," Mike explained, heading for a nearby offramp. Noah had never used this ramp before, so like a large portion of their trek through the city, he'd have to rely on Mike's innate knowledge of the cityscape and its streets.

Noah had expected to see a line of immobile cars on the ramp, but there was none. It made sense the more he thought about it. Why would people come *to* the city to escape a disaster-level event? The answer was that they wouldn't. They'd head to Brooklyn, like Noah and the others were.

Which means the Brooklyn exits are probably a mess, he thought.

"This sucks," Kyle moaned as they marched uphill.

"Sure does, kid," Mike said.

Noah felt it in his knees as they slowly, slowly climbed up the incline of the offramp. If Noah were hiking, and in the wilderness, he wouldn't have thought anything of it. There was plenty to distract you when surrounded by nature. It was the exact reason he hated running. Playing sports was fine because you were doing other things besides getting from Point A to Point B. Just running... That was brutal.

Like now, all Noah could see was more concrete and asphalt. Had he been in the woods, he would've been searching for wildlife and listening to the birds. Noah looked up, seeing other winged creatures in the sky. Pterosaurs of all kinds soared overhead, but none were close enough to worry about. One animal had a tail protruding from its rear. Noah had seen something similar outside the museum, when he had gotten his first proper look at the transformed world in and above Central Park.

There were no flying reptiles, that he knew of—that the scientific community knew of—that possessed long tails during the Cretaceous Period. Evolution had gotten rid of them millions of years prior to it. He hated not knowing what they were, though he had a couple of ideas based on their size and shape.

They made it up to where the bridge exit forked. The right-hand lane took commuters to northbound FDR Drive. The left-hand exit was the one they had just used.

"Almost...there..." Mike said, breathing hard.

Noah was too. The roadway leveled out for the moment, but banked aggressively to the left as it wrapped around and connected to the bridge itself. As they turned their backs on the city and made their way around the turn, the ambience grew quiet. The roars of an uncountable number of prehistoric creatures, the shouts of people, even the report of echoing gunshots—they all fell away. The only consistent sound now was the footsteps of Noah and his group.

"Whoa," Sarah said, slowing as they made it to 'bridge level.' Noah shared her astonishment. "There's so many!"

Hundreds of people had flocked to the Brooklyn Bridge entrance and were just beginning their exodus across it. This was the single largest gathering of people any of them had seen since the event had taken place. The mass gathering gave Noah hope, but it also worried him. There were predators out there that would be able to smell a *herd* of this magnitude—hear them too. Then there were the dangers from above. The bridge offered nothing in terms of cover—zero protection at all.

But Noah, Mike, Sarah, Kyle, and Becca were here. They had made it. Now, all they had to do was blend in with the crowd and make the trek over the East River and to Brooklyn. A tandem of deeper squawks caused Noah to freeze in place. The last time he had heard the noise had been during the charter bus fiasco with...

"*Quetzalcoatlus*," he said, turning and looking up. "It's back."

"And it's not alone," Sarah said. She jabbed a finger to the northwest. "Look!"

Two immense flyers were coming in low behind them. Even from here, Noah recognized the lead behemoth. Parts of its head, neck, and chest had been painted white by fire extinguisher residue.

"Run," Noah said, looking around at the crowd. Some of them had spotted the incoming creatures. It pained him to utter his next words, but he saw it as the only way to survive. "Keep to the crowd. Don't stray from it."

Mike backpedaled into a woman. She turned to berate him, but followed his line of sight back and up, then screamed at the top of her lungs. That triggered everyone, and the entire crowd, the herd of prey, began to panic and run.

Noah picked up Becca, swinging her around to his back, piggyback-style. She clutched his shoulders and squeezed his sides with her knees.

"Go," Noah said, "and remember, whatever happens, stay in the crowd."

Everyone nodded and got moving. Mike acted as their cow pusher and made a lane for the rest. Sarah and Kyle gripped hands and kept up with him, as did Noah and Becca.

"Hang on tight, okay?" he said. "Don't let go."

"I won't," she squeaked.

Luckily, Becca was slight in frame. Noah wouldn't be able to carry her the entire way, just long enough to make it further out onto the bridge, and away from the pursuing pterosaur giants.

Someone screamed behind them. Noah looked over his shoulder, and around Becca, to see a man get plucked from the crowd thirty feet further back. Then, the second *Quetzalcoatlus*, the one Noah had sprayed, snagged a woman. Both catches were lifted into the sky, then unceremoniously dropped from sixty feet up. Then, the flyers came back for another round.

Oh, my God, Noah thought. He had never seen such a method of hunting before: kill or injure your prey by dropping them from a great height, then come back at your leisure.

"Noah!" Becca shouted as she was lifted off his shoulders. The painted demon cawed in Noah's face, gripping Becca's shoulder with one of its clawed feet.

Not this time!

He quickly drew his pistol, forgoing his earlier apprehension of not killing the animal, and shot it twice in the chest. Noah didn't stop there, and he quickly sent a third shot into its long neck. The next noise the *Quetzalcoatlus* made was a gag as it coughed, unable to catch its breath. It released Becca, and she fell from ten feet up. But Noah was right there, catching her with a grunt.

The immense pterosaur managed to gain some altitude as it angled toward the East River. It struggled as it flew, veering left and right, until it couldn't continue. The apex hunter fell from the sky, disappearing from view. Noah was too far away to hear it splashdown in the river, but he knew it had. Mike, Sarah, and Kyle rushed over to Noah and Becca as they watched the second *Quetzalcoatlus* bellow into the air, no doubt saddened by the death of its mate. Luckily, it didn't continue its attack on the crowd. Instead, the carnivore banked west and headed back toward the city.

"Becca!" Sarah shouted, hugging her *and* Noah. She wrapped her arms around him, pinning Becca between them. "Noah, thank you!" She looked up and kissed Noah again. "Thank you."

"Um, you're welcome," he said, feeling his cheeks blush, his skin break out in goosebumps. He looked down at Becca. "You okay?"

She nodded, but moaned and said, "Can't...breathe..."

"Oh," Sarah said, releasing Noah and stepping back.

Noah set Becca down and let mother and daughter hug it out

on their own.

"You did good, my man," Mike said, patting Noah's shoulder. "Showed that bird who's boss."

"Didn't feel good doing it, though."

Mike squeezed Noah's shoulder then stepped away. "I know, but it was either Becca or it."

Noah agreed with a nod of his head.

"Thank you, Noah," Kyle said. Then he leaned in close. "Look, my mom really likes you, as I'm sure you can tell. Just...don't do anything to screw it up, okay? Becca—I—"

"I won't," Noah said quickly. "I promise."

He couldn't imagine how hard it had been for Kyle to say what he had. Noah knew how much the kid still missed his father, and seeing his mom begin to move on must've been a lot to handle. Even if things between Noah and Sarah worked out for the best, Kyle would always miss his father.

"I'm good to go, you?" Mike asked.

Noah looked around, seeing that the crowd had calmed. "Sure am."

The mass of people moved at different paces, using different paths to cross the bridge. Noah and his group stuck to the northbound lane. It featured a two-lane road, as well as a two-lane bike lane tucked into the inside and protected by a concrete divider and chain-link fencing. People gladly used both avenues. Then there was the southbound lane. It was similar to the northbound lane, but three lanes wide, and no bike lane. The third option was pretty ballsy considering they had just been attacked by something that could fly.

The Brooklyn Bridge Promenade was a pedestrian walkway that spanned the entire length of the bridge. It was elevated too, standing eighteen feet above the road. Noah gave the promenade another look as they continued further and further out onto the bridge. Cables ran along the entire length of bridge, and therefore, the walkway, acting as a sort of cage. In retrospect, the promenade would be perfect at keeping winged predators at bay.

Too late now, he thought, though he figured they could climb up to it if they had to.

He'd keep that option in his back pocket.

They came across a handful of cars on the bridge. Some were wrecked with others. Some were just flat-out abandoned. He watched as a few people checked them over. Conversation arose as six people piled inside another vehicle and pulled away, idling through the crowd.

"Lucky," Becca said, huffing next to Noah.

"We'll be fine," he said. "Just keep moving."

36

They were nearly halfway across the Brooklyn Bridge. The kids were exhausted and had slowed their pace considerably. Noah didn't say anything about it. He just allowed the adults to fall in line with them and take the rest of the trek in stride. They were now towards the rear of the main mass of people.

Then, something odd happened. Voices among the crowd picked up further ahead, then spread back to Noah and the others. It wasn't conversation, either. The tone was confused, but also angry.

Then a car horn blared.

"What on earth?" Sarah said, looking to Noah for answers.

He was taller than she was, and Mike, but he still couldn't make heads or tails of what was going on. There was obviously a car somewhere nearby, but why was the driver honking so feverishly? The crowd grew louder, then one by one, they began to part down the middle. Now it all made sense.

"Move!" Noah shouted, spreading his arms out wide and guiding his people toward the bike lane. But there was nowhere else to go because of the waist-high concrete wall and chain-fencing mounted atop it. "Climb!"

Thankfully, his people responded without question and they climbed, just as screams and honks grew to a fever pitch. Noah was the last one up and he got there just in time. He gripped the fence and lifted his feet as high as he could as the same car from earlier came zooming past. It scraped against the barrier, kicking up sparks beneath Noah's butt as it headed back toward the city.

"What the hell are they doing?" Mike asked, dropping to the road.

The car answered with a screech of tires and a crunch. The crowd parted enough for Noah to see that the driver had overcorrected after hitting the concrete divider, smashing into the outside wall of the bridge, crumpling the front end. The car must've been a total loss because its occupants spilled out of it and took off running.

"They're going back?" Sarah asked. "But why?"

"I don't—"

A chorus of screams cut him off, originating from further ahead. The bridge's central hump made it impossible to see what was coming at them. Whatever it was, it must've been a legitimate threat, because it made everyone turn and flee back toward the hellhole of Lower Manhattan. Noah had no plan of retreating, but nor did he want to stand and fight.

He spun, looking for somewhere to hide, just in case. His eyes landed on the wrecked car. It was close, and if they could get to it, they might just be able to hide inside of it.

"The car—go!" he said sharply.

"We aren't running?" Kyle asked, following Noah and his mother.

Noah glanced down at him, seeing the fear in the young man's eyes. He gripped his shoulder as they moved and looked deep into his eyes. "No, we aren't. We are getting across this bridge."

"But the car looks toast," Becca said from behind.

"Doesn't matter. We aren't driving it anywhere."

Mike understood what Noah was thinking. "We're using it as cover, Becca. We'll hole up in it and wait for whatever is coming to pass us by."

"But what if it doesn't just pass by?" Sarah asked.

Noah looked behind them, but still couldn't see what was chasing all these people. "I... It will."

"But, what—" Kyle started.

Noah snapped his head around at him. "It. Will."

Kyle quieted and nodded. "Okay, I... Whatever you say, Noah."

A primal, carnal roar sent a shockwave of fear through everyone still present. Dozens yelped. Several more flat-out shrieked. The creature was enormous, that much Noah was confident in. He searched his memory bank for other apex predators that dominated the Cretaceous Period. But he was too distracted to come up with anything that made sense.

The group piled into the car. The windows were all factory tinted, which meant that the back doors and windows were much darker than front-doors and windows, including the windshield. Noah and Mike sat up front, exposed and facing in the opposite direction of the beast. The Rakestraws huddled low in the back seat. Noah slouched as low as he could get, stopping only when his knees struck the dashboard connected to the steering wheel. Mike could get lower, mostly because of his height, but also because he had fewer restrictions in the passenger seat.

A handful of people still rushed by, but the human herd had most definitely thinned until the last person was long gone. Noah, Mike, Sarah, Kyle, and Becca were alone near the middle of the Brooklyn Bridge, with God knows what kind of monster stomping up behind them.

Another scream was let loose. This time, it was dampened by the car windows.

"Becca, no," Sarah said.

Noah glanced up in the overhead mirror and found Becca on one knee and staring out through the back window. It was clear that she wanted to see what was coming. Noah dragged his eyes off the back of Becca's head and froze as the animal crested the bridge's central hump.

It was enormous.

The first thing Noah saw was the sail on its back. Then, as it continued forward, toward Manhattan, its crocodilian snout came into view. Next was its fully articulating, semi-elongated forelimbs. The brown-gray behemoth finished the reveal with a powerful body and a long, muscular tail that was taller than it was wide; perfect for a semiaquatic lifestyle.

"What is it?" Mike asked, still tucked low in his seat.

Noah swallowed down his fear and twisted around in his seat to get a crystal-clear look at it.

"Noah?" Mike asked. "What—?"

"*Spinosaurus aegyptiacus*," he replied, "the largest land predator ever known."

Mike sat up in his seat, then paled when he looked behind them. "Oh, crap." He slumped down even lower in his seat. "And here we are, wrapped up like a dino-Lunchables."

Noah glanced at Mike. "Does it help if I say the *Spinosaurus* preferred fish?"

Mike shrugged. "A little."

"He's right," Becca said, finally turning and sitting.

"I am?" Mike asked, staying low.

Becca shook her head. "No, Noah. *Spinosaurus* loved fish. You can tell by its conical teeth—used them to spear its prey, instead of tearing and ripping."

"Lovely," Mike said, looking like he was about to vomit.

"Stay with me, Detective," Noah said.

Mike nodded and blew out a long breath. "Yeah, I know. I'm, you know, just a little spooked."

"You and me both, brother."

Spinosaurus aegyptiacus measured somewhere north of fifty feet long from snout to tail. Some experts believed they could reach lengths of nearly sixty feet if given the right conditions; plenty of food and good health. The one coming toward them was every bit of sixty feet long. Noah recalled both the rex and the *Carcharodontosaurus*. Each measured forty-ish feet in length. This *Spinosaurus* was easily fifteen feet longer.

Yet T. rex was still somehow heavier, he thought. It was truly a brute, thick and powerful where it mattered most. Rex's stout build and bone-crunching bite more than made up for its mostly ineffective forelimbs.

"Nobody move," he said, dipping low in his seat.

"Can it see us?" Mike asked.

Noah glanced at him. "Absolutely." He then shifted his gaze

to the road and watched as the group of people continued their retreat.

"If it can see us, then why are we just sitting here?" Sarah asked from the middle of the back seat.

"Because I'm hoping it's too distracted by the other people to care about us, especially since we aren't moving."

Mike looked up at him from low in his seat. "Let's hope you're right."

Noah met Mike's worried eyes, but didn't say anything. He was hoping for the same, but had no reassurances. Hiding in the car would either save them, or doom them. The creature grumbled, then let out an annoyed grunt. It wasn't rushing after the people attempting to evade it. If anything, the *Spinosaurus* wanted nothing to do with them.

As it stomped up next to the car, Noah noticed some pretty serious looking battle damage. The carnivore was bleeding from several wounds along the base of its neck, as well as its shoulder. It paused and leaned in close to the car, inhaling deeply. Noah looked away, as if he were hiding from it. The car was bumped, causing his stomach to churn. But he *had* to look. Slowly, he turned his head as the monster's snout pressed against the hood, denting it. Noah watched as it dragged its *nose* along the hood, toward the windshield. It breathed in deeply, then exhaled a long blast of air, fogging the windshield and sending a spray of snot.

"It's the engine," Noah whispered. "It doesn't like the fumes."

"Best news I've heard all day," Mike choked out.

It growled, then swung its head forward and stomped off. As it did, Noah also spotted a couple of, what were obviously, bite marks near the base of its tail, near where the animal's tall spinal sail ended. Whether it had won or lost the fight was impossible to tell, but it had fought valiantly. It was still alive, after all.

"What on Earth could do that?" Mike asked quietly.

"I don't know," Noah replied. He glanced at the fleeing people, who were now far enough away that Noah could barely make them out. Beat up or not, *Spinosaurus* should've been able to catch the slower of the prey.

That's when it hit Noah. "It's not hunting... It's fleeing."

"It's running away?" Kyle asked. "From what?"

Noah examined its injuries again. "From whatever kicked the crap out of it."

No one spoke another word until the animal was a hundred feet away. Noah waited for it to look back at the car and spot him in the driver's seat. But it didn't. Like the *Spinosaurus*, Noah took in a deep breath, letting it out slowly. His hands shook as he continued to hold the steering wheel in a death grip. He hadn't even noticed that he was gripping it so hard until now. He let go and flexed his hands. His knuckles were white and the underside of his fingers were red and sweaty.

"That was intense," Becca said.

"That's one way to describe it," Mike said, sitting up.

Noah just sat and stared at the creature. He couldn't help but be impressed by its majesty, at how something could ever grow so big, particularly a land-based carnivore. Marine animals routinely grew to impressive lengths and weights, but not land animals. Seeing it up close, with flesh and blood, was truly something to behold.

The *Spinosaurus* suddenly stopped. It sniffed the air and slowly turned within the confines of the northbound lane. To the five humans, the passage was plenty big, but not for something as large as the beast before them.

"No..." Noah said.

He waited for the super predator to charge them, but it didn't. It just got into what had become the typical threatening posture for a theropod; head low, hind legs wide, tail up. It was preparing for a fight—another one. Noah was confused, so he turned and discovered a pair of armored herbivores barreling straight for them.

"You've gotta be kidding me," he said, getting everyone's attention.

They all turned.

"*Ankylosaurus*, the 'living tank,'" Becca announced. "But why are they coming this way?" She turned and faced Noah. "There's no way that *Ankylosaurus* created those wounds."

She was right, of course. *Ankylosaurus* was known for using its clubbed tail as a weapon. And the animal's low center of gravity made it nearly impossible to upend. The only way to hurt the herbivore was to get to its unarmored underside. Its back was an evolutionary marvel, densely plated, hence Becca calling it a 'living tank.' Noah had also heard many of his colleagues call it that, so she'd been spot on.

Armored, armed, twenty-five feet long and 14,000 pounds... It wasn't a bull *Triceratops,* but it was damn close.

The two *Ankylosaurus* finally noticed the *Spinosaurus,* but they didn't stop. They only slowed. Noah didn't like this. It wasn't right. *Ankylosaurus* was tough, but choosing to fight something as enormous as the carnivore further ahead was insane.

"Unless they're running too," he said aloud, but to himself.

"What?" Sarah asked, leaning forward in the back seat. "What was that?"

Noah dropped his eyes down from the incoming herbivores. He stared at Sarah and repeated what he had said, only louder. "Unless they're running too..." he turned and pointed at the *Spinosaurus*, "from whatever caused that."

The bigger of the two *Ankylosaurus* waddled past the car. Another feature besides its hard, defensive back plates were the spikes that jutted out from its sides. Those same spikes scraped across the driver's side of the car, kicking out a chorus of metallic shrieks. The second herbivore stopped twenty feet behind the car. Noah winced when the animal's tail swayed toward them as it moved. It smacked the car's front, left quarter panel, crushing it like a tin can. Noah couldn't imagine what kind of damage the animal could do if it had actually tried to destroy the car.

The lead *Ankylosaurus* stopped thirty feet in front of Noah and the others. It too got into an aggressive posture.

"What the hell is going on, Noah?" Sarah asked. "Even I know this shouldn't be happening."

"I told you, they're running too."

Kyle reached forward and gripped Noah's shoulder. "But from what?"

That's when the most recognizable animalistic roar, other than a lion maybe, trumpeted behind them. Everyone looked outside—everyone except for Noah. He knew the noise well. Hollywood had actually been pretty spot on, which was impressive.

Noah slowly turned and saw the creature crest the bridge's hump. Then it stood tall and roared again, high into the air this time.

"From a *T. rex*."

37

"Another one?" Mike asked, spinning around in his seat.

Noah could only shrug. "Yep—bigger than the one from Central Park too."

"It's pretty beat up," Sarah said. Then she turned and looked at Noah. "I think we found the culprit."

Noah nodded. "Yeah, looks like."

"But the other one, the *Spinosaurus*, is so much bigger," Kyle said, looking back and forth between the two carnivores.

"Longer and slightly taller, yes," Becca replied. "But *Tyrannosaurs rex* weighed almost 5,000 pounds more. Even it could—can—push around an animal as big as *Spinosaurus aegyptiacus*."

"Becca's right," Noah said. "People always talk about rex's bite force, but what they always fail to mention is how strong its base is. Rex's actual power comes from its lower half."

"That's why I never skip leg day," Mike said under his breath.

The comment got looks from everyone. "What? You should *never* skip leg day."

Now, Noah and the others were stuck inside an immobile car, with an *Ankylosaurus* and *Spinosaurus* in front of them, and a second *Ankylosaurus*, as well as a *Tyrannosaurus rex* behind them.

"This may have been the worst idea yet," Noah said sadly. "I'm sorry."

"No," Sarah said, "it was the right call. It's the situation that's all wrong."

Mike patted Noah's arm. "She's right. This was our best option at the time." He looked around, then knocked on the ceiling. "Still might be if this thing can hold up."

"Hold up?" Kyle asked.

Mike nodded. "Yeah, kid. I have a feeling that things are about to get rough."

Just then, the rex and the *Spinosaurus* roared and charged. The *Ankylosaurus* duo got even lower in their stances, raising their tails higher as they angled themselves sideways a little. This was clearly their species' way of getting into position to use their clubbed tails. Noah gauged the distance between them and both herbivores. If they backed up at all, the car would be in their impact zone. The first *Ankylosaurus* had only tapped the front corner of the car, and it had caved it in. If the animal wound up and swung with all its might...

"Here we go," Noah said, gripping the steering wheel as hard as he could.

"Buckle in!" Mike shouted.

Noah let go of the wheel and tried to buckle in, but was thankful he hadn't. He dove right, into Mike's lap as the tail struck his door. It crushed inward, blowing out the window. Had Noah been sitting there, strapped in place by his seatbelt, he would've taken the shrapnel directly to the face instead of the back.

He pushed off Mike and fell into his seat, feeling shards of glass poke at his butt and legs as he did. He leaned away from the buckled door, as well as the fight taking place next to him. The *Ankylosaurus* grunted, dipped its head, and drove its thick, powerful legs forward, pushing the much bigger predator away. This was where a taller animal, like *Spinosaurus*, was at a serious disadvantage. It couldn't get low enough to counter the stout herbivore's maneuvers.

The carnivore stumbled back, then got its feet beneath it in time to take a clubbed tail to the left thigh. The impact staggered the carnivore, though Noah didn't think the connection had been solid enough to break anything. He imagined the carnivore had just received the world's worst dead leg. The *Spinosaurus* limped backward, snarling at the "living tank."

Noah turned and watched the second *Ankylosaurus* swing at the rex, but miss. The rex stepped back, dodging the attack, then pressed its own. It rushed the herbivore, getting its head low and shoving it right into the back of the car. The impact launched the vehicle forward ten feet, causing all of its occupants to yelp and hang on for dear life.

The collision with the car had also saved the herbivore's life. It had kept it upright, which meant the *T. rex* could do very little else to it. The *Ankylosaurus* recovered and turned. When it did, its clubbed tail *whooshed* right past the now blown-out rear windows.

The car had settled in the middle of the two-lane road,

having been removed from the right-hand guardrail by the jostling impact. Noah saw the next move before anyone else. The *Spinosaurus* stepped around the *Ankylosaurus*, now on the herbivore's left. As it did, the *Ankylosaurus* swung its tail around to meet the flanking predator, and instead of striking the *Spinosaurus* in the shins, the car took a direct strike from the full-power assault.

The passenger side crumpled inward on Mike and the car rolled. They were sent into and over the bike lane's low, concrete divider. The car shredded the chain-link fence and continued over onto its roof. Miraculously, Noah had *not* been thrown from the car. He did, however, end up crumpled on the inverted ceiling. There he lay, on his back, bleeding from a cut to his left temple. In his blurry, wavering vision, he saw that everyone else was suspended upside down by their seatbelts.

"Ugh," he moaned, seeing the battle outside rage on, but flipped 180 degrees.

From his lower vantage, he could see the top-half of the lead *Ankylosaurus* push forward, partially concealed by the broken remains of the concrete divider. It must've finally had enough. It huffed, lowered its head, and kept going, driving straight through the *Spinosaurus*. Seconds later, the second herbivore joined it and they disappeared from view. Now, it was just the two apex carnivores.

Spinosaurus aegyptiacus, the biggest ever—and *Tyrannosaurus rex*, the most powerful ever.

The super predators lined each other up.

North America's greatest versus Africa's greatest.

As Mike and Sarah unbuckled and fell to the ceiling, albeit with the ability to properly prep their landings, the two heavyweights charged.

The sound of them colliding made Noah, who was still slightly concussed, flinch. The *thump* had been impossibly loud. Rex roared as his combatant clawed at its neck and chest, while keeping rex's killer jaws at bay with the top of its own head by pushing them straight up. They looked like two tired boxers wrapping one another up at the end of a grueling match.

Becca scurried in next to Noah, leaning into him while watching the brawl with fascination. He unconsciously, protectively, wrapped his arm around her. When he realized what he'd done, he was shocked that she hadn't refused his touch. She just zoned out and stared—as did Noah.

Instead of pressing the assault, rex did the smart thing and backed off. With nothing left to push on, the *Spinosaurus* stumbled forward, exposing itself to an attack. The "Tyrant Lizard King" didn't waste the opening. Noah could see the fire in its pale, yellow eyes. It yawned open its mighty jaws and snapped them shut on the *Spinosaurus'* neck. Then, it applied what it was most famous for, its bone crunching bite force.

The thick skin and dense musculature making up the *Spinosaurus'* neck fought against the attack for a moment, but eventually, *T. rex* always won in these situations. The *Spinosaurus* gagged, its throat punctured. Blood flowed freely as the rex squeezed harder and harder, growling as it did. Noah flinched when he heard several pops.

The *Spinosaurus* went limp.

However, the *T. rex* did not let go. Its foe was dead, but it wasn't done. It squeezed even harder, causing several more vertebrae to shatter. Then, and only then, did it relinquish its hard-earned kill. Rex practically threw the deceased *Spinosaurus* to the roadway. Then, it tilted its massive head back, looked high into the sky, and roared, celebrating the victory in style.

Noah was amazed by what he had just witnessed, but he also knew that they needed to leave before the beast realized there were living creatures in the car. He looked south. They were in the bike lane now. The concrete divider could hide them if they stayed low enough.

There was also the elevated promenade.

Why not both? he thought.

He flipped onto his stomach and took in his people. He silently placed a finger on his lips, then tipped his head south, toward the back of the inverted car. No one asked him what his plan was. They just nodded and got moving.

One by one, they crawled outside, through the blown-out rear window, staying as close to the bike lane's divider as possible. Noah went as far as dragging his left shoulder along it to make sure he didn't stray too far. He glanced back to see that Sarah's face was barely a foot from his shoe bottoms. Becca and Kyle were next, with Mike bringing up the rear. Every so often, when Noah glanced back, he could see the rex's head pop up. And every time he saw the rex's head, it was covered in more and more blood.

"Spoils of war," he muttered, unable to hide his smile.

"You're enjoying this?" Sarah asked softly.

Noah shrugged. He couldn't help it. "Sue me."

When they were 200 feet away from the battleground, Noah stopped, rolled onto his side, and looked back at the others. He silently pointed up to the elevated walkway. Sarah, Becca, Kyle, then Mike all looked up at it with blank stares. It wasn't going to be easy, but there were plenty of hand and footholds to use thanks to a second chain-link fence. Beyond it were the bridge's supports, a maintenance catwalk...and water. A fall from this height might be a death sentence. The only obstruction above the fence was the promenade's reinforced handrail.

"Yeah, we can do this," Mike said, sounding like he was trying to talk himself into it.

"Then let's," Noah said.

A roar from the rex got them moving. Everyone leapt to their feet and threw themselves at the fence. They each picked a section and hurriedly scaled it like frightened squirrels, because to the rex, that's exactly what they were. Noah was nearly to the top when he watched the carnivore turn their way.

"Faster!" he shouted, doing exactly what he had just said.

Noah zoomed up the remaining fence, gripped the handrail, and pulled himself up the rest of the way. He kept watch on the rex as he did, dreading what he saw. The super predator was now stomping toward them.

"Hurry!" he shouted, waving the others forward.

Mike looked. "Oh, shit!" The sight of the creature coming for them lit a fire under his ass, and he rocketed up the rest of the way with little difficulty.

Kyle and Becca made it to the top quickly, partially thanks to their lighter bodyweights, but their mother didn't. Sarah was struggling with her injuries. Raising her arms high enough to pull herself up was proving painful and slowing her ascent.

"Sarah, you need to climb faster," Noah said, reaching down to her.

"I'm trying," she said, glancing at the rex as it continued toward them. "Oh, no..."

Noah pounded his fist on the handrail. "Hey, look at me!"

She did. "Climb."

She nodded and kept moving. Noah looked at the rex, then Mike. He grabbed Mike's shirt and shoved him toward Sarah's roundabout location.

"Help her."

"What are you doing?"

Noah backpedaled. "Getting the dino's attention."

He turned, drew his pistol, and ran to the north, toward the rex. He doubted a nine-millimeter bullet could do much else besides enrage the beast—and that's precisely what he needed. He kept to the opposite side of the eighteen-foot-wide walkway.

"Hey, Rexy!" he shouted, waving his empty hand. "Over here, you big brute!"

The animal slowed, eyeing him, but it didn't stop. Noah leveled his gun at the creature's shoulder, then pulled the trigger. The round struck the rex's hide. The wound bled, but barely.

Noah stepped closer and shouted, "I said, 'over here,' asshole!"

The carnivore stopped, pivoted, then roared right in Noah's face. Even though he was a good fifteen feet from it, Noah was slathered in fresh blood, tiny chunks of meat, and a whole-lot of spit. He was also pretty sure he just suffered significant hearing loss. The sound reminded him of the one time he'd stood too close to a jet turbine at an airshow. Noah stumbled backward into the opposite railing as the rex stood taller and snapped at him.

He hit the deck and covered his head with his hands. But the rex wasn't tall enough, or long enough, to reach him. Noah parted his hands and looked up to see the monster's snout ten feet from him. Its chin was resting on the handrail, and its head was turned sideways so that its left eye was staring right at Noah.

"Noah, come on!"

He forced himself to look away from the prehistoric giant. When he did, he found Sarah being dragged over the railing by Mike and her son. She was in rough shape from the looks of it. Noah blew out a long breath and crawled away. The rex snorted at him, then growled like a crocodile.

Noah couldn't take it. He jumped to his feet and ran.

"Go, go, go!" he yelled as the rex roared after him.

The experience of being face to face with a living *Tyrannosaurus rex*, as well as being in the middle of a battle royale for the ages, broke something in Noah. Tears streamed down his face, and he just kept on running, zipping past the others without another word.

"Wait!" Kyle shouted.

"Noah!" Mike yelled.

But he was gone. He just kept moving south until he could hardly breathe. A stitch in his side nearly made him collapse. He gripped the railing with his free hand, realizing that he was still clutching his pistol.

There, Noah leaned his back against the railing and slid down to his butt. Tears still flowed, but he didn't blubber. He wasn't crying out of sadness. He was crying because of fear, and what felt like an overload of adrenaline mixed with concussive shock. He just sat there and breathed. He'd never had a panic attack before, but he imagined this was what one felt like.

A familiar face appeared in front of him. Sarah knelt, then gently took the gun from him and set it down.

"You're okay, Noah." She motioned to everyone. "*We're* okay—thanks to you."

Noah nodded, then wiped his eyes. "Good," he mumbled. "That's...good." His hand went to his mouth, and he sniffed in, feeling his emotions begin to break down his dam.

He sobbed.

"Hey, it's okay," Sarah said, smiling softly. "It's okay," she cooed, leaning in. She took off his hat, reached forward, and forcibly tilted Noah's head down, so his forehead touched her own. She closed her eyes and softly repeated, "We're okay..."

38

As they continued along the Brooklyn Bridge Promenade, Noah was slowly coming out of his emotional funk. He rarely ever lost his cool—anger or otherwise. When he did, you could usually attribute it to exhaustion. And he was. Noah was tired... His nerves were frayed, and also fried.

At least the rex gave up, he thought, looking over his shoulder again. It had returned to its kill to feast.

The face-to-face encounter with North America's greatest predator had spiked his fear, while simultaneously causing his boyhood love for all things dinosaurs to launch into orbit. He'd been so close that he could've touched a real-life *Tyrannosaurus rex*. But if he had, it would've easily bitten off his arm. Rex wasn't his *Dreadnoughtus*, but it was the everlasting symbol, the mascot of prehistoric life, of dinosaurs. How could it not obliterate his emotional dam like it had? Anyone who loved dinosaurs loved *T. rex*.

Being eighteen feet off the road unnerved him greatly. Attack from above was possible, though not likely thanks to the bridge's network of support cables running alongside him. Noah trudged along then glanced to his right, looking out over the East River. He spotted a pier, and attached to it was a beautiful patch of green, a park from the looks of it. But that wasn't what had caught his eye first. The forty-seven-foot-long Coast Guard rescue boat pulling up to it was.

"Over there!" he shouted, pointing down to the incoming vessel. "We need to go there!"

"Hot damn," Mike said. "That's our ticket out of here."

Sarah wasn't so confident. "Can we get there before it leaves?"

"We're sure as hell going to try," Noah replied.

The thought of finally being safe—as safe as could be—reignited Noah's confidence. It also gave him a second wind or was it his fourth? He picked up his pace into a steady jog, eyeing the Coast Guard boat. It was still four hundred feet from shore. Noah gauged his party's position, estimating that they were roughly the same distance to shore themselves. Unfortunately, like before, when they had been at the Manhattan entrance to the Brooklyn Bridge, you couldn't just exit wherever you wanted.

"Where's the closest exit ramp?" Noah asked.

"Still another half a mile away," Sarah answered, getting his attention. "We used to live nearby. Moved upstate after Mark died."

Gotcha.

Noah didn't push for more information. He didn't need it, and she didn't need to relive it, not now. They were so close to freedom. They all needed to keep their heads straight from here on out. Plus, he already knew enough about what had happened to the Rakestraws, forcing them to relive the death of the man-of-the-household more than they already did on a daily basis wasn't needed. Noah knew they thought about Mark often. Noah thought about his own father all the time, every day.

I'm not a kid, either.

Dinosaurs began to pass them on either side. They were mostly herbivores, but he did spot some smaller carnivores dotted in here and there. To Noah, it resembled a grand migration. It made sense in a way. Brooklyn was an island, after all, the westernmost end of Long Island, in fact. If these creatures wanted to move to the mainland, the only way would be via the bridges that humanity had supplied. Of course, they'd also have to safely navigate Manhattan to get there.

"What about the *T. rex*?" Mike asked, leaning over the rail to watch a herd of ten, crested herbivores, *Parasaurolophus*, as he walked. The last time they'd seen one, it'd been killed by *Troodon*.

"That's not up to us," Noah replied. "Nature will do what nature does."

"Does that include us—people?" Kyle asked.

Noah thought over how to reply, and there was really only one thing he could say.

"Yes, it does." He was just being honest with Kyle, with everyone listening. "Mankind is powerful, and we are, still, undoubtably, the supreme species on this planet. What happened a couple of days ago has been a test to see if we still deserve dominion over Earth."

Mike laughed softly. "We have gotten kind of full of ourselves, haven't we?"

"Definitely," Sarah said, "but I wish there'd been another way for us to realize it."

"That's humans in a nutshell, though, right?" Noah asked. "We are the living embodiment of contentedness. We live and breathe comfortability."

"We're spoiled," Becca added.

Mike laughed harder now. "Okay, yeah, sure, I can't argue with that. But like Sarah said, I wish there had been a better way to test us than an all-out prehistoric blitzkrieg."

"We don't get to choose," Kyle said, laying down a profound statement.

Noah knew he was also talking about his father. He wanted to console the young man, but didn't know what else he could say that Kyle hadn't already heard.

"You're right," Mike said, breaking the tension Kyle's words had created. "We don't. Well, not always. I didn't have to save your asses from that feathered bastard, and Noah here didn't have to help Sarah find you two." He gave Kyle and Becca a quick look. "But we did. We might not have full control over our lives, but we do have the ability to make some of those choices ourselves."

"Nicely said," Noah said.

"Thanks."

Kyle gave Mike's shoulder a light punch. "Yeah, man."

Two, horned *Carnotaurus* stomped by on their left, toward the Brooklyn Bridge battleground. The migration was in full swing. Noah wondered if all of New York's bridges looked the same way. Luckily, none of the animals had approached via the promenade. Noah and the others had been given an uninterrupted, mobile, dinosaur showcase while they finished their trek across the bridge.

"Stay alert," Mike said, drawing his pistol. "We don't know how many of them are waiting for us at the end."

Noah drew his pistol again. He had gathered and holstered it once he'd gotten himself under control. He spotted an exit up ahead.

"That it?" he asked.

"Yep," Sarah replied.

Everyone climbed over the railing and onto the pavement. They had arrived in Brooklyn.

"What's that?" Sarah asked, pointing further down the road.

Noah had also noticed the lumps coming at them, but hadn't been able to make them out. Whatever they were, they were bounding right at them, moving fast. It reminded him of a herd of American bison moving across the Great Plains. Noah slowed, squinted, then pushed everyone forward and to the right.

"Faster, we need to get off the bridge, now!"

Everyone picked up their pace, but the exit was still two hundred feet away. The incoming horde was closer and coming in with a full head of steam.

As they neared their exit ramp, the sign above it pointed them towards the Brooklyn-Queens Expressway and a road called Cadman Plaza West. Noah had no idea what either were, but he trusted in Sarah's directions. The road branched, forking into three lanes. Two exited, and one stayed straight and true, deeper into Brooklyn. That was where the animals were coming from.

"Holy cow!" Becca shouted just as a gigantic herd of *Triceratops* galloped past them.

The humans darted right, running as fast as their tired legs could move. One of the animals lowered its head and bulldozed through a foursome of highway sand barrels, or "impact attenuators." The *Triceratops* grunted loudly as it decimated the barrels, covering it and the road, with sand. Noah stumbled to a stop and watched the herbivore aggressively shake the sand free from its head, looking very much like the world's largest dog. A breeze carried some of the sand toward Noah's group, and they couldn't help but cry out in laughter as they turned away and shut their eyes.

One by one, they opened their eyes and looked at one another. Mike had gotten the worst of it. He just stood there, still as a statue with sand covering him from head to toe.

He spat and grumbled, "Coulda really done without that." Then he waved at the vanishing herd. "Thanks."

Kyle snickered.

"Watch it, kid!" Mike said, jabbing a finger at him. But even Mike couldn't hold back his smile.

"Come on, Mike," Kyle said, "who doesn't love the beach?"

Mike reached for Kyle's throat but stopped when the telltale sound of a ship horn let loose.

The Coast Guard rescue vessel had successfully come ashore. No one said a word as they took off at a near sprint. The downward banking exit ramp only aided their footspeed as they headed around the curving thoroughfare and to street level.

As much as they wanted to keep pushing forward, they didn't. Brooklyn was much more open than Manhattan was. The buildings here were shorter and the roads and sidewalks were less cramped.

"Where are we?" Noah asked, panting hard.

"Middagh Street," Sarah replied. She pointed forward. "Dead ends in a couple of blocks. We take it until we can't."

Noah nodded, then blew out a long breath. "Alright, west it

is."

Middagh Street was of the one-way variety, but that hadn't stopped people from driving the wrong way when the event had occurred. Head-on collisions were plentiful, as were three-and-four-car pileups—fender benders galore. But because of the more "open floorplan" that was Brooklyn, there was still plenty of room to move. Bicycles zipped around, their riders heading to who-knows-where. Brooklyn, in its current state, did not get it as bad as the city had. Not that there weren't clear signs of death.

Bodies littered the sidewalks. Now days old, they were attracting the attention of scavengers. Noah had seen the same thing back in Manhattan. He thought back to what he had told the group, that "Nature will do what nature does." He still wholeheartedly believed that, but it made him sick to think of humanity as just another part of the food chain now, and not perched comfortably at its peak.

Noah must've been lost in his own head for quite a while, because he got a nudge from Sarah. "You still with us?"

"Most of the time," Noah replied with a wink.

"I know," she said, looking around, "it's a lot to take in. I don't blame you for thinking about it all the time." She slowed as they passed a boarded-up store. The sight caused Sarah to frown. "That was our favorite ice cream parlor. They had the best mint chocolate chip."

"I'm a peanut butter cup kind of guy."

She smiled softly. "That was Mark's favorite too." She blinked out of the memory. "And it was *really* good."

"I'm sorry that he keeps getting brought up," Noah said. "I don't want to keep forcing you guys to talk about him, not if you don't want to."

"Thanks," she said, "but it's okay. It's been long enough for us to have accepted what happened. The pain of losing him will always be there, and it's something we'll have to live with."

Noah nodded. "I know the feeling. When I got the call that my dad had finally passed away, I was gutted. We knew it was coming, but I still wasn't prepared for it when it did come."

"You two were obviously very close."

"We were. He was my best friend, not just 'Dad.' He was also my partner in crime, and my mentor." He looked away from her. "I never had a family; no kids or wife. I've barely dated since college. All I've had for the last two decades is my work."

"What about your mother?"

Noah shook his head. "Mom died ten years ago in a plane crash. Small puddle jumper got blindsided by a storm and went down in Canada."

"For work?"

"No, she was heading up to see her sister. It was supposed to be a routine vacation for her." He sighed. "Dad was supposed to go with her, but he came down with a bad cold and decided that flying wasn't a good idea."

Sarah shrugged. "I guess there's some silver lining. You got a few more years with your father that you wouldn't have gotten otherwise."

"Yeah, that's what I've always told myself, Dad too."

"How'd he take it? Was he understanding...?" Noah glanced at her. "You know what I mean."

He nodded. "Yeah, he understood that his life had been spared, but I think he would've rather been there with her in the end. Before he got sick, he once told me that he had wished to have gone down with her just so she wasn't alone when she died. I know, kind of morbid, but still..."

"Wow," Sarah said. "Sounds like they loved each other a lot."

"They did. High school sweethearts. They had eyes for one another from the time they were both fourteen."

Sarah chuckled. "Holy smokes. I'm honestly jealous."

"Same. They were something else sometimes."

A mid-sized carnivore popped out at the next intersection, coming from the north. Noah saw it first and quickly ushered everyone behind a box truck. He kept to its back, left edge so he could watch it, another *Dryptosaurus*. The other one they had seen had been stuck in a bus. And like the first one, this one also sported elongated forelimbs. They wouldn't be as feeble as the *T. rex's* arms were. It was lightly built too. Even at twenty-five-feet long, it'd be able to move fast. It showed off its maneuverability when it snapped its head around to the east and ran right toward Noah, down Middagh Street.

"Go around," he whispered, motioning for them to head to the right side of the truck.

With all traffic halted, it was easy to pick up on the animal's footsteps as it approached the box truck. It slowed, sniffing the air.

Shit, Noah thought as he knelt. He watched the carnivore from beneath the truck. The predator stepped closer to it, inhaling deeply. Then it pointed itself at the back of it and pursued the scent it had found.

Us.

Its prey backed away, toward the front of the truck. They all ducked around the front end just as the *Dryptosaurus'* head emerged and took in the empty sidewalk.

"Noah," Mike whispered.

He looked at Mike and noticed that between the time it took for them to hide and now, he had unzipped his pack and dug out a water bottle. Noah gave him a curious look, then understood what Mike wanted him to do. Noah nodded and took the bottle. Then, he stepped back and threw it as far as he could, over the truck, and the dinosaur. It landed with a *thump* somewhere out of sight. Noah couldn't see where the carnivore was, but Kyle could. He was lying on his stomach, watching it as Noah had.

Three seconds later, he gave them a thumbs up and climbed to his feet. The group lightly stepped heel-to-toe, keeping cars between them and the prowling carnivore. Once they made it to the intersection the *Dryptosaurus* had just used, the one at Middagh and Hicks, they switched on the afterburners and sprinted the rest of the way until they came to the dead end Sarah had mentioned earlier.

39

Middagh Street, indeed, ended up ahead, and it did so at a small footpath that ran alongside a gated playground. Based on the way Sarah eyed the playground, Noah guessed she had brought her kids there in the past.

They quickly crossed a tight one-lane road called Columbia Heights and entered a fenced entrance to Squibb Park Bridge. As they descended the entry ramp, Noah got a good look at the walkway. It was, in essence, a smaller version of the Brooklyn Bridge Promenade. The elevated, pedestrian-only footpath continued at the same level as the ground beneath it fell away, now thirty feet off the ground. They marched beneath a handful of tall trees, then popped out over Furman Street as it cut northwest. Then, the bridge turned due west and continued between two identical, nine-story-tall, luxury apartment buildings. Everything here looked brand-new, or at least, recently remodeled.

Noah looked over the northern edge and watched people funnel out of one of the apartment building's subterranean parking garages. He stopped, stared, and waited. Then, what he expected to happen, did. A group of small, puppy-sized predators rushed out after the people, chasing them down one by one. Mike saw it, immediately drew his pistol, and fired two shots into the air. The reports echoed back and forth between the buildings, spooking, and chasing away the predators. Several of the people below looked up and gave Mike a thankful wave. He returned it and got the group moving again.

But Noah couldn't just leave these people high and dry. "There's a rescue boat!" he shouted. "Near..." he said, not knowing the dock's name.

"Fulton Ferry Landing!" Sarah quickly added.

The tip was replied with nods and waves all around.

"I hope I didn't just give our seats away," Noah said.

Mike shrugged. "I agree, but it was the right thing to do."

Squibb Park Bridge cut ninety degrees to the north once it cleared the back of the apartment buildings. It began to descend too. A foghorn-like bellow started up in the greenery to the south of their destination. Brooklyn Bridge Park was a handsome slice of nature on the western edge of the New York City borough. Lush trees dominated the park grounds, though Noah could see a pair of open lawns where the trees weren't. Other than that, he couldn't see what had made the noise. The canopy was just too dense.

"Any idea what that was?" Sarah asked.

Noah shook his head. "No."

"Down we go," Mike said, quickly descending the stairs at the bottom of the rampway.

Squibb Park Bridge ended at the Brooklyn Bridge Park Greenway. They used the walkway for the next 150 feet, until the foghorn bellow, like that of an immense cow, started up again. Noah slowed and peered through the heavy brush that was used as a natural barrier between the walkway and the park. He squinted against the sun, then saw movement. He stared long and hard, then the creature bellowed again.

That's when the thickest tree trunks started to move. Noah's eyes opened wide, and he hurried down one of several, quaint, park entry paths.

"Noah!" Sarah shouted after him.

He skidded to a stop and returned to the group only to hold out his hand to Becca. "You need to see this."

Becca didn't bat an eyelash. She accepted Noah's hand and the two dinosaur nerds rushed headlong into Brooklyn Bridge Park. Sarah and Mike shouted after them, but Noah and Becca didn't stop. Noah led her offroad, through the shrubs and tall grass separating them from what he knew would be the most magnificent creature they'd seen thus far.

"You ready?" he asked.

"For what?"

Noah smiled as they exited the trees and stepped out into the open Bridge View Lawn. As they did, the beast raised its long neck and immense head into the sky and bellowed again.

"That... *Dreadnoughtus*," Noah said, marveling at the dinosaur—his dinosaur.

"Oh, my gosh!" Becca cheered. "Noah, it's beautiful!"

He grunted as he got down on one knee. There, he sat and watched. Becca stood next to him with her hand on his shoulder. They just observed in silence as the 100-foot-long, purple and black titan fed on the surrounding foliage.

"It's so much bigger than I expected," Becca said.

Noah nodded. "I know. Dad and I always thought that ours wasn't fully grown. Look at its colors too! Never in my wildest dreams did I expect...*this*!"

"Your dad would've loved to have been here, wouldn't he?"

"Yeah," Noah said, smiling softly, "he would've."

Becca released his shoulder and faced Noah. Because he was kneeling, he was currently shorter than her and had to look up at her to meet her gaze.

"Thank you," she said.

"No problem, kiddo," he said, shrugging. "I figured you'd want to see it too."

Becca shook her head. "No, I mean, thank you." Noah was surprised when Becca leaned in and hugged him. He'd held her hand and had carried her everywhere, but she had yet to work up the courage to hug him—until now. "Thank you, for everything you've done for us."

Sarah was the first to find them, and when she did, her hands went to her mouth in shock. Noah winked and smiled, but spoke to Becca. "You're welcome."

Mike and Kyle were too transfixed on the giant sauropod to give Noah and Becca the time of day.

"Oh, wow," Mike said. He finally looked at Noah but pointed up at the *Dreadnoughtus*. "That your dino?"

Noah smiled wide and stood. "It is."

Mike raised his hand and Noah slapped it. "Right on! Congrats, *Doc*!"

It took some convincing, but eventually, Noah was forced away from the dominating form of *Dreadnoughtus schrani*.

316

They hurried along the edge of the park, giving the behemoth as much space as it required. But then it suddenly swung its head around and began feeding on the leaves directly above the group. Noah slowed and looked straight up as they passed beneath its outstretched neck. Becca yanked on his arm, pulling him along, but even she couldn't look away.

Soon, they exited the park, losing sight of the animal in the process. That broke Noah's heart, but he knew they had to keep moving if they wanted to catch the Coast Guard boat before it left. Just to the north of the park was the entrance to Fulton Ferry Landing. It stood in the shadow of the Brooklyn Bridge. Everything around them looked miniscule to this feat of engineering. It dominated the surrounding landscape.

At the end of the wide, wooden platform was their escape vessel. It was still there! They ran for it, not accepting defeat now. They got the kids up the rampway first. Then Sarah and Mike. Noah was last to board. He gave the area one last look, then climbed aboard. They were the last ones too. Not seconds after Noah boarded did the sailor remove the ramp and yell into his walkie talkie.

"We're clear!"

"*Copy that, heading out,*" came a reply.

Noah shook his hand. "Thank you."

He nodded. "Just doing what we can."

They headed south, for deeper water, but still kept as close to the shoreline as possible. Noah wasn't sure why, but he wasn't curious enough to ask. He counted three dozen other people, and they were all crowded on the top deck.

Feels like a lot, he thought, unsure what the passenger capacity of this type of boat would be.

Dreadnoughtus bellowed again, raising its head high enough for them to see from the boat.

Noah caught the Coast Guardsman gawking at the big herbivore. "Amazing, isn't it?"

The other man nodded quickly. "Yeah, you could say that."

They pushed south, further down the East River, following the shore, and heading for the 400-foot-wide passage of water that ran between Brooklyn and Governors Island. The island itself held two out-of-service military forts, Fort Jay and Castle Williams, as well as several parks, and a bevy of historical buildings.

"Buttermilk Channel," Sarah said, materializing next to him. "Common ferry route."

"Um, what's that?" the sailor asked.

Noah turned and found him pointing into the water along their starboard side. He hurried over from the port side and looked down to see an absolutely humongous form slashing its way through the water, just beneath the surface. Its long triangular snout, thick body, four, paddle-like appendages, and swooshing crocodilian tail were immediately recognized by anyone who enjoyed the subject of dinosaurs, and in this case, their marine reptile cousins.

"That..." Noah replied with a sigh, "is a *Mosasaurus*."

The whine of a small engine caught Noah's attention as it passed further out to starboard. The motorboat was packed with people, but was much smaller than the vessel Noah was on. He dropped his eyes back down to the water, but the creature was gone.

"Oh, no," he said.

Suddenly, the twenty-foot-boat exploded from beneath as

the *Mosasaurus* rose. It exited the water like a breaching whale, showing off more than half of its true size.

Mosasaurus hoffmannii was the largest species of Mosasaur to ever exist, measuring in at a whopping forty-nine-feet long, and weighing in at 18,000 pounds. But based on what the animal had just shown Noah, he guessed that this one was easily eight to ten feet longer than the commonly accepted max-length of forty-nine feet. The boat had been splintered, and those that had survived the initial attack floundered, shouting and waving their arms wildly. But the *Mosasaurus* wasn't there for the boat. It wanted the food that had been aboard it.

One by one, the passengers disappeared beneath the surface, and the only thing the people aboard the Coast Guard boat, including its crew, could do was watch.

The sailor he'd talked to earlier rejoined Noah. "That thing is easily ten feet longer than our boat."

"Yeah, I know," Noah said.

"Think it can sink us?"

Noah looked around, kept his voice down, and said, "If it wants to, yes. Don't suppose you have any weapons on board?"

"Well, yeah, but nothing that'll kill that...*thing*."

"So, no torpedoes?"

The sailor's face blanked. He quickly shook his head, then hurried away, toward the wheelhouse, leaving Noah alone with his thoughts. His chin hit his chest, and he closed his eyes.

We were so close.

40

"What do we do?" Sarah asked.

Her question spurred Noah into action. He turned and marched straight toward the crewman. He saw Noah coming over, finished up with another passenger, then faced him.

"We need to go faster," Noah said, stating the obvious.

The sailor pulled him aside and softly said, "We can't. We're overloaded. We're only rated for thirty passengers." He glanced around. What he saw dissolved what little confidence he had left. "We're close to forty right now. We could capsize if we push any harder than we already are."

Noah didn't accept that there was nothing they could do. They passed several piers on the port side of the boat. Noah headed for the railing and looked for anything that could help. They were nearly at the entrance to Buttermilk Channel. The *Mosasaurus* would have a field day with them in the tight confines of the waterway. The sea beast was built to maneuver in the water. Humanity, even with all its creations, was not. Even the most advanced watercraft in the world was limited in what it could do.

A light caught his eye. There, floating aimlessly by itself along their port side, was a twenty-five-foot motorboat. They were so close to it that Noah had been blinded by the reflection of the sun bouncing off its windshield. As they drew nearer, the boat slowly spun. Noah's eyes opened wide when he saw them. The boat's keys were already in the ignition.

This was his chance to save everyone.

"There," he said, pointing at the boat. "Get me close, and I'll lead it away."

"No!" Becca shouted, grabbing his wrist and squeezing. "You will not be leaving us!" Sarah, Kyle, and Mike were right behind her, but Noah paid them no attention. He knelt and looked into Becca's eyes. "I have to, kiddo. It's the only chance all these people have—you too." He stood. "I'm sorry."

The crewman nodded his thanks, then radioed the pilot to slow and bring them closer to the derelict watercraft coming in along their port side.

"Good luck," the sailor said, "and thank you."

He held out his hand. Noah shook it—and immediately had a handcuff snap around his wrist. Then Mike shoved the bewildered Noah into the portside railing and attached the other end of the cuffs to it. Noah was confused—and angry.

"What the hell, Mike?"

Mike pulled a set of keys out of his pocket and held them out to...Sarah. He faced her. "Only when I'm far enough away."

Tears rolled down Sarah's eyes, but she took the keys, keeping them out of reach of Noah. "Thank you."

"Dammit, Mike," Noah protested, "don't do—"

"Let me," he interrupted. "To protect and serve, right? Besides..." he looked at the Rakestraws, ending on Becca, "they need you."

The crewman cleared his throat. "We're here. Whatever is happening needs to happen *now*."

Mike cracked his neck, then stepped up to the railing. He gripped it as Noah pulled on the cuff link to try and free himself. But once it was clear that there was nothing he could do to get free, he stopped, shoulders sagging.

"See you around, Dr. Clark," Mike said. Then he looked at Sarah. "Take care of our boy, will ya?"

Noah saw her nod out of the corner of his eye. He turned and watched two crewmen with a life preserver ring step up next to Mike. The floating ring was tied off somewhere.

"We can lower you down with this," the sailor said.

Mike gave him a nod, then glanced at Noah.

Finally, Noah gave up. "Good luck."

With that, Mike climbed over the railing and rappelled down to the unmanned boat. As soon as he landed, he released the ring, gripped the keys, and started it up. The dual engines roared to life. He gave the Coast Guardsmen a wave, then another to Noah and the others. Noah returned it with a subtle salute.

Sarah unlocked Noah's cuff, then backed off, unable to look at him.

"I could've helped him," Noah said.

"What about us?" Sarah asked.

Becca reached out and squeezed Noah's hand. "We need you too."

Kyle placed his hands on his sister's shoulders and nodded his agreement.

Mike pulled away as they began their entry into Buttermilk Channel. Soon, they'd lose visual on him as he pushed his boat west into deeper water. He blasted the boat's horn as he did and swerved around like mad. Behind the Coast Guard vessel, the *Mosasaurus* breached to breathe. Noah wasn't sure who it was more interested in at first, but then it turned toward the smaller prey and went under.

"He did it," the sailor said. "He saved us all."

Noah sighed. "He sure did…"

Another passenger joined them, speaking to the Coast Guard crewman. "Excuse me, but where are you taking us exactly?"

"To our station in Staten Island," he replied. "The National Guard has already cleared it out." He patted the passenger's arm. "You're safe now. Please, go, sit and relax."

Before the sailor headed back to the wheelhouse, he gave Noah a nervous look. The man truly had no idea if they would be safe, and neither did Noah, quite frankly. Mike may have only delayed the inevitable. The *Mosasaurus* might sink his boat then come back and do the same to them. Noah snapped his head around to the north, across the water to the southern tip of Manhattan. Even from here, he could see the Staten Island Ferry terminal.

That reminded him…

"Hang on," Noah said, getting the crewman's attention. The other man had been halfway across the deck. Noah hurried over.

"Yes?"

"There are survivors at Whitehall Terminal." He pictured the older man they had met, the one who had just missed the last ferry. "Some can't make it on their own."

The sailor nodded. "More boats are coming in a couple of hours. We're heading back out too, as soon as we unload. As I'm sure you can understand, things have gone haywire over the last couple of days. But the Coast Guard *and* the Navy are personally taking care of it. Those people will be out of there soon."

That relieved Noah some.

"Great," he said, "that's nice to hear. Thank you."

The crewman nodded and left, leaving Noah alone in the middle of the deck. But as they pushed south, multiple sets of footsteps announced the arrival of the Rakestraws. He looked west, just in time to see Mike's boat one last time before it disappeared behind Governors Island. What happened to Mike now was anyone's guess, but Noah had faith that his friend would somehow survive.

"See you around, buddy."

"You okay?" Sarah asked, gently stroking his right biceps.

Noah gave the family another look, then smiled. "Yeah, actually. I am." His eyes narrowed, focusing on the strap of the backpack Kyle now carried. "What's that?"

Kyle looked at the water. "Mike's backpack. He must've accidentally left it behind when he, you know..."

But Noah knew better than that. Mike did not *accidentally* leave it behind. He'd purposely given it, and the small fortune inside, to Noah and the Rakestraws.

You really were one of the good ones, weren't you?

"So, what happens now?" Becca asked, looking as unsure as Noah felt. "Where do we go from here?"

"Honestly, I have no idea, but," Noah replied, looking into Sarah's eyes. Then, he recalled a conversation he had with Mike, about this being a now-or-never moment with Sarah—and her kids, for that matter. He looked at Kyle and gripped his shoulder, then put his other arm around Sarah, causing her to blush, "...I'll be here if you need me, okay?"

Becca jumped into the air and squealed with joy. Then she latched herself onto Noah's waist and squeezed.

Sarah looked him in the eyes and smiled. Noah slowly leaned in and kissed her on the forehead. But that wasn't enough for Sarah. She raised herself up on her tiptoes and planted a passion-filled kiss on his lips, much to the disgust of her children, especially Kyle.

"Ugh, come on, you guys, really?"

Epilogue

Mike thought about driving with the throttle pushed all the way forward. He'd survive if he could outrun the beast. But what about the others? If he got too far ahead of the *Mosasaurus*, it would probably just give up and return to the rescue boat. The idea of him *not* trying to actively escape death filled him with anger, but it also made his heart swell with pride. He allowed himself to admit as much, especially since he was more than likely about to die.

"Here fishy, fishy, fishy!" he called out, jerking the wheel hard to the right.

The water to his left exploded as the monster breached, jaws agape. The sight made Mike completely forget what he was doing. All he could do was stare in awe over the size of the thing. Noah and the crewman had said that it was ten feet longer than the forty-seven foot Coast Guard vessel, placing it at around sixty feet in length.

"Holy shit," he said, blinking hard.

He shook his head, then got back to dodging the prehistoric Moby Dick. He looked down at the throttle and itched to shove it forward more. He restrained himself, but only for a couple more minutes. He didn't have a death wish. He just really wanted those people, including Noah and the Rakestraws, to get to safety.

"Okay, Mike, where the hell are you going?"

He looked around, landing his eyes on the Statue of Liberty. He knew it well, but it was an island. An island wouldn't help him right now. He traced his eyes north and found Ellis Island.

"Bingo," he said. Yes, Ellis Island was also an island, but it also had a bridge to New Jersey.

He cranked the wheel back to the left, angling for the water belonging to the Hudson River—but was nearly capsized when the creature breached again. Mike quickly abandoned the Ellis Island idea and pointed his boat north. He gave the boat a little more gas, then thought against it.

"Dammit," he cursed, slowing.

He went back to swerving like mad, trying not to fall into a rhythm that would make his movements easy to track. The water behind him burst to life, and when he looked back, he gawked at what he saw. The *Mosasaurus* had breached again, but this time it stayed on the surface, pursuing him like a surface torpedo with teeth.

"Wow, you're ugly!"

Caught up in the moment, Mike powered down the boat, causing the fast-moving predator to collide face first into the back of it. The impact made it snort and grunt, which Mike was thrilled to witness.

Stupid fish, he thought.

He quickly powered the boat up, but got a cough out of one of two engines. Mike instantly regretted his decision to antagonize an animal that was already fueled by untamable violence—and hunger. Black smoke poured out of the right-hand engine. It completely died seconds later.

He sighed. *Stupid human.*

Now moving much slower, he throttled up to compensate. He knew he was straining the second engine, but he didn't have a choice. His foolish actions had caused his predicament and nothing more. So, here he was, blazing a trail of smoke behind him with a fearsome sea monster chasing his wounded motorboat.

"Right, landfall—now!"

Coming in from the southeast, he yanked the wheel to the left, sending his boat beelining for the Liberty State Park peninsula, its many docks, and the Central Railroad Museum. That's when Mike remembered that the park had a marina on the northern side of it, in the Morris Canal. *That* was his ticket to safety, so was the murky water and the smell of fuel. He doubted the *Mosasaurus* could see or smell him with all the other sensory distractions.

He gave the boat more power, gritting his teeth as the single engine began to whine. It may have also been damaged in the collision. Still, he pushed it harder, coming closer and closer to freedom with every foot traveled. But within sixty feet to shore, the second engine popped and died. Now, it too poured out black smoke.

"Oh, damn," he said, releasing the wheel and turning in time to watch the animal go under.

Mike rushed back and forth from starboard to port, looking down into the water for any sign of the water demon, his own personal executioner. He waited and waited, but nothing happened.

"Maybe it left?"

Mike, and his boat, were lifted off the surface of the Hudson River. Mike went flipping into the air like a ragdoll. He splashed down so hard, and on his chest, that he lost his breath. There, he waded in the murky waters of the Hudson River, with a sixty-foot *Mosasaurus* prowling somewhere beneath him. But what if it couldn't find him?

With no other option, Mike flipped onto his back and floated, allowing the sloshing current to carry him along. He knew that splashing like a wounded seal would only draw the animal's attention to him, and he seriously doubted it could see anything.

The boat's remaining engine popped somewhere nearby. Mike lifted his head high enough to see that it had somehow restarted following the attack. Then he was even more surprised when the boat began to lazily chug back out to open water. He was lifted higher by a wake. Its creator was unseen, because its creator was directly beneath him. Mike blinked, then turned his head to find the tip of the *Mosasaurus'* tail flick two feet from his face. The motion splashed water right into his eyes and mouth. Mike gagged, but didn't complain. He just lay there and waited for it, and the mostly deceased boat, to continue east.

Suddenly, Mike's head struck something hard. He winced and felt for the object, touching something rough and cylindrical. He took his eyes off the vanishing sea monster and looked straight up into the face of a curious pelican. It was sitting on the edge of a dock and gazing down at him, perplexed by what he was doing.

"Shoo," Mike said, realizing what had happened.

He had been thrown to the west, toward his destination. Then, he had floated the rest of the way and clunked his head against one of the dock's concrete supports. Mike lifted his head again and found a ladder ten feet away. His eyes lit up. Forgoing any more caution, he righted himself, kicked as hard as he could, and climbed the ladder. Once on solid ground, he collapsed, thanking his lucky stars while trying to catch his breath.

"I'm alive... I'm alive?" He jumped to his feet and shouted, "I'm alive!"

The scream of a woman startled him, and he nearly fell back into the Hudson River. Mike spun around and spotted the voice's owner. She was being chased down a long dock over at the northern marina. At least, he thought it was a she. The person's head was covered by a hat of some kind—a sock hat, or perhaps a beret.

"Oh, come on!" he yelled. Nevertheless, he took off running after her.

Mike stumbled and nearly fell twice while en route to the distressed stranger. When he drew closer, he realized that she wasn't alone. Three small theropods were right behind her. Whatever they were, they weren't any larger than a rooster, but that didn't mean they still couldn't hurt someone—maybe even kill a person.

He made it to the dock entrance and went to draw his gun but found his holster empty. He'd lost the weapon in the river. Mike quickly looked around for anything to use, finding a large pipe wrench half-buried beneath a pile of sodden towels.

Good enough, he thought, snagging the heavy tool and hustling down the dock.

He made it halfway to the first of three pint-sized dinosaurs before his presence was discovered. The closest animal turned, hissed, then took the wrench across the side of the head. The force of the blow, combined with the creature's slight build, sent it flailing into the water. Mike didn't care if the thing could swim, or if it was even conscious. He was a man on a mission.

The second and third carnivore were further down the dock, still chasing the shouting woman. Mike hurried forward, yelling at the animals to gain their attention.

"Hey, you! Over here!"

It worked, and at the perfect moment, because just then, the stranger rolled her ankle and went down hard. Had he not gotten their attention, they would've swarmed her immediately. And yes, it was a *she*. He could clearly see her face now.

Both carnivores turned and hissed at him like a rodent would. When they did, they revealed dozens of tiny, needle-like teeth. This newest discovery caused Mike to take a moment and reevaluate the situation. He was bigger and stronger than them, but they were no doubt faster and more agile. Plus, who knew what kind of infection he could contract if they bit him.

Slowly, he edged forward, holding the pipe wrench out in front of him lengthwise. It gave him another three feet of reach, and he doubted the predators knew what it was. The pair squared him up, standing side by side with the woman behind them. She edged back, sliding on her butt toward the end of the dock, as well as a gigantic superyacht that dwarfed every other boat in sight. But he paid it very little attention, focusing on the two creatures instead. Still, not in a million years, had Mike ever thought that a superyacht would be the backdrop of a battle with a pair of real-life dinosaurs.

"Shoo!" he yelled, poking at one with the end of the wrench. "Go on, get!"

One of them snapped at the wrench, latching onto it. It let out a high-pitch whine as it tried to tear flesh from the metal tool. When it let go, it stepped back and chirped at its buddy.

"That's right, you can't hurt me." Mike grinned. "I'm made of metal, asshole." He swung the pipe around to the other dinosaur and jammed the end in its face. "How 'bout you, wanna give it a try?"

But the second animal was just as perplexed as the first. That's when Mike made his move. He raised the wrench over his head, and roared at them with every ounce of gusto he could muster. Then he charged, shrieking like a man possessed.

"Ahhh!" he shouted, launching himself forward. He slammed the end of the wrench down on the dock, then swung it around in a wide arc.

The two remaining carnivores squealed and bolted for the dock exit. Once they were gone, he dropped the pipe wrench, and faced the dinosaurs' would-be dinner. She was leaning away from him, though not because she was afraid of him. She was still stuck in the pose she had taken after she had fallen. She was locked in fear, staring wide-eyed at the world behind Mike.

He calmed and knelt directly in her line of sight. His presence forced her to refocus her attention on him and not the dock. He waited to say anything. She needed to come down from the adrenaline high first.

She let out a long breath and said, "Thank you."

Mike cocked his head to the side. The woman's words carried

a heavy Irish accent. She was beautiful, with light freckling across her nose and cheeks.

"You're safe now," Mike said, standing and holding out his hand. "Let me help you up."

She nodded and took Mike's hand. He gently pulled her to her feet, waiting for her to test her ankle. She hobbled a little but didn't seem seriously injured. He had rolled his ankle many times like that before, while playing basketball or by stepping wrong off a curb.

"You okay? My name is... *Wow*." Her eyes... They were the prettiest shade of green he'd ever seen.

The Irishwoman grinned with amusement. "Your name is 'Wow?'"

"Huh, what?" he asked, blinking. "Oh, no, it's Mike—Dillon—Detective Mike Dillon, NYPD."

"Well, it's a pleasure to meet you, Mike Dillon." She tore off her beret to reveal lush orange-red hair. "My name is Kelly Sullivan." A pair of screeches from above caused Mike and Kelly to reflexively duck their heads a few inches. She eyed Mike, fear creeping back onto her face. "Don't suppose we can finish our introductions aboard my boat?"

Mike stood tall and stared at the 100-foot-long superyacht. It was white with classy golden accents. An Irish flag billowed in the breeze, attached to the *boat's* stern. Mike lowered his eyes to the yacht's flank, reading its name to himself.

Irish Gold.

"This is yours?" he asked.

Kelly gave him a playful pout. "What, you don't like it?"

"No, it's great!" He blurted. Then he locked eyes with her. "It's beautiful."

"Come now, Detective Dillon, we only just met. Least you can do is buy me dinner before being this forward."

Mike blushed hard. Kelly was something else, for sure. More screeches picked up overhead.

"So, my boat?" she asked.

Mike nodded. "Let's go."

They hurriedly untied it, then boarded, heading up to the third floor, to what Mike figured was the wheelhouse. The watercraft's amenities were that of the most luxurious hotel he had ever seen. But there were also décor items pertaining to the movie trilogy of *The Lord of the Rings*, including a wall filled with official replica swords made by United Cutlery. Few knew how much Mike loved that series. If there was one thing that he nerded out on, it was those movies.

This must be a dream—or am I dead? Is this Heaven?

"There's only one problem," Kelly said, breaking him from his thoughts.

"What's that?" he asked, feeling his heart race.

She stopped at the top of the stairs and looked back at him. "I haven't been able to get in contact with my pilot. I fear he didn't make it."

"Do we need him?"

She shrugged. "I know how to get her started, but I'm a lousy pilot."

Mike grinned. "Let me worry about that."

"You have experience behind the wheel of a boat this big?"

"No, and please, if you could, it's not a boat. It's a floating mansion. Floating mansions are *not* boats."

She smiled, then turned and continued higher. "Fair enough."

"Look, we'll figure it out together, okay?"

Kelly nodded her head as they entered the wheelhouse. As Mike had expected, it was ultra-modern and contained all the bells and whistles a superyacht was known for. But Mike only had eyes for the captain's chair. He sat and got acquainted with the controls.

A superyacht is still a boat. How hard can this be?

"You sure we can do this?" she asked.

Mike didn't want to lie to her. "Yeah, probably."

"Good enough, I suppose. Oh, and Detective, thank you for saving my life."

Mike shrugged, then waved her off. "You're welcome, and please, just Mike."

She smiled. "Okay, *Just* Mike."

He rolled his eyes and looked out to deeper water, seeing several places he had recently visited on his way, well, here.

Battery Park, Whitehall Terminal, Brooklyn Bridge, Brooklyn Bridge Park...

He never wanted to see any of them ever again.

"Is this safe to do right now—with everything that's happened?"

Mike faced Kelly, and again, he decided to be completely honest with her. "I'd be lying if I said it was, *but* I promise I'll do everything I can to keep you out of harm's way."

She nodded and gave him a soft smile. "Thank you for being honest. I'm not sure why, but as soon as I met you, I knew I could trust you." She turned and eyed a panel to her right, giving Mike time to throw a fist into the air in celebration. "You alright?"

He was caught. He swallowed down his embarrassment and started the mansion-of-the-seas, *Irish Gold*. Somewhere belowdecks the engines rumbled to life. He sighed and stared through the windshield.

"Mike, you alright?"

He looked away from the world outside and gave Kelly the biggest smile. "Everything is perfect." Kelly blushed and tucked a loose strand of her gorgeous red hair behind her ear. Mike gave New York City's skyline another look, then breathed easy for the first time in days. "Everything is perfect."

CREATURE DATABASE: INTRODUCTION

Note: if these descriptions are a hair off from what I used in the story, that's because there is a lot of debate throughout academia, including the year these animals became recognized by the scientific community. I did my best, compiled the incredibly dense data, and combined information where it was needed to make it work. Also, new discoveries are constantly being made, so some of these might become outdated as time goes by.

Either way, I hope you enjoyed *Fracture*. I know I had a blast writing it.

—Matt

Ankylosaurus magniventris
Meaning: "Fused lizard with a great belly"
Diet: Herbivore
Region Lived: North America
Year First Discovered: 1906
Estimated Size: 25 feet long, 14,000 lbs.
Physical Description: Armored dinosaur with a massive club-like tail, bony plates, and a low, squat body designed for defense.

Carcharodontosaurus saharicus
Meaning: "Shark-toothed lizard from the Sahara"
Diet: Carnivore
Region Lived: North Africa
Year First Discovered: 1927
Estimated Size: 42 feet long, 14,000 lbs.
Physical Description: Large theropod with serrated teeth, a powerful, athletic build, and a long, narrow skull designed for slicing prey.

Carnotaurus sastrei
Meaning: "Sastre's Meat-Eating Bull" (first found on a farm named Pocho Sastre)
Diet: Carnivore
Region Lived: South America
Year First Discovered: 1984
Estimated Size: 25 feet long, 5,000 lbs.
Physical Description: Bipedal predator with a slender body, long legs, and distinct forward-facing horns above its eyes. Unusually deep skull with small, peg-like teeth, and extremely short arms.

Dreadnoughtus schrani
Meaning: "Fears nothing, named after Adam Schran"
Diet: Herbivore
Region Lived: South America
Year First Discovered: 2014
Estimated Size: 85 feet long, 114,000 lbs.
Physical Description: Massive sauropod with a long neck and tail, heavily built limbs, and a barrel-shaped body.

Dryptosaurus aquilunguis
Meaning: "Tearing Lizard with Eagle Claws"
Diet: Carnivore
Region Lived: North America
Year First Discovered: 1866
Estimated Size: 25 feet long, 3,000 lbs.
Physical Description: Lightly built theropod with long, powerful legs adapted for speed, large hand claws, and a robust skull with serrated teeth.

Edmontosaurus regalis
Meaning: "Regal lizard from Edmonton"
Diet: Herbivore
Region Lived: North America
Year First Discovered: 1917
Estimated Size: 40 feet long, 12,000 lbs.
Physical Description: Large, duck-billed dinosaur with a broad, flat snout, strong legs, and a muscular tail.

Elasmosaurus platyurus

Meaning: "Flat-Tailed Thin-Plated Lizard"
Diet: Carnivore
Region Lived: North America
Year First Discovered: 1868
Estimated Size: 35 feet long, 4,000 lbs.
Physical Description: Marine reptile with an extremely elongated neck making up more than half its total length, small head, sharp teeth, and large paddle-like flippers.

Gallimimus bullatus
Meaning: "Chicken mimic with a bulla (bulbous structure)"
Diet: Omnivore
Region Lived: Asia
Year First Discovered: 1972
Estimated Size: 20 feet long, 900 lbs.
Physical Description: Ostrich-like dinosaur with long legs, a slender body, and a toothless beak adapted for speed and versatility in diet.

Majungasaurus crenatissimus
Meaning: "Crenulated Mahajanga Lizard" (named after the Mahajanga region of Madagascar)
Diet: Carnivore
Region Lived: Madagascar
Year First Discovered: 1896
Estimated Size: 25 feet long, 2,000 lbs.
Physical Description: Stocky, bipedal theropod with short arms, a short snout, small crests on its skull, and robust teeth designed for crushing.

Moros intrepidus
Meaning: "Harbinger of doom, intrepid"
Diet: Carnivore
Region Lived: North America
Year First Discovered: 2019
Estimated Size: 9 feet long, 170 lbs.
Physical Description: Small, fast theropod with feathers, long legs for speed, and sharp teeth for hunting.

Mosasaurus hoffmannii
Meaning: "Lizard of the Meuse River, named after Johan Leonard Hoffmann"
Diet: Carnivore
Region Lived: Europe
Year First Discovered: 1764
Estimated Size: 49 feet long, 18,000 lbs.
Physical Description: Massive marine reptile with a streamlined body, paddle-like limbs, and a powerful tail.

Parasaurolophus walkeri
Meaning: "Near-crested lizard, named after Sir Byron Edmund Walker"
Diet: Herbivore
Region Lived: North America
Year First Discovered: 1922
Estimated Size: 31 feet long, 10,000 lbs.
Physical Description: Duck-billed dinosaur with teeth, a distinctive elongated, backward-curving crest on its skull, likely used for sound or display.

Piksi barbarulna
Meaning: "Strange elbowed chicken"
Diet: Carnivore
Region Lived: North America
Year First Discovered: 2004
Estimated Size: 3-foot wingspan, 2 lbs.
Physical Description: Small pterosaur or bird that fed mostly on insects.

Pteranodon longiceps
Meaning: "Winged without teeth and long-headed"
Diet: Carnivore
Region Lived: North America
Year First Discovered: 1876
Estimated Size: 20-foot wingspan, 110 lbs.
Physical Description: Large flying reptile with a toothless beak, lightweight bones, and a pronounced cranial crest for stability in flight.

Quetzalcoatlus northropi
Meaning: "Northrop's Feathered Serpent" (named after the Aztec god Quetzalcoatl and aviation pioneer John Northrop)
Diet: Carnivore
Region Lived: North America
Year First Discovered: 1971
Estimated Size: 40-foot wingspan, 500 lbs.
Physical Description: One of the largest known flying animals in recorded history. Elongated, toothless beak, long legs, a lightweight but powerful frame, stood as tall as a giraffe when on the ground.

Spinosaurus aegyptiacus
Meaning: "Spined Lizard from Egypt"
Diet: Carnivore
Region Lived: North Africa
Year First Discovered: 1912
Estimated Size: 55 feet long, 18,000 lbs.
Physical Description: Largest known theropod, elongated, crocodile-like skull with conical teeth, a distinctive sail on its back, a paddle-like tail, and webbed feet to hunt in rivers and lakes.

Stygimoloch spinifer
Meaning: "Horned demon from the Styx"
Diet: Herbivore
Region Lived: North America
Year First Discovered: 1983
Estimated Size: 10 feet long, 180 lbs.
Physical Description: Small, bipedal dinosaur with a thick, domed skull adorned with long, spiky horns. Fast and agile, possibly used headbutting for defense.

Thanatosdrakon amaru
Meaning: "Dragon of death, named after Amaru (a serpent/dragon from Inca mythology)"
Diet: Carnivore
Region Lived: South America
Year First Discovered: 2022
Estimated Size: 30-foot wingspan, 550 lbs.
Physical Description: Enormous flying reptile with elongated

wings, a streamlined skull, and robust limbs for gliding.

Triceratops prorsus
Meaning: "Three-horned face, forward-pointing"
Diet: Herbivore
Region Lived: North America
Year First Discovered: 1889
Estimated Size: 30 feet long, 24,000 lbs.
Physical Description: Large herbivore with three facial horns, a parrot-like beak, and a broad frill protecting its neck.

Troodon formosus
Meaning: "Wounding tooth, graceful"
Diet: Omnivore
Region Lived: North America
Year First Discovered: 1855
Estimated Size: 7 feet long, 110 lbs.
Physical Description: Small, slender dinosaur with large eyes, and serrated teeth.

Tyrannosaurus rex
Meaning: "Tyrant lizard king"
Diet: Carnivore
Region Lived: North America
Year First Discovered: 1905
Estimated Size: 40 feet long, 22,000 lbs.
Physical Description: Massive predator with powerful jaws, sharp teeth, and a robust body balanced by a long tail.

Velociraptor mongoliensis

Meaning: "Swift thief from Mongolia"

Diet: Carnivore

Region Lived: Asia

Year First Discovered: 1924

Estimated Size: 7 feet long, 45 lbs.

Physical Description: Small, agile predator with a sickle-shaped claw on each foot.

About the Author

MATT JAMES is the international bestselling author of forty action-packed titles, including the fan-favorite Jack Reilly series, *The Cursed Thief*, *The Blood King*, and *Dark Island*. He specializes in globetrotting thrillers that fans of James Rollins, Steve Berry, and Ernest Dempsey will devour!

He lives twenty minutes from the beach in sunny South Florida with his amazing wife, three beautiful children, a lovable pooch, and an overly dramatic black cat.

Go to **MattJamesAuthor.com** and subscribe to his newsletter for early and exclusive news and updates! You will NOT be mercilessly spammed with junk mail. And don't forget to click the **FOLLOW** button on his Amazon page to receive new release alerts!

YOU CAN VISIT MATT AT:

Website: **MattJamesAuthor.com**
Newsletter: **MattJamesAuthor.com/Newsletter**
Facebook: **Facebook.com/MattJamesAuthor**
Facebook: **Facebook.com/groups/MattJamesReaderGroup**